LAND OF THE
TWILIGHT MIST

BY

CAROL WEAKLAND

This book is a work of fiction. Places, events, and situations in this story are purely fictional. Any resemblance to actual persons, living or dead, is coincidental.

ISBN-10: 1466440880
ISBN-13: 978-1466440883

Printed in the United States of America

DEDICATION

For my mother,
my father, who now dances with the angels,
and my little brother, Denny.

I would also like to offer a very special thank you to
Jonathan, my guide.

CHAPTER 1

"I don't care what they say! It must be true! I believe —I believe—I believe," Diana Sherwood whispered into the feathery depths of her captive pillow. The nightmare was upon her once more, offering little peace.

Diana was running, running as fast as her spindly legs would manage down a rough, uneven pathway. The heavy presence of some unknown pursuant nipped incessantly at her heals. Onward she raced through an endless maze of darkness, fleeing that which could not be seen.

Suddenly, the familiar touch of mist kissed Diana's brow. That meant Crescent Lake could not be far away! Somehow, she managed a tiny burst of speed; but it was to no avail. The unknown tormentor only increased its maddening pace. Faster and faster it came, never speaking, never making any demands. What could it possibly want? Diana already knew the answer. She must become one with the darkness. Only then would it be satisfied.

Something hard hit Diana's tender shoulder. Casting a quick glance back, she saw Kelly Branwell's golden hair, blazing against the night sky like so many tongues of flame. The fearsome apparition was pelting stones at her!

"You're a liar, Diana Sherwood! Admit it!"

"No!" Diana tried to scream, but the voiceless cry stuck in her throat.

Invisible hands thoughtlessly seized her from all sides. They were lifting her higher and higher, hissing venomous taunts that grew so loud it seemed her eardrums must crack. It was no use. Crescent Lake's dark waves consumed her body before she could even scream.

Caught within this watery prison, Diana floated downward, wondering what she clutched so tightly in her hands. She was about to identify its source when the sandy lakebed brushed her cheek. Alone and afraid, she wondered why life must end this way. Was there not something else she must do?

A mysterious light appeared in answer, pulsating ever so slightly. Diana knew she must move toward it, but her stubborn limbs remained frozen. One thought alone whispered repeatedly inside her brain.

"I believe...I believe...I believe..." it said, then the darkness came.

At the same moment that Diana struggled to free herself from the recurring nightmare, two figures materialized. Their lithesome bodies appeared ethereal, almost fairy- like, as they hovered over misty Crescent Lake. Silently, they skimmed the still waters, unmindful of the difficulty this task would impose upon most beings.

Upon reaching the shoreline, the pair began to converse in a strange airy dialect, similar to the whispering wind. Even more spellbinding was the fact that their tiny feet never touched the ground.

"I like it not, my lady," began the more animated of the two beings, his elfin features forever in a state of mischievous flux. "Perhaps you are wrong about her. If so, what will we do?"

His lovely companion flashed a warning glance, then allowed him to continue.

"If she is the one, then he must already know about her. We should leave now, while there is still time—or all our plans could come to naught!"

"York, you know I am right about this."

The beautiful creature raised her hand in warning, anticipating an all too predictable response. York could be frustratingly persistent. Perhaps that was part of his magic. Everything about him spoke of charm. Indeed, his dark,

2

elfin locks remained perpetually mussed, heightened always by the mischievous gleam that lit his eyes. There was a restlessness about York, reminiscent of a firefly trapped within a child's mason jar, ever anticipating that moment when grubby fingers would unwind the top and set him free.

"Lady Selene," he twittered in a voice meant more to amuse, than reproach for daydreaming. This was his own precious guardian, beautiful beyond compare. How could he consent to a plan that might very well bring about her destruction?

"Please, hear me, my lady," he began, kneeling before her respectfully. "If you—we are wrong about this, many people will be hurt—including the girl. Are you willing to risk that? Are you willing to risk everything we have worked for all these years?"

A single strand of auburn hair brushed Selene's cheek as the night wind sent it dancing to and fro. When she did reply, it was through thought alone—thought that transferred effortlessly into York's mind.

"We will succeed—no matter what he throws our way. It is our right. Come, we have stalled long enough. There is work to be done. Great work. Through this girl, we will accomplish the miracle and reclaim our reason for existence."

"Listen to that which you are saying!" barked the impish lad. "If she is the one spoken of—the one who will bring us out of the mist—then you must leave. There can be only one Selene!"

Selene turned her luminous gaze upon him and offered up a heartfelt smile.

"York, you know I do not belong here."

"But, my lady," barked the disgruntled elf, shuffling his tiny feet across the dew-moistened grass, "you have become so very special to us all. I—we could not bear to be parted from you."

Selene straightened her willowy frame into its most regal bearing, then said, "When the time comes, York, you must be ready. I can rely on you alone to prepare her for the future. I will not be there—no matter how much I wish otherwise. My destiny lies along another path. She is the one who needs your guidance, not I."

"I understand, my lady. I will be ready when the time comes," proclaimed the little elf, his head bowed in sorrow.

Selene gently smoothed a lock of hair away from his elfin brow. It was then she noticed that he was trembling. There was little she could do but offer a solemn blessing.

"May the Spirit protect you, York. Do not be so downcast. Remember who she is."

Selene raised York's chin with her translucent fingertips, forcing him to meet her eyes. She held that gaze for a moment until his lips revealed the enchanting smile she loved so well.

"It is time," came her voiceless urging. "Follow me."

Silently, they approached the tiny cottage where Diana slept. After pausing outside the bedroom window that overlooked Crescent Lake, they nodded to one another, then proceeded to meld through the restrictive screening.

Once inside, Selene could not help but notice the peaceful look blanketing the young girl's face. Doubt was no longer possible. She had made the right choice. If only her companion might see—

"Look at Diana. She was born for this purpose. Believe me, I know."

York flashed a reluctant smile at his guardian captor. He was about to answer forthright when Selene silenced him with a wave of her hand.

"Use thoughts only, York. It is not yet time to reveal ourselves to them."

Sighing impatiently, York happened upon the girl's brother, lodged within a tiny bed that lay on the opposite side of the room.

"Do not disregard Daniel," Selene continued, reading his thoughts. "He is also destined to play a role in the miracle."

"He looks brave enough," York conceded, with a wry nod of his head. He then turned his attention on the sleeping girl. Selene saw the recognition flash across his features and trembled despite her best intentions to remain calm.

"I know her!"

The words tumbled out before York fully realized he had spoken.

"Hush!" came Selene's firm command.

Fortunately, the house remained blissfully unaware of the outburst, and its inhabitants slept on.

York continued to stare at Diana with wide eyes.

"Stay with me, Little Elf!"

"Do not call me that, my lady!" cried the offended York, his face turning a painful red. "You know how I hate to be called that name!" His tiny frame began to hop up and down as if powered by rapid bursts of electricity.

"Then stop acting like one. I need you to remain focused."

Selene's strict tone lasted only a moment before melting into its normally peaceful strains. "Remember, the father is a fine, brave man. He is also a believer, yet fate has determined that he should take little part in the creation of our miracle. No, Michael Sherwood will suffer the great loss once more, and with this passing—rediscover the meaning of true happiness."

Selene drifted off on a swift current of thought, little imagining that her elfin friend would slip away. Once she had consciously returned from those private musings, it, therefore, came as some surprise that York had deserted his post.

Gazing through the tiny network that comprised the window screen, Selene caught sight of the mischievous sprite carelessly skipping back and forth across Crescent

Lake. His motions, magical to behold, were riveted with unspoken joy. Oh, how she wanted to laugh and smile at his clever antics, but it was not to be.

"Little Elf!" she cried so loud that a pair of barred owls screeched before seeking cover.

The startled York gave a shriek, struggling valiantly not to jump out of his translucent skin.

Once again, Selene suppressed the laugh that rose to her lips. "Off with you. Attend to the matters at hand."

"I am always at your service, my lady," York faithfully pledged with a well meaning, if not overly dramatic bow.

"Thank you, York. Prepare the others for what is to come."

The air born York executed a perfect somersault, then cried, "Never fear, my lady. I obey you in this as in all things!" A peal of laughter echoed through the air, long after its owner had faded from view.

Selene smiled to herself. She trusted York implicitly with this sacred task. Indeed, there was no other that could hope to fulfill his part.

Brimming with hope, she willed herself once more unto Diana's side. The delicate form was shuddering at those unseen horrors that so often colored her dreams. It was time to set the miracle into motion.

"Diana, daughter of light," she whispered, gently stroking the child's silken locks, "you are about to undertake a great quest—one that will be difficult beyond imagining. Few would contemplate such a journey. You, dear child, are different. Never forget that you already possess the gifts necessary to accomplish this miracle. Listen to the teachings of your inner voice, Diana, and you will not fail. Blessings be upon you, dear one."

A single tear slipped from Selene's lashes as she stooped to kiss Diana's brow. Unwilling to risk detection, she melded with the morning air.

Diana stirred as the soft droplet moistened her cheek. The first thought that crossed her groggy mind was that it must be drizzling outside. Suddenly, the poor child sat bolt upright in bed. Something strange had just happened. A presence both mysterious and yet familiar had called her from the land of dreams. Opening her eyes, she quickly scanned the room for any sign of intrusion, but no hint of magic could be found anywhere. Everything appeared just as it had before she drifted off to sleep.

"I must have been dreaming about Selene and the angels of the twilight mist again," mused the lovely child as she shuffled over to the window seat, her body stiff with unfinished sleep. "What would Kelly Branwell and her friends say if they knew?"

Still wrapped in dream-spell, Diana absentmindedly wiped the midnight dew from the sill with the palm of her hand. "They'd call me daydreaming Diana as always. I can hear them laughing even now," she said with a sigh.

After easing herself onto the window seat's well-worn cushion, she turned her blurry gaze toward the moonlit lake.

"Well, let them laugh. I never said she was a fairy or a ghost. No, Selene is something greater than that—much greater."

Diana's weary head began to nod, as the last traces of moonlight slowly faded from view. "I wish I could see her," she softly whispered against the cuff of her sleeve.

"Perhaps one day you will," an elfin voice replied.

Diana shook her head. "Who said that?"

The poor girl never heard an answer for within seconds, she had returned to the land of dreams.

York studied his new ward, as he perched merrily upon a pine bough that offered optimum viewing of the bedroom window. A final beam of moonlight caught her angelic face, illuminating silvery highlights on her brow.

"Perhaps one day I will…" she whispered. "Perhaps one day I will…"

CHAPTER 2

The first determined rays of sunlight easily slipped past an intricate pine bough barricade on route to their target: the Sherwood cottage. Fortunately, this proved far easier than usual as the children's window appeared conveniently naked of curtain or blind.

Daniel Sherwood stirred in his bed, letting out a faint groan. Saturday was the single day he could enjoy the simple pleasure of sleeping late. It seemed only natural that he take full advantage of the situation.

This particular morning, the task was easily accomplished by placing a trusty pillow over both eyes and sinking his face down into the cottony depths of his mattress. The world of dreams beckoned, awaiting his summons. Soon scores of images whisked through his eager mind. When Daniel's senses finally cleared, a massive battlefield stretched before him. Ancient it was, not to mention dark in hue. Heavily armored knights were fighting a wide range of elemental foes, composed of fire, water, wind and earthquake. Through it all, lightning blazed fiercely overhead. Daniel was confused. Why were knights engaging the elements? More importantly, who had unleashed such forces upon the hapless warriors?

A great raven appeared on the horizon, offering answer with each beat of its enormous wings. At that moment everything became clear. It was Bran! Bran, the malevolent wizard known for his unscrupulous dealings in black magic. He had sent the elements to destroy Camelot and the table round. This would be a relatively easy task to accomplish since Merlin was gone and the King remained captive.

The harsh sound of laughter brought Daniel to the side of Sir Lancelot, who had been struck down by a wicked shaft of lightning. What could a young man do amidst such atrocity? Daniel silently trembled at the thought that Lancelot might already be dead. Thankfully, a slight rise and fall of the good knight's chest quieted Daniel's fears. There was no time to lose. Excalibur must be called into action. Nothing short of the sacred blade could defeat such a powerful foe. Daniel felt certain King Arthur would not mind if he wielded her in defense of Camelot.

Unexpectedly, the longed-for blade appeared in Daniel's hands. Grasping the hilt, he allowed a great rush of energy to carry him forward. He was about to face Bran when a far off voice diverted his attention.

"The time is near…It will happen soon…"

"Who said that?" wondered Daniel. "Was it you, Bran? Yes, the time is near for you to die!" he cried, swiftly bringing the sword down upon its mark.

"Will I be ready when it comes?"

"Huh? You're supposed to be dead! What are you up to now?"

"Will I be ready? Will I? Will I?"

Daniel shook his head in confusion. The voice obviously belonged to someone other than Bran. Curiosity demanded that he uncover its true source. Carefully lifting the corner of his pillow ever so slightly, the young Sherwood met with a blinding stream of sunlight. Both eyes instinctively squeezed shut against the rude assault. At that moment the mysterious voice rang out again. This time, Daniel tore the pillow from his eyes only to find Diana propped against the window sill, apparently sound asleep.

"I'll get her good," he snickered to himself.

Unable to resist what seemed to be an instinctive reflex, he flung the pillow toward his unsuspecting sister.

The soft missile took Diana completely unprepared as it landed upon her brow. What was going on? Daniel's ringing laughter quickly helped her evaluate the situation. She had fallen victim to yet another of her brother's devilish pranks.

"Danny, you scared me half to death!"

"What'd you expect? Talking in your sleep again. You should have heard yourself," Daniel teased as he fell to his knees, melodramatically. "Will I be ready when it comes?"

Resuming his own voice and demeanor, he cried, "Well, I decided to find out just how ready you were and 'bam!' you were not ready when it came! You jumped so high—you should have seen yourself!"

Daniel collapsed back against his tangled bed sheets, roaring with laughter.

There was nothing Diana could do but give into his contagious mirth. She knew from a vast range of experience that it was impossible to remain angry at Daniel for long. He was one of those rare children who could execute the perfect practical joke, yet somehow always managed to befriend his victims. His personality was so likable that it felt wrong to call him offensive. Diana adored Daniel, but she also knew that he must answer for his crime.

"So, you think it's funny, do you? We'll see about that!"

Before Daniel could respond, Diana hurled the delinquent pillow back at him—the force of which knocked him even further into the depths of his mattress.

"Not bad, Di, not bad," Daniel chuckled appraisingly. He shook his head from side to side, hoping to regain some equilibrium, then allowed his feet to dangle over the edge of the bed. Oh, how he wanted to ask Diana about her dream, yet somehow she always managed to dodge the issue. One thing was in his favor this time: her unusual post at the window. It couldn't hurt to ask about that. Maybe then, she would tell him the truth.

"What made you sleep next to the window last night?"

Diana's tiny, pink lips twitched nervously, as if contemplating an appropriate response. "I don't know," she finally offered. "What was I saying?"

"Something about—'It will happen soon. Will I be ready when it comes?' You know, the unusual stuff," Daniel added with just the hint of a smile. "Only this time you were sitting at the window—like you were waiting for someone."

Diana's thoughts turned inward. Her dreams had been filled with nighttime terrors. Dare she tell Daniel about that?

"Earth to Di, earth to Di."

Diana snapped out of her trance. "What is it, Danny?"

"You didn't answer me. Who were you waiting for? Was it the dashing Lancelot? Was he going to carry you off to Camelot?"

After receiving no response, Daniel decided that his initial means of attack would prove far more successful. Diana could not help but respond when the pillow hit her face!

"Oooh, you take that!" she cried, rapidly returning fire. "If I were expecting someone, it would not be the treasonous Lancelot. It would be Arthur himself—the noblest of them all!" Instantly, she had procured her own pillow and flung it in a display of dazzling succession. The double force caught Daniel off guard and down he went.

"He's out for the count!" cheered the victorious Diana.

Daniel rose slowly, taking time to calculate his response. "Now you've asked for it. Direct combat. No mercy. First, you insult my good friend, the heroic Lancelot—"

"He's a womanizer—"

"And second—second of all—"

"Yes, Sir Laugh-a-lot," Diana teased, edging him on, "You were saying—second of all?"

This time Daniel was ready for her. "Second of all, Arthur would never come for you, because you are too

11

much like his sister Morgan Le Fay and would always be playing tricks on him—so there!" Daniel quipped with pride. All those stories father told them about the Knights of the Round Table came in handy at times.

"You realize, Princess Morgan, an insult of such magnitude may only be answered with a duel!" Daniel exclaimed, gallantly throwing Diana her pillow. "Your weapon, dear princess."

Diana could do little but giggle as Daniel slipped into his comic warrior mode. His grand sense of adventure even amidst the smallest games never ceased to amaze her. At nearly fourteen years of age she was still willing to play along. Mirroring Daniel's stance, she moved into battle position.

"On guard—and no magic!" Daniel cried, raising his pillow overhead.

"Against you—magic won't be necessary!" Diana challenged, with a flare of her steely, gray eyes.

Diana's insult quickly achieved its desired effect; for Daniel charged and the assault began. The blows proved erratic at best, allowing Diana to gain control over the enemy pillow by tickling her unsuspecting brother when he least expected it.

Daniel dropped to his knees, desperately striving to reclaim his lost foil that remained firmly lodged under Diana's foot. When this failed, he further retaliated by tickling her big toe. Necessity urged her to leap aside so she might avoid further abuse from his nimble fingers. With a flourish, he easily reclaimed the cherished weapon, delivering several perfect volleys before she could return fire.

After regaining control over her own most hallowed pillow, Diana leapt onto the whimpering mattress and began aggressively deflecting a steady stream of blows. The old bed frame could not help but utter a series of moans and groans that made Diana fear it might cave in altogether. She had little time to ponder the possibility of such a disaster, however, for Daniel soon drove her from the unstable perch.

Brother and sister wove across the room as tell tale feathers flew in all directions, leaving no space untouched by the fray.

"Take that—and that—and this—you enchantress!" howled Daniel, flinging the trusty pillow at his unyielding foe.

"Your sword is no match for me, Sir Laugh-a-lot! See how I turn your fine steel into mere fluff!" she chimed, as another hit sent showers of goose feather's raining down upon them.

"Fluff? Fluff? I'll show you fluff!" Daniel cried, bounding across the room. His new plan involved attacking Diana's left flank. Using a perfect combination of timing and coordination, he succeeded not only in knocking the pillow from her hand, but also in landing himself flat upon the floor.

A wave of tenderness swept through Diana, as she knelt beside her seemingly unconscious brother. "Are you badly wounded, Sir Laugh-a-lot?"

Daniel remained deathly still for a moment, then responded by blowing a stray feather onto the crest of his sister's nose. They stared at each other with an air of dreadful seriousness before breaking into fits of laughter.

Without the slightest hint or warning, Michael Sherwood stepped into this chaotic world of feathers and fluff. At first glance, it was easy to misinterpret the patriarch's look. Most people found him difficult: an observation that did not fall too far off the mark. Dark and brooding, as best befits a reclusive artist, Michael did little to sway such opinion. Hailed as a painter of the highest rank, many of his oils drew top bids across the country. While this pleased him, he had little taste for celebrity. In fact, more often than not, the fans got on his nerves. At times they begged—no demanded—that he move to the city so his work might be more accessible.

Michael typically listened to these suggestions with a polite outward expression, yet inside his mind raged. He would never leave his home at Whispering Pines. Never. It connected him to the past. As long as he remained lodged at the cottage in the glen, a part of Cynthia still lived. How could he ever consider cutting that fragile cord that bound them throughout time?

Ten, long years had passed since Cynthia Sherwood's death, and Michael still felt the ache. Indeed, it filled him with a kind of torment to think that Daniel and Diana had never really known their mother. Somehow, amidst all the heart break, Michael had managed to raise them alone. Although this elevated eyebrows amongst the local gossips, no one could deny that he was a good father. Michael taught the children about life the only way he knew how: through art. Imaginative stories were created to explain the hidden meaning behind his work. Each canvas served as a springboard for teaching lessons about life, drawing attention to all the wonders and fears it had to offer. Often these stories were embellished with further tales about knights rescuing victims from terrible fates: the kind of tidbits on which Daniel and Diana thrived. Upon surveying the battle-scarred room, however, Michael wished he had invented tales that promoted tidiness.

"What's all this?" he asked in a tone that was meant to convey anger but only succeeded in making Diana laugh.

"We were pillow dueling, father," Daniel replied, instantly springing to attention.

A smile threatened to break through Michael's tightly gritted teeth. "Pillow dueling?" he questioned. "Is that a new form of medieval combat I'm not familiar with?"

"Oh, yes," Diana beamed, "brand new, father. You see, it's much safer than dueling with swords."

"And much sloppier," Michael chuckled.

"Now you've done it, sis," Daniel said with a groan.

"You started it!" quipped Diana.

"—Waking me up from such a great dream with all that mumbling!"

Daniel whispered just loud enough for Diana to hear, "She was having those weird dreams again."

A look of genuine concern flooded Michael's brow. "Were you, Diana?"

"Yes," she reluctantly replied. "I was dreaming about Selene. Did you know that she was here last night?"

"Here?" questioned Michael.

Diana was aware of the little catch in his breath. She quickly met his eyes and read the uncertainty behind them. "In my dreams, of course," she suggested, realizing this was not the right time to say anything more.

"Double, double, toil and trouble!" Daniel mischievously cackled with hag-like glee.

"Danny stop!" You know Selene is not a witch! Father, tell him!"

"Calm down. I was only kidding, Di. You know how I love to tease you."

Michael picked up a few, stray feathers and rubbed them between his fingers. There were many things he needed to tell Diana about the past—things that could easily affect her future.

"The moon was like a crescent last night," he finally began. "You know what that means."

"The angels of the twilight mist were out in force!" Daniel exclaimed, drumming his heals against the floor.

Michael offered a warm smile. "It is possible one of them visited you."

"I think it was Selene herself, father," Diana volunteered with growing enthusiasm.

"That is unlikely, Diana. It is very unusual for her to visit humans, even children like you, for she is needed everywhere. You remember the story—"

15

Diana immediately picked up on her cue. "Tell us again!"

"First we must start thinking about breakfast," countered Michael. "A prospective buyer is coming to look at some paintings."

Diana was instantly on her feet. "Oh, I forgot about breakfast!" she cried, thrusting her feet into a pair of well-worn slippers.

As she skid across the floor, Daniel thought they did little but impede her progress.

"Not to worry," Michael announced with a sense of pride. "I made breakfast this morning. So prepare yourselves for a real treat!"

Daniel could not resist the urge to moan, "See what you got us into, Di? Remember what happened the last time he made breakfast?"

Michael hit his son square across the chest with what was left of the makeshift pillow. "I'll let you get away with that for now, young man, but next time you will not be so lucky! I expect this room to be in top shape by afternoon." Michael took one last look at the full extent of damage, then added with a sorry shake of his head, "If that is humanly possible." He further punctuated the remark by strolling out the door.

"Ugh, what a mess," sighed Daniel.

"Should have thought of that before you threw the first pillow," came the giggled response.

This brief exchange of remarks was all it took to set Daniel off. In no time at all, he was flinging handfuls of feathers at his sister once more.

Aware that the situation was hopeless, Diana naturally returned fire.

CHAPTER 3

It proved no small endeavor for Daniel and Diana to tidy up the splendidly well-feathered room. Once accomplished, however, they managed to wash and dress in record time, surprising Michael with their early arrival. When questioned about this miraculous event, brother and sister merely exchanged knowing glances.

"Call it teamwork," Daniel suggested as he lifted a piece of bacon from the pan.

Michael knew it was useless to press the issue any further. Settling down into his chair, he watched Diana serve the morning repast.

Back and forth she trotted, arms laden with morning delicacies. No sooner had Diana deposited the glasses and juice, then she set out for further offerings. On and on she trod, humming a merry tune, until the table was stocked full with delicious edibles. Diana could not help but muse how very lucky they were to enjoy their meals in such a lovely setting. Whether or not Daniel and Michael took this view, she could hardly imagine. Indeed, they were strangely mute upon the subject.

Glancing once more at the beautiful surroundings, a smile rose to her lips. Why, the very table itself was a work of art. Liberally adorned with pine boughs, it boasted a length of knotty cones gently carved along the glossy outer lip. Who the artist was, Diana never knew. Still, it was altogether certain he or she had spent hours crafting it to perfection.

All meals at the Sherwood cottage were enjoyed in this—the largest of four rooms. Although Michael often housed a multitude of paintings in this area, it was also used as a dining room and kitchen. Daniel and Diana thought it more of an eclectic art studio. Indeed, canvases could be found in every available nook and cranny. Somehow the room never appeared cluttered, simply captivating.

Moving out of this central area, a narrow hallway offered entrance into the bulk of the remaining living quarters. Small and intimately compact, it came as little surprise that the cottage boasted only three additional rooms. Brother and sister split the largest between them by means of a curtained divider, leaving the lesser unit available for Michael. A tiny bath completed the homestead tour.

Those who were lucky enough to visit the Sherwood cottage always found it neat and charming. Still, there was something about this structure that was not easily defined, something capable of drawing the visitor in for a closer look. Whoever had crafted the wooden beams and carved the intricate furnishings—had done so with great skill. Throughout each and every chamber, the discerning eye could catch some little embellishment, here or there, that seemed to have its own private story to tell.

Diana often beckoned the oaken beams to offer up their secrets but had never yet heard a reply. And so she moved through the cottage, waiting, wondering when the truth might be revealed to her satisfaction.

After serving the meal, that consisted of oatmeal, bacon, toast and orange juice, Diana casually took her seat. Offering a brief nod to Michael, who was waiting patiently, and Daniel, who was contemplating the bacon with hungry eyes, she folded her hands.

"Thank you, Great Creator, for the food we are about to receive," Michael began, "for the beauty of the earth— well, at least the beauty here at Whispering Pines—"

Daniel giggled but Diana promptly checked him with a swift elbow to the ribs.

"And for the love of this family. May we never be far from each other. May we never falter in our belief of You or ourselves. Amen."

Michael kept his head bowed until he heard Daniel and Diana reply in unison, Amen."

The morning ritual completed, Daniel attacked his bacon with great zeal. He had worked up quite an appetite while feather dueling and needed to refuel post haste.

"Tell us about who is coming to see your paintings, father," Diana prompted just as Michael began to munch on a piece of bacon.

"Well," he replied, after hastily swallowing, "this may surprise you, but it is none other than our esteemed Senator.

"Really? You mean Senator Branwell?" Diana asked, eyes wide with astonishment.

"Yes, believe me, I'm just as surprised as you are. It's not often the Senator leaves Washington to visit his hometown of Canfield, Ohio."

There was a wry expression on his face that set the Sherwood children giggling.

"It is rather hard to believe that he might actually waste precious time viewing some frivolous piece of art," Michael grumbled in a voice not unlike the Senator's own.

Diana fell into a heady laughter, amused at her father's impression of the man. She agreed that Branwell seemed a very conceited individual who thought highly of himself and little of everyone else, unless that someone happened to be his precious daughter, Kelly. This incessant doting left the young Miss Branwell very spoiled. In his eyes, she could do no wrong.

"His daughter saw my exhibition at the National Gallery and has been hounding him about a painting she must have—or else."

Michael punctuated this remark by pounding his fists on the table until the room echoed with laughter.

"What else could he do but pay me a visit?

Diana began to fidget, her smile melting into a frown. "Does that mean Kelly is coming with him?"

"Yes, she is. Aren't we lucky?" Michael replied, still unaware of Diana's sudden change of expression.

Diana spoke not a word, a misty glaze filtering across her soft, gray eyes.

At that moment Michael caught the look. "What's wrong, Diana?"

"Kelly makes fun of Diana at school," Daniel volunteered.

"Is that true, Diana?" Michael tenderly asked.

"Yes," she softly said, casually avoiding his gaze.

"That Diana Sherwood is nothing but a daydreamer," Daniel trilled in a high-pitched whine not unlike that which belonged to Kelly. "She'll never amount to anything—just wait and see."

Poor Diana sought to hide the flush that spread across her face behind a veil of hands, but Michael saw it all.

"Why didn't you tell me this before?" he carefully asked.

Diana paused for a moment, uncertain how to reply. It seemed impossible to speak the words that he was not yet ready to hear. Perhaps if she created a diversion...

"Kelly really doesn't matter all that much. She only teases me to get Danny's attention."

"Really?" Michael asked, rather hopefully.

"Last week, I heard Kelly tell a friend that she thinks Danny's cute, even if he is too young for her."

Daniel's face twisted into a sour grimace. "Ugh, she's a witch—and too old for me anyway."

That did it. Daniel's strong display of dislike brought laughter to his father's lips. "Really, Daniel, you must learn to stop encouraging those older women."

The youngest Sherwood made another face, then continued attacking his oatmeal.

Once she had successfully navigated through the rocky moment, Diana decided it was time to remind her father of his promise. "You were going to tell us about Selene."

"Don't you think you've already heard that story too many times?" Michael teased with a knowing grin.

"No, I don't," Diana eagerly replied. Of all the stories Michael Sherwood told his imaginative daughter—this was her favorite. Snuggling back into her wooden chair, she found the most comfortable spot possible and waited for the magic to begin.

"Long ago, when the earth was still young, the Creator dreamed of a haven known as Whispering Pines. It would be one of the most beautiful places on earth—"

"Go ahead, Dad, just put in another plug for Whispering Pines," Daniel chimed mischievously.

"—For it had a very important function to fulfill," he continued, ignoring Daniel's remark. "Here the earthbound angels would dwell. What are earthbound angels you ask?" he paused before answering the unspoken question. "Human beings—like us—that were cut down early in life —well before their time."

A frown darkened Daniel's characteristically sunny brow, "It must be terrible to die before your time."

This was a delicate topic. Michael knew he must tread carefully, else the question of Cynthia might arise.

"Most earthbound angels take delight in performing great acts of kindness. That is their true reason for being. Why, then, should they mourn the loss of mortal existence?"

Diana remained silent, positively transfixed by the tale. Aware that Daniel always asked the appropriate questions, she allowed him to do so without interruption of any kind.

"So, exactly where is this land, Dad?"

Diana smiled to herself. She knew he would ask that one.

"That's hard to say, Danny. All the tales have been handed down by storytellers—like myself. No human has ever seen the land—at least no human I've ever heard about."

"Maybe someone has," Daniel interjected, with growing enthusiasm. "Maybe someone we have never met."

Michael offered a rich, warm smile. "Maybe so, Danny. Maybe so…"

His voice trailed off into nothingness, eyes staring past that which Daniel and Diana could not see.

After a time, he blinked, then resumed in a whisper, "When daylight ebbs to a close and the mists rise from Crescent Lake, the twilight season begins. It is at this precise moment that the gateway opens between our worlds, and the two become one."

Leaning across the table so that he was no more than a few inches away, Michael offered this confession. "I think the doorway lies somewhere between Crescent Lake and Whispering Pines. Sadly enough, I have never found it. Even if I did—it would do me little good. Only earthbound angels can pass through to the other side."

"So everything you are telling us is just a guess, right?" Daniel grinned before receiving an elbow in the ribs from Diana.

"True. It is all a matter of belief."

"Tell us what you believe then, father," Diana suggested, urging him on.

"I believe the secret lies within the lake itself. Do you remember how it was formed?"

"Just go on!" brother and sister cried in perfect harmony.

"One night, as the moon gazed down upon Crescent Lake, she became entranced by her own reflection. It was then she decided to leave behind a permanent reminder for all to see. Kissing the shimmering waters, she created the crescent shape that remains to this day."

Diana anxiously waited for Daniel to resume his former line of questioning, but when his lips remained silent, she cried, "Well, go on—tell us about Selene!"

"As you know, Selene is the Lady of the Twilight Mist —a sort of queen or guardian. The stories tell us that she was once a young woman who regularly visited the lake. Perhaps, like the rest of us, she found it to be the most beautiful place on earth. In any case, the moon saw the girl's lovely reflection and became extremely jealous—so jealous that she sent down a great fog that lasted well into morning. The woman was never seen again."

Aware that Diana was close to tears, Michael kissed the palm of her hand. "Don't worry. Mankind may not have witnessed her disappearance, but the Creator took pity on her plight. Selene possessed special qualities that set her apart from the others. The Creator could see that right away. Soon she was placed above all the earthbound angels. As guardian, she keeps her wards safe from the evil that lurks just beyond Whispering Pines."

As Michael continued with the tale, Diana rose from her seat and walked directly toward one of his paintings. Acknowledged as his personal favorite, it was the only piece that held a permanent spot in the room. The beautiful oil remained delicately perched upon a polished easel just beyond the old, green sofa that sported plush if not slightly tattered cushions. Silently, Diana gazed at the familiar colors, as if viewing them for the first time.

"This is Selene. I'm sure of it," she whispered, pointing at the lovely, red-haired woman in the painting. A soft, blue light filtered across her vision as she slowly turned back to face her father. When she finally spoke, the voice that issued from her lips sounded far deeper than her own. "How did you know what she looks like?"

A flash of surprise registered in Michael's dark eyes. What had prompted her to ask such a question? His thoughts were cut short by a crisp knock at the door.

"What did I tell you. They are always talking about fairies and witches—and that sort of thing," declared an unusually high-pitched voice that could be equated with nothing more pleasant than the scrape of fingernails against a fresh chalkboard.

"Well, Kelly, that's really none of our business," followed a deep, resonant reply. It was easy to hear that this man was used to making speeches for a living.

Michael could not refrain from rolling his eyes. "Let's get this over with," he whispered to the children.

"Good morning, Senator. Kelly. Welcome to Whispering Pines. Please come in." Michael hoped the greeting did not sound as forced as it felt.

Few could dispute that Stuart Branwell was an arresting figure. Tall and almost forcibly lean in build, the Senator took control of a room the moment he crossed its threshold. Upon sizing up the reclusive artist that stood before him, however, Branwell recognized a man who would not easily relinquish power, especially in his own home.

"Thank you, Sherwood. It is lovely out here. Very lovely. How strange that I have never visited this area before. But I can't be everywhere, can I?" he articulated with a politically correct shake of Michael's hand.

"No, I suppose not," came Michael's rather flat reply. "Yes, it is beautiful out here—close as we are to the lake and the forest. It must bring out my artistic abilities. I don't seem to paint well anywhere else."

The Senator's lips twisted into a half-smile, "Oh, come now, Sherwood. There are certainly other places that could inspire the muse in you. If you would take more time to visit D.C., for instance, I know you would agree."

Diana noticed that as Branwell smiled the edges of his mouth curled up ever so slightly. Something about the action was unsettling to say the least. His dark eyes gleamed as they latched onto Michael's paintings, obviously impressed with what they saw.

"Your paintings are quite good," he volunteered after receiving no response. "Unfortunately, I have never had the opportunity to properly view them before. It was Kelly that brought me to you."

Kelly instantly picked up the cue, her delicate, pink lips breaking into a smile. No one could argue with the fact that Kelly Branwell was a beautiful girl. Her soft, golden locks framed a perfectly oval face that boasted skin lightly kissed by the sun.

"Hello, Daniel. Hi Diana—seen any fairies lately?"

"That will do, Kelly," Branwell reprimanded, his cheeks splashed with crimson. He did not approve of the sarcastic remarks his daughter often made in public. Sherwood was a constituent; and as a junior Senator, Branwell could not afford to look bad.

Michael quickly decided that it would be best to offer his daughter some mode of escape from Kelly's deft claws.

"Diana," he began in a casual voice," will you fetch me some water from the lake? I need to soak these new brushes."

"Sure we will," Daniel eagerly volunteered, as he caught hold of a pail in one hand and secured his sister with the other. He had also been searching for a means of exit ever since the Branwell's arrival. "We were just getting ready to go anyway," he called out, eagerly pushing Diana through the open door.

Can I come along?" Kelly asked, rushing after the pair.

"Oh, I wouldn't, if I were you. A city girl—like yourself—might slip and fall into the lake—if she wasn't too careful," Diana volunteered in a sweet voice. She flashed a meaningful smile at Kelly then raced after Daniel before any further words could be exchanged.

"Direct hit, Di!" Daniel crowed with glee. "You really got her that time. Come on, let's get the fishing poles and have some fun! Last one there has to take all those feathers out of the hamper and put them back into the pillows tonight!" he cried, racing toward the storage shed.

"You're on!" came Diana's enthusiastic reply. In a flash she was hot upon his trail, never bothering to look back at the solitary girl who stood watching from the cottage window—never bothering to see the singular look of sorrow painted on her lovely face. The race was on! Diana willed the excitement to carry her forward and forgot everything else.

CHAPTER 4

As the noon sun proudly shone, a certain heaviness dampened the air, offering little doubt that Indian Summer had arrived. Daniel and Diana watched the morning slip away from their stony perch on Crescent Lake's eastern shore. Lookout Point it was called and for good reason. This large rock formation boasted the highest peak along the lake's two mile perimeter, well celebrated for its excellent view. An occasional splash of greenery could be found peppered here and there, demonstrating some hint at life; but all in all, Lookout Point was surprisingly devoid of color. One aged, oak tree, dangerously near the end of its existence, completed the charmed, albeit modest, setting. This year not a single leaf could be discovered amongst its gnarled branches. Only the occasional drip of sap proclaimed its will to survive.

Well satisfied with his generosity, self-proclaimed victor of the morning race, Daniel Sherwood, settled back against the dying tree. He had graciously agreed to a draw and that pleased him. In truth, the thought of Diana stuffing feathers into pillows all night long proved rather unappealing. Soon his attention wavered, fluctuating between the lazy fishing line, that had not entertained a single bite since morning, and the heat rising from the lake. Perhaps it was too hot for even the fish to stir. Checking the sky, he spotted a few dark clouds on the horizon. This was a good sign. Whispering Pines had been dry for almost a month. Any hint of rain was a reason to celebrate. He was about to express this hope, when Diana spoke instead.

"Saturdays are so wonderful. I wish they could last forever. No one to interfere with dreams or imagination…"

This blissful reverie was rudely interrupted by a deep throated croak from the resident bullfrog.

"No one except Mr. Bigmouth over there," quipped Daniel.

"Danny, you know what I mean," she sighed, dreamily propping herself up on one elbow. "Everything at school is so—organized. There is never any time for adventure or excitement. Here, you can imagine anything you wish."

"Oh, come on, Di. Did you really think you'd find adventure at school?" laughed Daniel, forcing himself to stand with the aid of a trusty fishing pole. It was time to reel in the unresponsive line.

"You love school, Di. You're at the top of the class. That's why Kelly is so mean. She wants to be best in everything."

"Well, she doesn't have to worry about beating me in math or science. Those are her areas to shine."

"Yeah, but think about it. You are first in everything else," he proclaimed, while struggling to release the half-drowned worm from the end of his fishing hook. "You also tell stories better than anybody I know—except Dad. Everybody loves to hear your stories. That has to count for something."

"Yeah, right. That's why they always laugh at me.

"I'll tell you a secret," he said, pausing briefly to bury the mangled corpse with a clump of parched soil. "Even when they laugh, they want to hear more."

Diana offered no response other than a skeptical raise of her eyebrow.

"I'm sure Kelly is the ring leader. They only laugh because of her."

"Do you really think so?" asked a still unconvinced Diana.

"Sure, I do. There is another reason," he suggested, waiting until he had her full attention.

"Well, go on."

"It's simple really. You're too pretty—that's all."

Diana was more than a little surprised to hear such a compliment escape her brother's lips. She had never thought of herself as being pretty, not even a little.

"Come off it," she exclaimed. "I'm just a red-haired shrimp with freckles."

"True," chuckled Daniel, as his eyes sparkled with mischief, "but you are bewitching as a fairy, my lady." He could do little but punctuate the wry compliment with a mock bow.

Diana threw a pinecone at him in retaliation. "Stop making fun of me!" she cried.

"No, I'm serious," Daniel tried to explain as he sought cover behind a rocky ledge. "Ask David—ask anybody! They'll tell you!"

Diana found herself surprised once again. "Do you mean David Moss?" she asked. "I thought he liked Kelly."

"That's just because she's a big Senator's daughter. You know, that's supposed to mean her family's important. Everyone wants to be on her good side, even David." Daniel saw that his commentary had done little but frustrate Diana even further. Perhaps if he made light of the situation, she might forget the whole thing.

"Let's think about something else," he quickly suggested, popping up from behind his stony barricade.

"Fine," Diana answered, absent-mindedly. Her thoughts had already begun to wander down a new path.

"Danny, do you think father ever gets lonely out here?"

Whatever Daniel had expected to come out of his sister's mouth, it was certainly not that. He frowned for a moment, then said, "I guess he does when we're at school, but he always has his painting to keep him busy."

"I mean since mother died."

"Oh," Daniel answered thoughtfully. "She died a long time ago. I can hardly remember her."

"You were only one year old then—but I was three. Sometimes at night, when I dream—I can almost see her face, but then—just as the mists clear—she slips away…"

Daniel could not help but notice the strange shadow that passed over Diana's features. He had always known that she was different from most people, but each time one of those odd moods occurred, it scared him.

"That was a long time ago. You were young too…"

A moment of understanding passed between brother and sister. Afterward, they remained silent for what seemed to be a very long time. Neither could break free of the spell that held them in the shadowy past.

Finally, Diana spoke, "Don't you think it's strange that father keeps no pictures of her anywhere?"

"No," replied Daniel, very softly.

"He's an artist, Danny. I'm sure he must have painted her at least once. She was his wife, and he loved her. Why would he hide something so important?"

"Maybe seeing her painting every day would hurt too much." Daniel bit down hard on his lip to keep it from trembling. Why were they discussing this topic on such a beautiful day?

Diana tossed her fishing pole and began burrowing into the parched earth with the heels of her tennis shoes. Why not just tell him what she believed to be true? Why was it always so hard for others to understand?

"Danny, don't even think of laughing at this," she offered in fair warning. "Sometimes when I dream of Selene—I feel certain she was our mother."

Daniel's expression twisted into a mask of doubt. Di was acting really weird. It was probably that dream working on her mind. Well, time to pull her out of it, he thought to himself.

"It's all in your head, Morgan le Fay," came the merciless taunt. Then, after realizing the tactic did little good, he added, "You just want to remember mom so much, that you imagine her, as your favorite fairy-tale character—"

"She's not a fairy-tale!" Diana cried. "You know that! Don't tell me after all this time you still refuse to believe?"

"I do believe. Really."

Diana's mouth twitched, ever so slightly. She wanted to smile but could not yet bring herself to do it.

"Swear on your sword, Sir Laugh-a-lot," she commanded, handing him the stray fishing pole for that express purpose. After all, there were no real swords to be found at Crescent Lake that day.

Daniel's expression broke into a grin. He had won a small victory, if only for the moment. Diana was her old self again. Kneeling with a dramatic flair, Daniel placed his hand upon the sacred fishing pole and said, "Princess Morgan, I swear by the sword Excalibur."

"You can't swear by Excalibur—that's Arthur's sword!"

"Don't you see?" he said, thrusting the fishing pole before her eyes, "I borrowed it for this special occasion."

"Very well, go on."

Daniel cleared his throat, then spoke with as much authority as his eleven-year old voice would allow, "I swear by the sword Excalibur that the Lady Selene is as real as you or I."

Into this magical theater of make believe strolled the ever-practical Kelly Branwell. She took one look at the scene unfolding before her eyes and snorted, "Oh, brother, now she has you believing that nonsense too."

Kelly's silent entrance caught Daniel somewhat off-guard. After making a valiant, if not awkward attempt to rise, his shoelaces met with the fishing line, and he landed with a resounding "thud" upon the ground. "What are you doing here?" he asked, amidst a peal of laughter.

"I was just wondering why it would take two such— intelligent people so long to get some stupid water," she said sarcastically. "You just wanted to get away from me. Admit it."

"You're absolutely right," chirped Diana, a little too sweetly. If Kelly wanted a fight, she would not deny her.

"I know why Diana hates me—" Kelly retorted. "She's afraid of me!"

"I am not!"

Feeling rather certain of success, Kelly shifted focus to her next victim. "But you, Daniel, I thought at least we could be friends," she sighed, allowing her perfect lips to quiver ever so slightly.

Daniel was not affected by this tactic. "Maybe when you stop acting like a witch, we will."

Kelly's cheek turned crimson and began to twitch. The Sherwoods had detected weakness in her and that was unforgivable. It was then the tears came. She tried to blink them back but to no avail. A wave of anger rushed through her veins. How could they be so cruel—staring at her in that way?

"You're as bad as she is, Daniel Sherwood!" Kelly cried. "I'll tell everyone what I saw here today—the crazy Sherwoods acting out fairy-tales!"

Kelly knew she had to escape before they began to laugh at her. How could she have blundered so terribly in such a short time? She had just set off toward the cottage when a strong arm arrested her in mid-flight.

"I've been looking for you everywhere," Senator Branwell exclaimed with concern.

Diana questioned where the Senator might have come from, for his path lay in a direction opposite the cottage. This made her pause. Could he really have been standing near the old, oak tree? If so, how much of their conversation had he actually heard?

Placing a protective arm around his daughter's shoulders, Branwell sought to quiet her trembling. "It's time to return home, Kelly."

"I see no reason to stay any longer," she responded with an air of outward calm.

Branwell glanced at his daughter, then turned his gaze on the Sherwoods. At that moment everything became deathly still. A soft breeze blew a dark lock of hair across his eyes, seemingly obstructing them from view.

Diana noticed that he was staring at her from behind those dancing locks. "It's a lovely day for a swim, isn't it?" he asked, slowly turning toward the shimmering waters.

The words were harmless enough, but there was something behind Branwell's tone that made Diana flinch. He was watching her again, dissecting every move, or perhaps, every thought. And then there was that smile.

"We don't go swimming here anymore," Daniel volunteered. "It's way too deep."

"Of course," Branwell replied; "Just as you told Kelly, someone might accidentally drown…"

"I never said anything about drowning—"

"Of course not," Branwell said, with an easy air, "but you were thinking that, weren't you?"

Diana shivered despite herself, then met the Senator's dark eyes once more. She was amazed to find that they appeared perfectly normal, almost sparkling in a friendly manner.

"Well, it doesn't matter, since no one swims here anymore," Branwell offered with a smile. He then patted Kelly on the shoulder and said his good-byes to the Sherwoods.

Brother and sister watched the Branwells' departure until they had safely disappeared behind the cottage. Ever punctual in his commentary, Daniel said, "Don't worry, Di. Looks like insanity runs in the family."

"I guess so," Diana replied half-heartedly. "Danny, I'm a little tired. Would you bring the poles back when you have finished? I'm going home."

Daniel stooped to pick up the stray lines, then thought better of it. He was about to protest Diana's decision to abandon him, when he discovered she had already gone.

CHAPTER 5

Michael sat poised on an old wooden bench, liberally marked with scratches, yet still dear for the years of faithful use it had supplied. His right hand appeared frozen, unable to begin the next stroke. It was not unusual for Michael to lose command of his work when the memories spoke, but today they would have to wait. Kelly Branwell's cruel visit still weighed heavily upon his mind.

Had he made matters worse by sending Diana away? What would Cynthia have done? A sigh escaped Michael's lips. He would never know the answer to that question. Cynthia was gone…

The age-old dialogue played upon his mind, leaving him caught between reality and dream-spell.

"Diana is different from other teen-agers," the voice began.

"Yes, I have always known that. She seems so close to understanding the mysteries of life, perhaps even more so than most adults."

Michael glanced around to make certain he was still alone. At times the inner voices sounded so real. The cabin offered a creak or two, but there was no further evidence of invasion, leaving him free to continue.

"This inner knowing makes Diana quiet and withdrawn; characteristics that are often misinterpreted as snobbery. Nothing could be farther from the truth. Diana is uniquely authentic. Is that really so difficult to understand?"

Michael stopped short of answering that question. No one had ever understood him, except for Cynthia and she was gone.

Vaguely aware that the screen door had opened, Michael willed his eyes to regain focus. Diana stood before him, a somewhat amused expression painted across her features.

"Well, father, you're not going to get much work done if you stand there daydreaming all afternoon."

Michael's embarrassed smile served as the perfect reply. Scanning the canvas of her face, he thought, "Everyday she becomes more like her mother."

"How did your meeting with Senator Branwell go?"

"I'm afraid our Senator is somewhat lacking in artistic taste," Michael chuckled good- naturedly. "He did seem interested in one painting though, which shows he has some promise. It was the one you call Selene."

Diana's heart began to race. He couldn't possibly sell Selene to the Branwells! After taking a deep breath, she said, "Of course, he did. Selene is your most beautiful piece. You're not going to sell it to him, are you?"

"I couldn't," Michael whispered. He was truly amazed she had even asked the question.

There was a slight trembling of the lips as she offered fair reply. "I know."

Michael felt her soft arms twine about his neck. "I am sorry Kelly makes fun of you because of this," he began, indicating Selene's picture. "I have often wondered if it was wise to fill your head with stories about the twilight mist. You might be happier today if I had not."

Diana sprang to her feet. "How can you say that?" she cried in disbelief.

A sigh escaped from the very depth of his being. "Be calm," he soothed, grasping hold of her delicate hand. "There is something I want to tell you. Why don't you sit down."

Diana reluctantly flopped onto the old, green sofa and waited for him to continue.

"I want you to listen carefully to everything I say—without becoming upset, all right?"

A brief nod was the only answer Michael received. It was obvious she awaited his announcement with a sense of dread. This puzzled him.

"Remember, I love you and that I'm proud of you. Nothing will ever change that…"

Michael paused. She looked so much like Cynthia, but he could not think about that.

"You, Diana, are such a magical child—now don't make faces—you're still a child to me. The problem is—you rely so much on make believe that you hardly seem at home in the real world."

No matter how hard she tried, Diana could not help but fidget in her seat. When had her father changed his ideals? He was the one who had taught her to appreciate the beauties of imagination and the mysteries of the unknown! Why the sudden transformation?

Aware that her father was still speaking, Diana realized that she had missed a great deal of what he had to say.

"I know this is my fault—telling you stories about spirits and other worlds only makes you want to slip farther away from everything that's real. Let's face it. Reality can be pretty boring sometimes."

Diana tried to chuckle, but instead, a moan escaped her lips.

"You are not like Kelly and the others that gossip all day at school and worry about who is wearing the most expensive outfit. You, Diana, are a beam of light shimmering through the darkness. Nothing can contain your spirit. You are so like your mother."

There was a sudden brightening of her expression. Michael had finally stumbled upon the one topic she did wish to discuss. "Tell me about her," she interjected before he could breathe another word.

37

"What would you like to know?" he asked, shifting his weight a little uncomfortably from leg to leg.

"Well, what did she look like?"

"She was very—" Michael fell silent, as a touch of red darkened his complexion. "I know we don't talk about her very often, but she was very much like you."

'Really?" Diana gasped, pleasantly surprised. "Why don't you keep any pictures of her around?"

"What makes you so certain that I don't?"

Diana noticed that Michael no longer met her steady gaze and that his movements had become almost agitated. It was obvious that he felt rather uncomfortable discussing the subject, but she had come too far to let it pass.

"I have never seen one," she continued, after a moment of silence.

An audible sigh of relief escaped Michael's lips. "Her beauty could not be captured on canvas," he offered in reply.

"But, you just said—!"

"I merely hinted that I may have painted her at one time."

This statement was issued with such finality that Michael felt certain his daughter would not press the issue any further.

"Then why not let me see," came the demand that all but crushed his previous hope.

"You must trust me. I know what's best for you."

"Father, I don't understand," Diana whispered, painfully aware that he would say no more on the subject.

"One day you will."

She had heard that response many times before. Sensing the hopelessness of the situation, Diana opted for a new course of action: one she felt certain could not fail.

"Do you miss her?"

"You know I do," he gently answered, his dark eyes pooling with tears.

"You will never marry again."

Diana made this statement with firm resolve. Indeed, she knew better than to ask such a foolish question. On this point, she had been able to read his heart.

"No. Does that upset you?"

Diana shook her head. "I know she meant everything to you—even more than your art."

Michael could not endure the exchange any longer, so he altered position and rose to his feet. Diana had scratched the one chink in his armor. How did she always manage to read his mind? Did she have any idea how much he was suffering at that moment? He wanted to answer, but fear held him in check. What would Cynthia have wished? The answer was quite simple: tell the truth no matter how much it hurt.

"Your mother was the one who encouraged me to paint," he finally offered. "She believed in my talent when no one else would."

"And now you repay her by using these paintings to help you forget the past—"

"Oh no," Michael said in earnest. "It is through my art that I remember and honor your mother. Every piece is dedicated to her; every stroke has her influence upon it. So, when I told you that at one time I painted her—that wasn't exactly true. You can see her in every picture I create—for she is a part of everything I do."

Diana gazed at the painting before her with a new sense of understanding. She eagerly explored the lovely colors, the perfect forms and the magical way in which they all combined to make a perfect whole. It was not hard to imagine how her mother had played so large a role in helping perfect his art. Gently, almost involuntarily, her fingers touched the frame that housed her favorite canvas.

"Do you see her, Diana? Michael softly whispered.

"Yes," she answered in a tear-choked voice.

Michael gently turned her until they stood face to face. "You have your mother's spirit. She is not dead, as long as you live."

Each soul waxed silent, trapped within their own private web of emotion.

When Diana spoke, it was to ask another question. "How did she die?"

Michael took a deep breath and pondered his response. Should he tell her? There was only one other person still alive that he could ask, and Michael had not seen him in a very long time.

"Forgive me, that's better left unsaid."

"But, I must know—"

"One day you will."

The screen door slammed back against its rusty hinges, heralding the entrance of the youngest Sherwood.

"Where have you been?" asked Michael, more than a little relieved by his wayward son's arrival.

"David Moss and his dad were just here," Daniel offered, with a wide grin.

"Reverend Moss was here? That's strange. I was just thinking about him. This must be our day for visitors."

"Yeah, listen to this—he wants to bring the church picnic to Crescent Lake tomorrow—if you say it's okay. I said you'd give him a call. Almost everyone from school is invited."

Upon seeing Diana's skeptical expression, he added, "Think of it, Di. We could have such fun tormenting Kelly Branwell!"

Daniel's suggestion brought forth a round of chuckles from the entire clan, until Michael remembered that he was supposed to be setting a good example for his children.

"Daniel, you wouldn't," he scolded in a none too convincing manner.

"Oh, yes, I would," rang the merry reply. "Now that you've met her, can you blame me?"

"No," Michael confessed, as he playfully boxed Daniel about the ears. "You realize, of course, that there will have to be several chaperones. I, for one, do not intend to hold down the entire castle by myself."

"Oh, yeah, I forgot to tell you. Reverend Moss will help you out."

"Will he now?" Michael asked with raised eyebrows. "Well, I guess you can count me in."

"You'll come too, won't you, Di?"

"I don't know," she replied, averting her eyes to an unattractive spot on the hard wood floor. Methodically, she tried to rub it away with the heel of her foot.

"Oh, come on," Daniel cried, as he grabbed her by the arm. "Think of it as an adventure. Without us, they'll get lost!"

"An adventure," whispered Diana, who was already warming to the idea.

"Yes, let's pretend we're Lancelot and Morgan frolicking amongst the unbelievers. You can cast a spell or two on them."

"Danny, what am I going to do with you?" she asked, reaching to pull at a stray lock of his disheveled hair.

"Ouch!" Daniel protested in momentary pain. "That means you'll come, right?"

"I think you should," Michael interjected.

"All right," Diana sighed, pretending to be much put upon, though secretly delighted by the prospect.

"David will be glad to see you," Daniel teased.

"David?" Michael questioned.

"David Moss. He likes Diana. I think she's the reason he wanted to have the picnic here!" Daniel did his best to dodge the string of blows that were being inflicted upon him by his embarrassed sister.

"Really, Diana?"

This bit of news greatly pleased Michael. It gave him hope for the future: Diana's future. Perhaps she was not so different from other teenagers after all.

"You never told me about this."

"Because it isn't true!" she cried, playfully chasing Daniel around the table.

"Careful, careful," Michael warned, as Daniel almost toppled into a spare canvas.

"You wouldn't be chasing me around the room if it weren't true!" Daniel quipped, before he ran out the door.

Diana was soon in hot pursuit. "You want an adventure, Daniel Sherwood? I'll show you an adventure!"

The screen door slammed shut behind her, locking Michael within once more. How he longed to jump up and race after them—to realize the childhood he had never known, but that was impossible. They were young and belonged to the wild. His place was there in the cottage, surrounded by his work and his memories.

"This is what she needs—to be with other children," he thought to himself. "I have been holding her back within my private world for far too long. Tomorrow, I will speak with Moss and hear what he has to say." Slowly, Michael walked back to the picture his daughter so lovingly called Selene and placed his work bench in front of it. Resting one knee on its withered exterior, he allowed himself to gaze into the depths of the painting.

"It was right for us to live like this, but Diana—Diana is too young. She must experience the real world first, then decide. Daniel is different. It is hard not to like him. In that way, he takes after you. You would be proud—proud of them both. I think you would approve."

CHAPTER 6

Although the threat of rain lingered over Crescent Lake that late October day, the picnic proved a memorable experience. Hot and muggy it was—without a hint of breeze to refresh the waning crowd. Some fifteen students were in attendance, delighted with the prospect of extending summer's calendar one weekend longer. Once evening arrived, however, the group began to thin out until only eight remained: a fact hardly due to the impending storm. Indeed, most students desired nothing better than to brave any tempest that might rock Crescent Lake. It was Kelly Branwell's cutting remarks that had sent them packing.

Stationed near the picnic baskets, Kelly and her best friend Jenny offered a running commentary on everyone and everything. It should be understood that Kelly was the ringleader in this exercise and that the thoughtless Jenny merely echoed her words. Soon seven people, including Daniel and Diana, decided it was much easier to leave rather than suffer her abusive tongue.

Few stopped to question the Sherwood's whereabouts. Certainly, Kelly and Jenny had more important things on their minds. David's radio had suddenly lost power, leaving the picnic without music—a fate worse than death, or so expressed the elegant Miss Branwell.

Michael quickly set off in search of batteries with Reverend Moss in tow. They had assured the other chaperone, Dr. Schilling, that the entire venture would only take a few minutes. After all, the cottage was within viewing distance. Hence, the poor Doctor was left to watch the pack out by the lake alone—a task not for the weary at heart.

"Hurry back, Michael," she whispered, thrusting both hands into her pockets.

Gazing out at the lake, she saw a great darkness coming, then rapidly blinked until twilight's purple hues came back into view. Surely, her eyes were playing a trick of some kind. It was still early evening—not some distant time of night. A shiver raced up her spine. The sooner they all left Crescent Lake—the better.

Near the water's edge stood brotherly twins with the Sherwood's fishing poles firmly clutched in hand. Each waved at Dr. Schilling, then commenced scavenging for worms. Eric and Marty were Daniel's best friends. One look at their roguish faces whispered that they too shared a great enthusiasm for adventure. Since the lazy fish suffered from the same lack of motivation as they exhibited on the previous day, Eric and Marty wisely turned their attention toward catching salamanders instead.

Every now and then, they turned their sights on the meadow and chuckled with amusement. The four remaining students were finding it rather difficult to dance without musical accompaniment of any kind. Eric and Marty held their tongues, thinking themselves lucky not to be a part of such silliness.

David Moss had grabbed Sandy Schilling by the hand and began to twirl her around the stiff, dry meadow. This shy, young woman, who had grown up in the shadow of her mother, the aforementioned pediatrician, rarely attended church functions. In fact, it was not often that she even allowed herself to have fun. After much in the way of prodding from her mother, Sandy had finally agreed to attend the picnic. At long last, she was glad about the decision. David was so funny, as he shuffled along, that she could not help but smile and follow his rambling steps.

The other dancers were a genuine couple, or so Kelly called them. Shirley and Craig had been dating for more than a few weeks. Craig was the star of the school track team, while Shirley ranked as a cheerleader on the varsity squad, along with Kelly and Jenny. Following David's awkward yet noble lead, they danced with as much grace as the pitted ground would allow.

It should come as no surprise that Kelly felt obligated to provide a running commentary on the proceedings.

"That was brilliant, David," she began in an irritated voice, "—forgetting to bring extra batteries. Do you realize how stupid you look—dancing without any music?"

"Come off it, Kelly. We're having fun, even if you're not," Sandy said without considering the possible consequences.

After making certain that Dr. Schilling was out of earshot, Kelly retorted, "Who asked you, Sandy?" Kelly leaned over to Jenny and remarked just loud enough for everyone to hear, "The mouse must think she is important or something—now that she's dancing with David."

Sandy's head drooped as a flash of crimson painted her cheek.

"Ignore her, Sandy," David said. "You k-n-n-now she's all talk. I'm glad you're having fun."

David Moss possessed a slight stutter, that often appeared when he least desired it. Most people overlooked this difficulty because David was so funny. They didn't see the pain and frustration stored up inside of him, waiting to surface at moments like this.

"Thanks," Sandy timidly replied.

David smiled, silently hoping that Mr. Sherwood would beat a hasty return before Kelly's scathing remarks caused any further damage.

Michael paused just short of opening the cabin door. This was the moment he had been waiting for all day long. Moss followed close behind him. Perhaps now he would find the answers to those questions that plagued his mind.

Reverend Moss followed Michael to the cottage in silence, stopping just short of the threshold. How many years had passed since their last meeting? Had he been wrong in waiting for Michael to come to him? Something told him that he was. Why else had he convinced Daniel to ask about holding the picnic at Crescent Lake? Gazing at his old friend from behind a pair of sad eyes, Moss decided that he should be the first to break the silence.

"It's been a long time since I've paid you a visit, Michael. The place hasn't changed a bit. Why, the cottage looks almost exactly the way she left it."

Michael felt his throat tighten. He didn't want to talk about her! Why did Moss have to broach the subject at all? More importantly, why did Michael feel as if he were about to explode? It was imperative that he think of Diana. This might be his only chance to speak with Moss. He could not allow another ten years to slip away.

"Why did you never come back to us, Michael—to your church? We wanted to be there for you and the children, but you shut us out at every turn. It couldn't have been easy raising them alone."

"You know why I didn't come back, Moss. How could I allow my children to attend a church where the minister accused their mother of running off with another man? How would that make them feel? It's bad enough the Creator took her from us—"

"Michael, I did not come here to fight with you—"

"Then what did you come here for?!"

Reverend Moss took a deep breath. He had anticipated this. Michael Sherwood was a man who held onto pain. He would have to tread carefully. "I came to have a picnic and to see my old friend," he finally replied.

Michael turned away, still struggling against the anger that threatened to consume his being.

The Reverend watched him carefully from behind a pair of bristling brows. Moss was a short man, who tended towards stockiness, but that seemed unimportant, for his eyes sparkled with a sense of compassion; and his gentle, moon-shaped face exuded love. He was no more than forty years of age, but heredity had added an extra ten years to his countenance. Intuition told him it was time to change the subject.

"Let me see your paintings," he simply said.

Michael opened the door and waited for the Reverend to enter. Moss was a patient man. Few others would have tolerated his outburst with such good grace.

After looking from painting to painting, while Michael pretended to search for batteries, Moss said, "I don't know how—but you have managed to improve upon your gift. Your paintings really speak to people. I understand they're everywhere—from our illustrious courthouse to the National Gallery. Still, I find this portrait of Cynthia has the most to say. You've captured her perfectly. She was always at home in nature surrounded by lakes and trees. Your daughter reminds me of her."

Michael flinched. Moss had made it easy for him. "That's something I'd like to speak with you about."

"Yes, Michael?" asked the Reverend, who instantly assumed a guarded position.

"Should I tell her the truth about that night?"

After offering much in the way of verbal abuse, Kelly had finally pushed the easy going David Moss a little too far. David was not the kind of person to strike back with words, even when wounded to the core. Instead, he opted to work on her mind in a far more subtle fashion. He would steal her precious audience away. Perhaps then she might actually leave. Yet, how was such an undertaking to be accomplished? How could he upstage the indomitable Kelly once and for all?

Suddenly and without prior contemplation, he began to whirl Sandy around and around, while humming a blatantly dramatic tune. The attitude was theatrical to say the least, even from the young Miss Schilling's perspective, and she began to giggle.

Kelly watched as Craig and Shirley followed suit. "Look, Jenny," she cried, "It's like watching Sesame Street! There's Big Bird dancing with the Cookie monster! Oh— wait! Did you hear that? It's ring around the rosy!"

Soon Jenny joined in the attack, singing in her throaty voice, "Ring around the rosie; David's such a posy; ashes, ashes, we all st-t-tutter now!" The two snobs promptly collapsed on their blanket, laughing until their sides ached with pain.

David valiantly ignored the insult.

"What's wrong with them?" Craig asked Shirley. He had never really met Kelly before and was unimpressed with what he saw.

"She's just mad because Daniel hasn't paid her any attention today," Shirley whispered in his ear. "She has this plan about making him fall for her—or something."

"Why would she do that? He's just a kid. He's what— twelve—?"

"Who knows why," Shirley interjected. "I think it has something to do with getting back at Diana."

Kelly saw the couple glance her way, then whisper amongst themselves. Forgetting that she had been using the same tactic all day, Kelly felt the hot flow of anger simmer around her temples.

"What are you two gabbing about?" she literally shrieked across the meadow.

"That's none of your business, "Shirley replied with a toss of her dark curls.

"Watch it, airhead. Toss that head too many times and there won't be anything left!"

"You watch it, Kelly," Craig warned, "I don't care who you are. Mind your own business." After allowing his temper to cool, he added on a lighter note, "Hey, what's wrong with you anyway? Does this have anything to do with the fact that Daniel doesn't know you exist?"

Kelly's face grew red. "No, it does not!" she cried. "It's just that this picnic is sooo boring. I don't know why I even bothered to come all the way out here to no man's land. None of the really cool people showed."

"Well, I'm still glad I showed up," Sandy whispered to David, as she gently squeezed his hand.

"Thanks, Sandy," David gallantly replied. "Let's waltz!"

"Waltz?" laughed Kelly. "Get real, David."

"I'd love to," Sandy quickly replied.

A series of waltz steps were awkwardly managed by the valiant duo, as each sought to inflict their own private tempo upon the other. After this period of trial and error, they eventually settled into a cautious, if not counted pace. David had little idea that his face clearly betrayed the inner calculations of 1,2,3, and 1,2,3. Everyone in the group seemed highly amused, that is everyone but Kelly. Even Jenny offered the hint of a smile, and the tension eased, ever so slightly.

From somewhere beyond the glen, a voice rose on the evening air, a voice almost haunting in its purity. Everyone fell silent as they listened to the magical sound that mingled with the distant strains of a recorder.

At that moment, Diana appeared through the eastern fringe of pines, with the ever faithful Daniel at her side. It had been the combination of her voice and his recorder that ultimately drew the quarreling students into a lull.

"Don't stop just because of us!" Daniel cried in delight. "You wanted music, didn't you? Well, now you've got it!"

The students slowly formed a circle around the Sherwoods without offering insult or comment of any kind. As they began to dance, each adopted the style and flavor of

Diana's song. No one seemed concerned with the fact that it looked as if they belonged to some distant place and time.

Aware that this unexpected change bought her an element of time, Dr. Schilling slipped off toward the cottage, hoping to bring Michael and the Reverend back before things once again turned sour.

Diana pressed on, allowing the rush of words to flow through her body as the song continued. Something far beyond her own self was in control at that moment. She was merely a vessel—a channel speaking of forgotten mysteries to those who would hear.

"The moon shines;
The mists climb;
Twilight fills the air.
The waters weep;
While children sleep;
Many questions they do share.
The pines know;
The stars glow;
Through darkness gleams despair.
Daylight brings;
Eternal wings;
That they alone can share."

As the song drew to a close, Diana became aware that all eyes were upon her. Most appeared puzzled, almost distant in their gaze, haunted by some long forgotten knowledge. Even the ever practical Kelly stood entranced.

It was David's voice that finally broke the spell. "That was great, Diana. Where did you learn to sing like that? Dad sure could use you in his choir."

Daniel quickly responded with a quip. "Didn't you know Di is the fairy queen of Whispering Pines?"

That did it. Everyone awoke with a start, breaking the spell as they began to twitter. Although the laughter appeared to be good-natured, Diana feared the ill-timed remark would set Kelly off again.

"Danny—" she warned, through a set of tightly, clenched teeth.

"It's her way of casting a spell on you," he continued teasing, oblivious to his sister's concerns.

Diana's temper got the better of her, and soon she was chasing Daniel along the lakeshore.

"See what happens when Di gets mad? She's not a red-head for nothing!" he crowed with wild glee.

There was no stopping Daniel when the mischief took hold. It never once entered his mind that he might actually be embarrassing Diana.

The poor girl's face turned crimson as she continued the chase, still oblivious to the fact that it was she and her wayward brother who had brought the picnic back to life. Everyone was enjoying the friendly battle; that is everyone but Kelly.

"Oh, when will you just grow up?" the Senator's daughter cried, struggling to draw attention back to herself.

"Never, if I have to be like you," came Diana's firm reply.

"Listen to her," Kelly sneered to Jenny, "Little Miss Make-Believe!" Both girls laughed cruelly at the jest.

"L-L-Leave her alone, Kelly!" David exclaimed, in the hope of rescuing Diana from any further embarrassment.

"W-W-What are you going to do about it, D-D-David?" challenged Kelly in a thoughtless tone.

"Someone ought to teach Kelly a lesson," Marty suggested with a grin.

"And we know just the guy to do it," added Eric, offering Daniel a handful of snails. The twins quickly scaled Lookout Point to insure the best seats for what undoubtedly would prove the highlight of the day.

"Hey, Kelly," Daniel said in an angelic voice; "I have something for you."

Kelly's eyes registered surprise of a most pleasant kind. "You do?" she asked in an uncharacteristically sweet voice.

"Yes," replied Daniel, never showing a trace of his true intent, "close your eyes and hold out your hands."

"All right," cooed Kelly. Perhaps her plan was finally working. If Daniel developed a crush on her—Diana would totally lose it. She took a moment to adjust the golden scarf, that elegantly held her pony-tale in place, then offered two perfectly manicured hands.

One look at Daniel's face told Diana he was up to no good. Regardless of her dislike for Kelly, she thought it best to offer warning of some kind.

"Kelly, I don't think you should—"

"This is my surprise, Diana," came Kelly's firm rebuff.

"It certainly is," said Daniel, basking in the glow of almost certain success.

Diana was about to intercede one, last time, when she stopped short. Something inside told her to let it happen, and so she did.

There was a moment of uncertainly as all eyes turned toward Daniel in anticipation of what the renowned prankster might do.

Rising to the challenge, Daniel gently poured the slimy snails into Kelly's marble smooth hands and crowed with glee, "Just what you've always wanted, Kelly! Just what you deserve!"

Kelly remained deathly still for a moment, unable to fully comprehend what had just happened. Everyone was pointing at her, laughing in an almost grotesque fashion. Slowly, the blood began to drain from her face. She could feel the snails oozing slime on her hands.

"How could you, Daniel Sherwood?" she sobbed bitterly, pausing only to fling the snails at his face.

Luckily, Daniel ducked just in time to avoid impact. He watched as the poor snails flew overhead, before landing in a heap upon the ground.

The laughter only increased in its intensity as Kelly tore the golden scarf from her hair, vigorously rubbing each soiled hand against its silken threads. They were all staring at her; waiting for her to act. There was something monstrous about each ruddy face as it distorted with glee. Escape was the only option, so Kelly began to run. The scarf, no longer necessary or important, fell to the ground unheeded. Soon Eric and Marty appeared hot on her heals with a fresh batch of slimy friends.

"Well, I guess she finally got hers," Shirley declared with a proud toss of her dark locks. Craig could not help but agree.

"Danny," reprimanded Diana, "You shouldn't have done that. She'll tell her father and then—"

"I don't care, Di. Whatever happens—it was worth it."

Diana could not help but notice that her brother was still grinning from ear to ear.

"That was your best one yet, Dan! She ran off like a shot into the woods!" Eric whooped, as he and Marty jogged back into the meadow, free from their surplus supply of snails.

Jenny had not spoken a single word throughout the entire ordeal. She simply stared at the others in disbelief. It was not until the echoing sound of thunder registered in her brain that she seemed to snap back into reality.

Casting a wary glance overhead, she cried, "What happened to Kelly? Where is she now?"

"We lost her just beyond the edge of the forest. There's lots of places to hide," crooned Eric, still pleased with himself for thinking up the whole scheme.

"You mean you left her out there alone? She doesn't know her way around here!"

"Jenny's right," said Diana, observing the shift in weather. How could the storm have crept up so quickly without her noticing it? "Kelly doesn't know these woods." There was no response. Apparently no one seemed concerned about Kelly's predicament.

"Look, its getting late and a storm's coming in! If she dies out there, Daniel Sherwood, it's your fault!"

Daniel sighed. Jenny was right. This time he had gone too far. "Don't worry, Jen," he said, "Whispering Pines is safe."

"But all the stories Diana tells about those spirits out there—what if they're true?"

Diana secretly smiled to herself. Perhaps they did believe. The wind lifted her hair until it danced about her shoulders. It wouldn't hurt to explain the truth to them now.

"Jenny, the angels of the twilight mist only use their powers for good. If Kelly meets any kind of danger, they'll watch over her."

Jenny stared back at her unconvinced. Without voicing another word, she continued to gaze at the darkening sky. There was nothing left to do but begin a search and hope that Kelly wanted to be found.

"Eric, Marty, could you climb those trees and see if there is any sign of her?" asked a hopeful Diana.

The nimble duo quickly swung up between two adjoining oaks. Together, they scanned the darkened forest for any sign of the Senator's daughter but were obliged to return in defeat. "Not a sign of her anywhere, Di! We could go on the trails!" Marty suggested as his feet touched the ground.

"You don't know the forest like we do," Diana said with a sigh. "Danny and I will find her."

"We'll wait here until you get back," David called out as brother and sister headed for the woods.

"No, David," Diana cried over her shoulder, "find my Dad! Tell him what's happened, and make sure everyone gets back to the cottage until their parents arrive!"

"—But I want to help!"

"Please, David, it's our fault—Danny's and mine—that she's lost. Help us by getting everyone inside."

"All right," David reluctantly replied. "Come on, let's find my dad."

Daniel and Diana pressed on into the forest as fast as their tired feet could manage.

"I have a funny feeling about this, Di," muttered Daniel under his breath. "I think we should turn around and go back."

"Daniel Sherwood—I'm surprised at you! You wanted an adventure—well, here it is!"

"This isn't exactly what I had in mind."

"But that's what makes an adventure exciting. You never know how it will turn out—or what lies ahead. Come on!" Diana cried, as she ran deep into the forest.

Daniel paused a moment before offering pursuit. A sharp chill was slowly weaving its way up the length of his spine. After shaking off the uncomfortable sensation, he set off into the darkness, hoping it was merely a trick of his imagination.

CHAPTER 7

Within the fragile quarter of an hour, a storm of unexpected fury swept through Whispering Pines. This was no ordinary rain shower. Even the squirrels, nestled in their customary hollows, could see that at a glance. Silently, they watched the heavens blacken overhead as the tempest gained in power.

Diana cast a wary glance at the ebony sky. It could be no later than seven o'clock, yet the bitter darkness seemed far more appropriate to midnight. "The witching hour," she whispered under her breath. The moon offered a brief glimpse of her silvery orb before retreating behind a mask of clouds. When she appeared again, her broad, expansive disc grew in size until it nearly eclipsed the sky. Suddenly, Diana felt very uneasy. What was happening? What were her senses trying to communicate? In a flash, the moon was gone, and darkness fell around her once more.

Aware that Daniel stood shivering nearby, Diana quietly mused how very pleasant it would be back at home. She imagined them all huddled around the fireplace, listening to the familiar crackle and snap of the flames as Michael told his favorite stories. The ones about witches and vampires seemed especially appropriate for such a night. It would be so easy to seek shelter in the cottage, but that was impossible. Kelly still remained lost in the woods.

A fierce wind gust caught Diana off guard, assaulting her tiny frame with all the intensity of a human fist. Disoriented and confused, the poor girl fell to her knees, un- able to draw breath. There was a haunting quality about that moment, whispering strains of doubt. Once it had passed, however, Diana knew there was little else to do but continue searching for Kelly. Everything about the night seemed so alive. Even the air appeared to be boiling all around her in mad glee.

"Kelly—Kelly—where are you?" Diana cried, into the seething night. Unfortunately, the sound was swallowed within a deep roll of thunder. No one could have possibly heard her through the mayhem unless they stood nearby.

Daniel approached, shaking his head. "Maybe she doubled back to the cottage!" he suggested in the hope that they might depart without further delay.

"Do you think she could find her way?"

"I don't know," came the faint, but honest reply.

There was another flash of silver lightening. Daniel and Diana looked up at the same time to see a spectacle of horror take shape. A shattered limb broke free from the majestic pine overhead and began a downward spiral in direct line with where they stood. Somehow, Diana managed to shove Daniel out of the way before throwing herself in the opposite direction. The charred branch narrowly missed its target, landing with a hollow thud upon the very spot they had occupied only a moment earlier. It trembled, then became deathly still, as smoke billowed from its severed arteries. Thus fell the storm's first victim.

Peering intently across the smoldering apparition that separated her from Daniel, Diana noticed how everything seemed to blur into one shade of black. Did that mean she was actually going to faint?

Daniel also felt disoriented. The trees, the ground, the sky—all appeared fuzzy, like he was looking through the lens of a camera that was terribly out of focus. Blinking rapidly, he questioned whether or not this was a very vivid dream—for Diana actually appeared to be fading in and out of view. A violent shiver ripped through his frame. He could not pass out at a time like this. Mercifully, a cold gust of wind came to the rescue, offering solace as it caressed his throbbing temple.

"The storm must really be messing with my mind," he muttered, while clearing a pathway through the thick tangle of branches that kept them apart.

Upon finally reaching his sister's side, Daniel enveloped her in a broad bear hug. "Thanks sis," he said. "You really saved my skin that time."

Diana felt the familiar sting of tears grace her eyes. This will be the last time, she thought without quite knowing why. Her fragile grip tightened around Daniel's shoulders, stubbornly refusing to let go.

"We'd better get back now, Di, before—"

A stream of light fell across Daniel's brow, cutting him off in mid-sentence. Where it had originated from—it was impossible to say. One glance revealed that Diana was also enveloped in the beautiful, blue glow.

Even more startling was the fact that this light revealed a trail that had previously escaped their notice. Hypnotic it was, beckoning them forward, heedless of care or worry. As they stepped onto the bluish plane, all sight and sound faded away, leaving each intoxicated with its purity.

"The moon shines;

The mists climb;

Twilight fills the air…"

"Listen, Di," Daniel cried through a set of trembling lips, "that's your song! Maybe its Kelly! Quick—let's follow and see!"

Diana remained perfectly still. "It's Selene," she whispered to Daniel, never once doubting the validity of this claim.

"How do you know?"

"I just do."

Following the voice through an endless tangle of weeds and brambles, the Sherwoods pressed on until a series of familiar markings signaled that they had almost reached home. It was impossible to stay tears of relief as they stumbled onto the much-loved glen. So close were they—so utterly near—that the fireplace clearly blazed a heady welcome through the un-shuttered window. Indeed, a mere fifty paces separated them from the front door! They had only to move forward and close the gap. Yet somewhere in the night, Crescent Lake also waited with glistening eyes.

Daniel had almost touched foot to cottage threshold when a bright explosion caught his attention. It was the lightning again. This time something made him turn toward the lake. Another flare, brighter in hue, illuminated the weather battered form of Kelly Branwell. A mass of pale hair streamed out behind her, conjuring images of a mythical siren trapped within the fury of her own spell.

A third blaze of lightning found Kelly even closer to the water's edge. She appeared to be reaching out toward something caught within the churning waves.

"It's Kelly!" Daniel cried as he began a mad bolt in the direction of Crescent Lake.

Chills began to course through Diana's exhausted frame. "I've seen this before," she thought to herself. "I know what will happen next…"

Suddenly, nothing seemed real any more. The dream had come to life. Another burst of light found her at Kelly's side.

"Thank God you're all right!" Diana cried. "We were so worried about you—"

Kelly never stopped to acknowledge the genuine concern in Diana's voice. Instead, she screamed wildly at the top of her lungs, "This is all your fault, Daniel Sherwood! Dad will kill me if I lose that scarf! It was his special gift!"

The frantic girl pointed toward a yellow scarf briefly dancing just beyond the outer lip of Lookout Point before it plunged head first amidst the churning waters.

A sharp stab of shame colored Daniel's features as he looked into Kelly's tear stained eyes. "I'll get it," he volunteered, carefully maneuvering across the rocky ledge. "Diana, bring me a branch or something!"

Another spasm lanced through Diana's spine. She watched her body move to the nearby oak and break off a long, thin branch from its withered exterior. Somehow the article found its way into Daniel's hands. The next sight Diana consciously recognized was that of her brother inching his way along the outer most edge of Lookout Point.

"Danny, be careful!" she yelled into the rushing wind. "This side of the lake is deep—and the wind is so strong tonight!"

"Don't worry!"

Diana knew she must not interfere. Everything would unfold of its own accord without her assistance. Daniel had anchored his left hand against the jutting ledge, while struggling to procure the lost article with his right. How calm he appeared—how utterly self-assured in each action. He was talking in a warm voice, trying to reassure Kelly.

"Could I allow Lady Branwell to be grounded forever on my account?"

Diana shook her head. This was the Daniel everyone loved so well. Even the somber Kelly could not help smiling, but there was little time to enjoy the sight. Indeed, the dream was about to become reality.

"Danny!"

"Don't worry, Di. This is my adventure!"

Daniel was interrupted by a great flash of lightning. Blinded for an instant, he lost all sense of bearing. A sharp crack ripped through his left arm, followed by the strange sensation of falling, almost like one experiences in the throws of a nightmare. He tried to cry out, but the waters closed around him.

"Danny!"

"Oh, God! I can't see him anywhere! I think he may have gone under!" cried an hysterical Kelly.

"Get my father!" rang Diana's desperate plea.

"He'll drown!" Kelly sobbed between gasps. "I'm sorry—so sorry!"

Diana slapped Kelly hard across the face. "Go now!" she cried, shoving the delirious girl toward the cottage. Aware that Kelly would find her father, Diana took it upon herself to save Daniel.

"Show me what to do. Help me save him," came her solemn prayer as she leapt into the churning waters. Liquid cold, the likes of which she had never experienced before, easily enveloped her being. A frozen dreamland it was beyond length and breadth of time. Diana forced herself to move forward even though her limbs felt unequal to the task. Where was Daniel? Why couldn't she see him? How strange that the entire surroundings appeared to blend into one shade of ebony. That was when the water took command, pouring into her nose and mouth until she was forced to gasp for air.

"Danny—Danny—where are you?" she screamed as a wave slapped against her face. A bitter length of silence proved her only response.

"Please—help me see him!" the plea echoed inside her brain.

Within the span of a heartbeat, a soft, familiar light filtered through the darkness. It folded Daniel in a warm embrace, illuminating his half-drowned silhouette. The poor soul was struggling to keep his head above water with the aid of his good arm. Diana's heart beat a little faster. The length of a few feet separated them from each other. She had but to narrow the gap and then—

"Diana!" Daniel gasped upon seeing his sister's approach. "You'll have to help me—I can't swim. I think I broke my arm!"

"Can you hold on to me with the other?"

Daniel tried to reach out, but his whole body felt as if it were devoid of muscle. He was just beginning to sink below the surface when Diana threw her arms around him. A thankful cough sputtered in appreciation was his only reply.

"You must help him to the shore," the bodiless voice supplied, spurring her onward.

"I can't see it!" the desperate girl cried. "Can you show me?"

The mysterious light answered her question by gently illuminating its mark. Thankfully, the rocky beach appeared to be no more than a few feet away. All that remained was for them to narrow the distance. With a great deal of effort, brother and sister slowly moved forward, struggling against the endless waves that pelted their tender skin.

Diana did all she could to keep Daniel's head clear of the water, for it soon became apparent that he had lost consciousness. The final yards seemed to last an eternity, but somehow she made it to the shoreline. It was then she recognized the pull of invisible hands upon her tiny frame. Utilizing every last bit of strength she possessed, Diana hoisted Daniel's sodden body out of the water. It was not until he collapsed on the muddy bank that she let go.

"Now I can relax. Now my work is done."

Down she drifted, down into the murky depths of Crescent Lake, seemingly lost and alone. It was cool there, and surprisingly still. The laws of science told her that she must be sinking toward the bottom. Why, then, did the journey take so long? Something she could not quite identify was slowing her progress. It was then she heard the familiar voice at her ear. Diana's eyes flashed open. Now she understood. A pair of hands controlled her very movements with graceful precision. The question was—to whom did they belong?

"Where am I? What is happening to me?" Diana knew she had not spoken the words, but still they screamed for answers within her brain.

"We are almost there, my lady," came a soothing, albeit unexpected reply.

Suddenly the hands released Diana, leaving her completely alone. It was then she saw the bright light found so often in dream-spell. Where it had come from—she could hardly tell. A subtle pricking at the back of her neck forced Diana to turn around. Instead of encountering her mysterious guide, she found a dark cavern completely devoid of light. It appeared to be the polar opposite of the familiar, blue glow she had come to know so well. Unlike the brilliant sphere, this yawning chasm took the liberty of pulling her forward toward its unseen recesses.

Diana demanded her release, unwilling to explore the hypnotic tunnel until she better understood this altered state of existence. Thankfully, it complied, and she found herself in command once more. Turning back toward the light, a new wonder met her eyes. The brilliant orb had begun to pulsate like the steady beating of a heart. How strange it appeared—how strange and utterly beautiful.

The light was actually whispering to Diana, telling her to enter. For some reason, it was imperative she do so. Unfortunately, Diana could not imagine how this feat might be accomplished—since there appeared to be no visible entrance. Should she simply walk in and hope for the best?

The light must have sensed her confusion, for it shot out to meet her hand, forcing Diana to flinch with its intensity. This was hardly an inappropriate reaction as the sensation stabbed much like a jolt of electricity. Feeling somewhat abashed, Diana asked the energy current to touch her again. This time, she allowed its power to filter through her very soul. There was the sense of rising, of lengthening, of undergoing an expansion that connected her with the whole of existence. She was one with the universe—one with creation, and now she could soar!

Diana opened her eyes. She was no longer beneath Crescent Lake, but above it. The invisible arms that had previously held her suddenly took shape and form, revealing a strange, young man that hovered at her side. Did her eyes deceive, or was he actually dancing in mid-air? A smile spilled across Diana's lips. How charming he was—how charming and utterly amiable. His dark hair rustled into wisps that often fell across a set of merry eyes. Everything about his demeanor made Diana want to giggle. Who was he?

"I am York," he exclaimed with a well-timed bow. A bright, musical lilt native to the British Isles colored his voice. Without another word, he whisked Diana off to the lake edge and would not let go until her tiny feet actually touched the ground.

Diana gazed upon her unusual companion with undisguised curiosity. "Is he real?" she silently pondered, "or am I dreaming again?"

York answered with a beaming smile that demonstrated just how real he actually was.

She stared at him intently, trying to unravel the mystery of his being. York seemed surprised by her reaction, but said nothing. Indeed, he merely indicated with a gesture of his hand that she should look toward a shimmering globe that hovered over the body of her unconscious brother.

"What's wrong with me? How could I have forgotten about Danny?" she cried in confusion. The light was trying to help him, just as it had helped her so many times in the past.

Suddenly, Diana appeared at her brother's side.

Sensing a new presence, the globe shot straight up into the air. Diana shuddered despite herself. This was definitely too real to be a dream. Indeed, the bright form began to pulsate as it had before. Diana could do little but gasp at the metamorphosis that transpired before her eyes. A pair of hands began to unfold from the blue light's core, accompanied by a full wing-like stretch of arms. Each breath brought forth some new characteristic, until all that remained was the ethereal image of Selene.

"It is you, Lady," Diana whispered as she knelt before the awesome presence. "How can I thank you for saving him?"

"There is no need to thank me, child. It was you who saved Daniel."

Although Selene's voice sounded warm and peaceful, her inner thoughts were far from tranquil. There was so much she wanted—needed to tell the girl, yet the restrictions of time made that impossible. Instead, she simply placed a translucent hand on Diana's brow and breathed the spirit of understanding into its receptive plane. It was vital the girl release all ties with the past, sever all connections with the land of the living before daylight touched the sky. Only then could she achieve her divine purpose.

"Diana, there is little time for us to share together. It is essential that you take leave of your brother."

"Leave?" Diana asked in confusion. "Where am I to go?"

"You are one of us, now," Selene gently soothed. "Go to him, child, and say your good-byes."

A burning sensation crept into Diana's eyes, but no tears formed to offer the much needed release. It was time to leave this world she knew so well—time to part with Daniel, perhaps forever. Kneeling beside him, she felt sharp waves of sorrow filter through her soul. They had spent all their young lives together, sharing moments of joy and pain.

Gently cradling Daniel in her arms, Diana remembered when they had nothing more important to worry about than pillow duels; and the mound of feathers left behind. A smile touched her lips as she remembered the zany adventures of Sir Laugh-a-lot. Soon Daniel would be well enough to revel in his silly pranks once more, but Diana—his long time companion—would no longer be at his side. It was time to leave behind the sweet, familiar world of youth and step forward into the mysterious unknown.

Diana's lips softly brushed against Daniel's cheek. "God bless you, dear brother," she whispered. "Try not to be sad. I will always be with you in spirit—if you only just believe."

An urgent sound of voices cut through the heavy air, rousing Diana from her parting. Suddenly, she noticed that everything was very still and that the storm had all but died away. Time was of the essence now. It was vital she leave immediately, for to remain might jeopardize all hope of future success. Diana never questioned how she achieved this realization. It was simply a part of her being.

Upon turning to Selene and York, she found they were welcoming her with open arms. The three beings of light joined hands and were instantly engulfed within the mysterious, blue globe.

"There he is!" cried a breathless Kelly as she broke onto the shoreline. Reverend Moss and the esteemed Senator followed directly at her heels. Michael pushed past them, racing along the muddy bank toward the stiff, unmoving figure of his son. All evening he had struggled against the fear that gripped his heart. Daniel and Diana—his children —were all he had left in the world.

A great sob escaped Michael's lips as he gathered the fragile bundle into his arms. Yes, he was breathing. At least that much was certain.

"Danny, I was so afraid I'd lost you," he whispered, gently rocking his son back and forth, like a new born babe.

The young Sherwood responded with a fitful moan.

Tears began to well up in Michael's eyes: tears he had kept painfully in check for far too long. He watched as they lightly fell upon Daniel's face, willing him back to life.

Soon the eyelids flickered with waking. There was something he had to remember—something very important that could no longer be denied...Diana! They had to find Diana!

Daniel's eyes flew open. He made a valiant attempt to speak, but his uncooperative lips fluttered silently against the coming dawn.

"Don't say anything just yet, Danny. It's all right," reassured Michael in a quivering voice. He wanted to crush the tiny form against his chest for fear it might slip away.

Daniel focused all his attention on the fist of his good, right hand. It felt frozen with stiffness, but somehow he caught hold of Michael's jacket. "Diana," he whispered, "You have to bring her back."

Michael felt the tightness in his heart take hold again. "Where is she?"

Daniel slowly nodded toward the lake.

"Oh, my God..."

The words drifted onto the rising wind. How could he have not understood?

"Moss!" Michael cried, ignoring the others congregated around him, "Watch Daniel!"

The minister was instantly in place, supplying much needed attention to the ailing child. Dr. Schilling was fast upon his heels with first aid kit in hand.

Michael could not believe this trick of fate. It was happening all over again, but this time to Diana and not Cynthia.

As he reached Lookout Point with Kelly and Senator Branwell in tow, his eyes were irresistibly drawn to a point just above the silent waters. It was at that moment he saw them: three figures engulfed within a shimmering light. Why—they almost seemed to be rising from the depths of Crescent Lake. An unforgiving chill raced up the length of his spine. Each of the beings was staring at him with compassion. Somehow he felt certain the others could not see them.

"There is no need to fear, Michael," soothed the soft, hypnotic voice he knew so well. "She is with me now."

CHAPTER 8

When Diana finally touched down upon her new world, she could not help but gasp with delight. The air was tinged with a soft, purple haze that stretched far as the eye could see. All the rocks, trees and plants were likewise colored. Even the lake, that was shaped remarkably like a crescent moon, and the nearby rock formation, that all but screamed Lookout Point, appeared wrapped in the same violet glow. How strange… how strange, yet utterly wonderful. All the stories whispered by candlelight were true.

"This is the Land of Twilight Mist, Diana. It is to be your new home."

What was it the Lady had just said? Diana struggled to refocus all attention on the ethereal presence before her. Selene's voice sounded so warm—so hypnotic. How beautiful she was, cloaked in a perfect cascade of amethyst tresses. In the Land of the Living, the waving locks had appeared red like Diana's own. There was a certain knowing about the wide, twilight eyes: a perfect understanding that went beyond mere words. If only one day, Diana might grasp a fraction of that knowledge, then she would feel lucky, indeed.

"I know you will come to love this place," Selene continued. "Indeed, you must—for there is great work to be done."

Diana blinked. Her eyes did not seem to be working properly. Either that or something strange was happening to her guardian. There was a certain frailty about Selene that had not been apparent before. In fact, the blue light that had acted as such a strong beacon appeared to fade a little more with each passing moment. What could possibly be wrong?

The light was so much a part of Selene. What would happen if it disappeared altogether?

"I know there are many questions you wish to ask: many things you need to understand. They will be revealed to you in the coming twilights."

"Thank you," Diana replied, as she struggled to match her tone with that of the mysterious lady.

Selene smiled then motioned for Diana to join her on the familiar edge of rock, not so unlike Lookout Point. "We have very little time left together, child."

A look of concern flashed in Diana's clear, gray eyes. "What do you mean, Lady?"

"Call me Selene, for the present. I see York has not fully explained why you were brought here," she said with a sigh. Her gaze fell on the impish young man, lightly admonishing him for some form of neglect.

"There was no time," Diana covered, sorry to see York punished on her account, "everything happened so quickly after we—I stepped through the light. First, I saw you, then I said goodbye to Danny—and now we are here."

Selene smiled, knowingly. "There is no need to defend his actions, child. I am really not angry with him."

Diana bowed her head and said no more.

A mixture of pride and sorrow drifted across Selene's features. "York, will you leave us for a moment?" she asked, not quite able to still the tremor in her voice.

The merry glow, that habitually bathed York's elfin features, instantly drained away. He promptly bit his lip, as if to ward off tears, then gave a sad nod of the head. His drooping form had already begun to fade when Selene added, "Do not stray too far. I—we will need you presently."

York's downcast face brightened a bit before he became one with the twilight air.

"I'm sure he didn't mean any harm," Diana offered a little too casually.

"Of course not," Selene answered with a smile. "York is a pure soul, but I must warn you that he can behave in a childish manner. I suppose that is part of his charm. The important thing to remember is that York does not always follow through with unpleasant tasks as quickly as you might wish. He is, however, honest and true. You may trust him completely, Diana. He will be your guide for a time."

"Oh," Diana sighed, unable to hide her disappointment. "I had hoped you would—" her voice trailed off into nothingness.

Using just the tips of her translucent fingers, Selene stroked Diana's cheek. Its perfect softness was reminiscent of butterfly wings. Their eyes met in silent blessing. It was then Diana realized that Selene's violet orbs had become noticeably dimmer.

"I would gladly be your guide, if that were possible. Do you see, even now, how the light gravitates toward you?"

Diana glanced down at her hands. Selene was right. The blue glow was now emanating from her own body. A wave of terror rushed through Diana's soul. "I—I don't understand!" she cried. "What is happening to me?"

"Be calm, Diana. It simply means that you have been chosen to take my place as guardian over the angels in this land."

"I? How can I ever be expected to take your place?"

"You were born for this purpose, Diana."

The poor girl shook her head in confusion, trying to make sense of it all. "What will happen to you?"

"I do not belong here," came the steady reply. "I was simply chosen to prepare the angels of the twilight mist for you. Now that you have arrived, I must move on."

Diana tried to clutch Selene's hand, but found it to be no more stable than the swirling mist. "Where—where will you go? How can I possibly hope to take your place?"

71

"The answers you seek are within. You must simply learn how to harvest them."

Selene slowly rose from her violet-hued perch. "Be strong, my child," she said. "You are the chosen one: the only being capable of bringing our angels out of this twilight prison."

The truth struck Diana hard. "Bring them out? Why would they want to leave?"

"Do you see how twilight covers everything here?"

"Well, yes, but—"

"We are always near darkness," Selene continued, her lovely voice faltering ever so slightly. "If things remain unchanged, we will never see daylight again. Our world merges with the Land of the Living when twilight falls." The lady paused for a moment to catch her breath, then continued rapidly, "We earthbound angels may only perform miracles at night. Do not ask me why—you will know soon enough. Diana, I need hardly tell you that it is vital we watch over mankind by day as well. You must find the way to bring this miracle about. Everyone here will help. Trust all the angels, especially York."

The low tones of her voice gained in power as she breathed a final warning, "Be careful, Diana. Beyond the woods lies an entity that will stand in your way. He is ancient—beyond imagining. He will do everything within his power to see you fail."

Selene's fragile body swayed to and fro as if it were in danger of collapse. Clutching the rock for support, she dutifully whispered York's name.

The elfin lad instantly appeared at her side. "Bless you, dear Lady," he cried, pausing only to kiss her outstretched hand.

"Now you must assist the rightful Lady in her search for the truth. Teach her everything you know, and the rest will follow, Little Elf."

Diana thought she saw York flinch slightly, before struggling to regain composure.

"Remember, York," echoed Selene's voice as she disappeared from view, "she is my daughter."

CHAPTER 9

Diana trembled despite her best intentions to remain calm. There was so much to think about: so much to explore. Soon she would meet the angels who depended on her for guidance. How could she ever lead them when she did not fully understand the gifts she supposedly possessed? If the answers were at her fingertips, why did she feel no wiser than before? What should she do? Where could she turn for help? Suddenly, the answer appeared full formed in her mind.

"York—yes, I'll call on York! He is, after all, supposed to be my guide—but where is he?"

A quick scan of the surroundings proved futile, for there was no trace of the little elf anywhere. What if he had deserted her? How could she ever succeed with only her own self to rely upon?

Diana slowly navigated the misty shore line, spurred on by the invisible tentacles that seemingly wrapped around her heart. Purple water splashed against her legs, yet she felt nothing of its moisture. Indeed, she could not sense anything beyond the terror growing inside. What was she doing? There was no place to run, no shelter large enough to shield her from the future. Finally, Diana's legs gave way, and she collapsed upon the lake bed.

"Mother," she whispered between sobs. "I want my mother."

Truly, Selene's spirit had fled with the fading mist.

Glancing down at the water, Diana was startled by the image that met her eye. There, rose a majestic figure enveloped in shimmering light. This was not a frightened young woman, but a noble lady suffering from some great sorrow, her face drawn in pain. The powerful, blue light emanating from her frame suggested that she was far from helpless. If this was, indeed, her own image, then why did she feel so weak? Frustrated and confused, she gave the earth a violent kick and watched as its fragments exploded in a bright blaze.

"Purple—everything here is purple! Everything except—"

Diana stopped short as her gaze fell upon the soft, blue glow that emanated from her wriggling toes. At that moment, she finally understood. *I am Selene now. This light proves that I am! All I need do is call my guide, and he will appear!*

"York!" she bellowed at the top of her lungs, "Will you—"

"I am here, my lady," he quickly replied, cutting her off in mid-phrase. York landed at her side with both index fingers tightly thrust into his delicate ears.

"There is no need to yell in the land, for we are never more than a thought away. Simply wish for me," the elfin guide suggested as he disappeared,"—and behold! I shall appear!"

York punctuated his boast by executing a perfect somersault, reappearing in mid-air.

"How wonderful!" exclaimed Diana. "Show me how you did that!"

"It is quite simple. Here, lend me your hand," the little elf chimed as he waited for her to comply. "All you need do is turn upside down—like this!"

Together they effortlessly tumbled through the air.

"No—" Diana giggled, noting how at ease she felt with her merry guide, "I meant, how do you disappear?"

"You ask the key to that which is the simplest trick of all. Simply think, and it shall be so. Observe—I am going to disappear." Without so much as a further word, York vanished from view. "See how easy it is?"

"York, where do you go when you disappear?"

"Oh, I am still here," he mischievously chuckled. "I can see you, but you cannot see me!"

"You can?" asked Diana, growing a bit uncomfortable.

"Aye!" he gleefully replied. "We all can!"

"All—?" Diana's voice fell to a hush. "Do you mean the other earthbound angels are here too?"

"I do!" his voice rang through the thinning mist. A perfect chorus of giggles accompanied him in time.

"Have they been here all along?" she asked, hoping against hope that her biggest fear would not be realized.

"Yes!" replied the chorus of cheerful voices.

Diana could not help but blush. They had witnessed her folly. Well, there was little else she could do but make the best of an awkward situation.

"Why not introduce me to them, York?"

"With pleasure, my lady," rang his most amiable reply.

Suddenly, the air over Crescent Lake was teeming with angels of all colors, shapes and sizes. One trait alone they held in common. Each and everyone of them appeared to be arrested in some phase of childhood.

"There are so many of you—" she cried, "How will I ever—?"

York never allowed her to finish the thought. "'Tis a hard task, but someone must undertake it!"

Diana was about to respond when she caught a good look at York's face. There was no way to reprimand her guide when his dimples were aglow.

"Don't listen to him, Lady!" chirped a tiny girl of about six and a half. Her golden curls bounced charmingly upon a set of narrow shoulders as she flew to Diana's side. "We're not so hard to take care of—after all, we are angels." The young beauty then whispered in Diana's ear, "York just likes to tease everyone."

"I heard that Ora," snapped York in mock anger.

"Your name is Ora?" asked Diana, charmed by the delicate beauty.

The little girl nodded, an action that set the ringlets into a merry dance. "I am the angel that brings light to anyone who is afraid of the dark," she proclaimed with a delightful bounce of her fair curls.

"So, you are the one who helped me through all those sleepless nights," Diana said as she patted Ora's golden locks with genuine tenderness. "Thank you, Ora, for your gift of light."

Diana was surprised to hear these words escape her lips, yet somehow knew the blessing was proper. Undoubtedly, it had been prompted by a higher source.

Ora curtsied sweetly, and though it hardly seemed possible, her cheerful face shone brighter than before.

Soon another spirit approached Diana. His demeanor appeared quite serious, almost somber, in comparison to the charming Ora. Straight and tall he was, nearly the height of an adult, yet one look at his face told Diana that he was not much older than Daniel. Peering beyond the purple haze, she saw that his skin was the color of pine bark newly kissed by the sun. When he finally spoke, his voice was no more than a whisper.

"My name is Forrest, Lady," he said, shyly averting his eyes from those of the new guardian.

"Can you guess why?" York devilishly chimed in, before Forrest could offer any further explanation. "He is the guardian of Whispering Pines!"

Forrest's eyes quickly sought the ground. This time, Diana noticed his expression was clouded with embarrassment.

Diana found it strange that angels could still experience emotions native to human beings, especially when they were unpleasant ones, like shyness. There was a lesson to be learned here.

"York, you remind me of my brother," she stated in a firm tone that almost took her by surprise. A quick glance at York proved that he was equally dismayed. "You always make a joke out of everything—without taking time to consider whether or not it might hurt someone's feelings."

"I am sorry, Forrest," the poor elf softly said. "Forgive me. It will not happen again."

"There is no need to be sad, York. Just learn from your mistakes," suggested the new Selene. How comfortable she was beginning to feel as a guardian!

"I will, my lady, "York replied, with a quick bob of his head.

When Diana turned her attention back on Forrest, she found that he was gone!

"Thank you, Forrest, for guiding my brother and me through the woods last night during that terrible storm."

The woodland angel instantly reappeared. This time, his face was shining with pleasure.

"The storm was so fierce," she continued, "we might never have found our way back without your help."

Diana watched as the corner's of Forrest's mouth quivered into a smile. She would have to tread very carefully around this sensitive angel.

"It was an honor, Lady," he whispered, then disappeared from view before Diana could breathe a reply.

"He's very shy," suggested Ora, "but I know you will like him."

"Of course I will!" Diana cried, as she threw her arms around the tiny angel. "I like all of you! What I mean is—I love all of you."

The angels were genuinely pleased with Diana's declaration, for they twittered and buzzed until another young comrade decided to introduce himself. Diana was taken aback when he stooped to kneel before her. What did this mean? Why would anyone kneel to her? Uncertain of how to respond, she scanned the angel's features, hoping they might offer some clue as to why he had chosen to greet her in that way.

The face bowed before her had a sculptured appearance, boasting high cheekbones that could only have been Native American in origin. A thick mass of black hair fell about his strong shoulders.

"I am Proudfoot," he proclaimed with great emotion, "the angel that watches over the earth."

"I see," replied the new Selene, still a little taken aback by Proudfoot's manner. "How do you help those in need—while you watch over the earth?"

The angels broke into another round of giggles, while Proudfoot's face took on an even ruddier tinge.

"I ask this question," Diana quickly interjected, hoping to spare Proudfoot some of the humiliation Forrest had suffered, "because I am new at being a guardian. There are many things I still do not understand."

The angels instantly fell silent, sorry to have hurt their friend.

"I watch the earth in times of danger, whether it be storm or drought," he said in a booming voice that Diana would forever associate with his name. "I see that people remain unharmed when the circle is broken and the earth becomes unbalanced."

"That is quite impressive, Proudfoot. I have much to thank you for as well."

After a brief nod, the bronzed angel returned to his place amongst the other spirits.

Diana could not help but feel more than a little overwhelmed by everything that was happening to her. Nothing had prepared her for this experience—nothing at all.

Out of the corner of her eye, Diana caught the image of a bright fire crackling and sputtering through the deepening twilight. There was something hypnotic about the flames as they swept forward, almost too quickly, stopping just short of herself. Inside the spectacular glow of orange and yellow, danced an ever-emerging form. It belonged to a tall, lanky girl of about sixteen. One glance at her smoldering eyes revealed a soul filled with anger.

Diana remained silent as the golden orbs narrowed into two points of yellow flame. She offered a kind introduction, but the fiery angel merely stomped about in reply. This put Diana on edge. It was essential that she put all negative feelings aside. Only then, could she guide this girl to the good that remained locked within. Perhaps some of the other spirits, like this firebrand, had also brought unresolved problems with them from the other world. If so, each must be dealt with before a true sense of peace could ever be achieved. Perhaps, Diana's first task was to help ease the torment of such a deeply troubled spirit.

"Call me Brenda—or Phoenix—whatever you feel like. I'm a guardian of fire," she blurted in a sharp staccato. "It's obvious what I do—help kids not get burnt. I haven't had much practice though. Its been quiet here on the fire scene."

"I am glad of that," Diana replied. "I hope your good fortune continues for a long time."

Brenda was about to sputter a reply when York interceded.

"As you know, my lady, I am York, otherwise hailed as the trickster," he declared, beaming with delight. "Hence, I watch over people when they enact foolish pranks and see that no harm comes to them."

"Really?" questioned Diana, with both eyebrows raised. "I never would have guessed.

"I shall also be your guide for a time, and it is my suggestion that we take leave of the angels at present."

A disappointed groan filled the air, as the angels realized they were about to be dismissed.

"The hours are passing very rapidly," York interjected, trying to ease the situation. "Soon it will be twilight, and our Lady still has much to learn."

"York is right," Diana sighed. "I do have much to learn. It doesn't seem possible that time could have passed so quickly. Believe me, I look forward to meeting each and every one of you. I know that we will become good friends."

The angels chattered in chorus once more, before disappearing amidst a clatter of good-byes.

"I am sorry to take you from them, my lady, but—"

"You did the right thing, York. I have so much to ask you—I do not know where to begin." Turning to face the merry guide, she was surprised to find that York was no longer stationed at her side. Instead, she found him dancing across the horizon, seemingly oblivious to her presence. Had he even heard a single word she said?

"Why not begin with your name," he suggested.

Diana nearly jumped at the sound of his voice. So, he had been paying attention!

"Do you know what it means?" he cheerfully asked.

"Yes, it means: of the moon."

"That's right, that's right!" came York's lilting reply. He darted in a perfect circle around her, then added, "As does your human name, Diana."

The similarity never occurred to her before. "What is my gift, then?" she whispered softly, almost afraid to hear his answer.

"See how you glow, my lady? Does it not remind you of the moon? Your glow acts as a beacon for the angels of the twilight mist. You are their guide between worlds. You make certain they always set forth at twilight and that they always return at dawn. Without you they—we would become lost and never find our way back home."

"Then, I am the gateway between worlds…"

"You become the gateway," clarified York.

"But, how do I—?"

"Through the light of the moon," came his unsettling reply. "You must look to the moon."

"What do you mean, York? I do not understand—"

"The light that shines from you is moonlight. With this special gift, you and the moon become one and the same."

Diana's features twisted in confusion.

"When moonbeams merge with your light, you beat like a heart. This is the sign which tells us to enter the gateway."

"So, the light I entered when I first came here was actually Selene—my mother," she whispered softly.

York understood Diana's feelings of regret. He had also loved Selene. "I swear we will speak of her at another time. Now, we must make ready for twilight."

"Already? How can you tell?" asked Diana. "I can not even see the moon yet."

"You never shall see it in this land, my lady. I know it is time because you are beginning to pulsate."

Diana glanced down at the small of her hand. The light surrounding it was ebbing and flowing like the tide. "What do I do now?"

"Never fear, my lady. It shall happen of its own accord. You need not do a thing. Remember, I shall always be at your side!"

CHAPTER 10

"So this is what it means to be Selene…"

No longer able to move, or even properly think, Diana felt the transformation eclipse her spirit. Quick it was, blinding in merciless precision. A sharp, electric current swept through her veins, forcing all senses to merge as one.

"How do I call the angels when I cannot see or hear them? How can I hope to guide them along the way?"

"Fear not, my lady. I am here to guide you." The answer surged deep within the Lady's core.

Selene experienced a number of similar jolts, indicating that the angels had arrived. Each stamped its own unique identity across her soul, creating a bond that connected them throughout time.

Once her senses had finally cleared, Diana realized that they were no longer in the world of twilight and mist. Indeed, she was sitting on an ancient rock known as Lookout Point, feet dangling over water, the ever-faithful York hovering at her side. Everything appeared finely tuned to the eye, as if she were peering through a large magnifying glass.

"How beautiful the world is at night," she sighed.

After receiving nothing in the way of a reply, Diana cast a glance in York's direction—the very sight of which made her pause. He was staring at her in a rather bizarre manner that made each pupil dance within its orb. Believing the absurdity to be a figment of her imagination, Diana closed both eyes then carefully reopened them. York's look was still unsettling. It appeared that he wished to say something yet held back. When he finally did give voice to his thoughts, they were quite harmless.

"How do you feel?" he gently asked.

"A little drained, but I guess that is to be expected—since I am new at this."

"You shall adapt to it very quickly," he said, with just the flash of a smile.

"I hope so. The whole experience was very strange—it almost made me feel awkward."

"You must never feel awkward around us," York proclaimed, as his mouth quivered in anticipation of what he was about to say. Oh, what an irresistible urge he had to ride the night breeze! In a flash he was one with the air, leaving Diana and his troubles far behind.

Finally, after countless loops around the lake, York dropped out of flight and marched directly toward Diana with a most determined stride. "We earthbound angels are indebted to you, Selene. Without your guidance, we would forever be lost in twilight. We could not create miracles, and our purpose would cease to be."

A frown wrinkled Diana's smooth brow. "I do not understand. The One Spirit made you and all earthbound angels with a purpose in mind. Why then, must I guide you into this world? Why must we perform miracles only when the sun sets? People need help during all hours of the day and night. Why would the Spirit place restrictions on us?"

York trembled ever so slightly: a movement just large enough to be detected by the Lady's keen eyes. He bit down on his lip with such force, that had he been alive, she felt certain the act would have drawn blood.

"Selene, your mother did not tell you about the one who lives beyond the forest—"

"She did mention him," Diana carefully interjected.

A wave of relief swept over York's brow.

"She said that I would have to learn about him on my own."

"That would be unwise," he sputtered, almost hastily. "It is essential you learn about him before the first meeting occurs."

He paused a moment to take a fortifying breath, then added, "I will tell you all I know."

Despite the seriousness of York's tone, Diana watched in amusement as he marched back and forth across Lookout Point like a tightly wound toy soldier preparing for battle.

"He is known by many names, but you may think of him as Nero—the Dark One. Nero is one of the other kind, if you understand me," York said, with a quick wink of his eye.

After looking about for a moment, he began to communicate without the aid of spoken words. Diana was surprised that she could read York's thoughts by simply staring into his deep, brown eyes.

"Nero is a spirit from the dark realm. His chief purpose is to cause us trouble. Do you realize what he has done?"

Diana shook her head in the negative, then urged York to continue.

"Nero is the being who closed the gateway between our worlds. Before he cursed us—we were able to work by daylight. At that time, the moon held no control over our movements. In fact, our worlds were joined as one. We merely remained invisible to those who did not believe."

Diana remained silent, choosing her next words very carefully. "How long have you been an earthbound angel, York?"

His eyes widened almost imperceptibly. "That is a topic for another time."

Noticing the obvious disappointment in Diana's expression, he added, "All right, I shall tell you this much— I lived and died in what you call the Dark Ages. Hence, I have not always been an earthbound angel."

This hurried confession only served to kindle Diana's curiosity. York must have grown up in Britain—his lilting accent gave that away—yet he spoke modern English very well. Had he lived during the time of King Arthur's reign in Camelot? Unable to control her anxious tongue, Diana blurted out, "You must tell me more!"

"Sh!" York cautioned, as he brought a trembling finger to his lips. He briefly paused to scan the surroundings then continued, "One day, I shall tell you all. Now we must concentrate on the matters at hand."

Feeling somewhat abashed, Diana fell silent and waited for him to continue.

"Nero came to us when we had no guardian. The One Spirit knew evil had entered our midst but decided not to intervene. That meant all earthbound angels were to be tested."

"Tested?"

"All beings, both of spirit and flesh, must undergo a series of trials to prove their worthiness—their loyalty. The One Spirit is perfectly willing to accept each individual by their own merits, but the Dark One demands that loyalty must be proven through an outward display."

"Go on," entreated Diana. "How did Nero shift the worlds apart? He must have great power to accomplish such a feat."

"Nero's power lies in his ability to locate the hidden weakness within others…"

"I see," Diana said, slowly turning from York so she might better gaze upon the water. There was a secret about Crescent Lake that had yet to be told—something that had to do with this "Dark One."

York met her eyes, then continued, "Nero tried every possible scheme to tempt the earthbound angels into joining his legions of darkness, but not one of us would give in. Years passed without a single sighting of his presence. We thought he had returned to his realm. Instead, Nero was formulating a plan by which he would gain control over all our movements. He knew the only way to defeat us would be through the torture of an innocent person."

Diana sensed a faltering in York's thoughts. It was evident that the process of reliving so violent a memory must necessarily cause him pain. Her whole being cried out to shelter him—to keep him from divulging the secret, yet something made her hold back. The story must be understood if she was to survive.

"Every night, Nero watched a beautiful, young woman draw water from Crescent Lake and take it to her family…" York paused as a stray moonbeam fell on Diana's twisted brow. "Can you guess the rest?"

"I think so. Please continue."

"Nero enlisted the moon's aid by blinding her with flattery. The celestial orb was so taken with this praise, that she remained completely unaware of his true intent. He told her that no one in heaven or on earth could match her perfect beauty. As you can imagine—she became quite vain. Little did she suspect what Nero had planned for her."

"He claimed her soul—" Diana whispered into the thickening night.

York offered a brief nod of his head. "One night, Nero told her that he had been mistaken—that there was someone more beautiful then she. The moon naturally demanded to see this maiden for herself. It was then Nero parted the misty heavens to reveal a glimpse of the lovely creature kneeling on the lake shore. Enraged, the moon created a storm of such fury that the woman was swept into the lake and drowned."

York briefly paused, for Diana was grasping his hand with vice-like intensity.

"In conclusion, her broken body was lifted from the liquid depths by Mara, guardian of the waters. Before they could reach the light, Nero demanded that the woman be released into his custody as a spoil of war. Together, the moon and Nero drained Mara's powers until they were able to seize the woman. This was the way he set about wounding the earthbound angels. The woman would be released if we agreed to enter the world of mankind only at night. He kindly offered the light of the moon as a gateway between dimensions. If the moon chose not to shine, we remained trapped in twilight. Such was Nero's offer. We had little choice but to accept his terms. That was when Selene—"

"My mother," Diana interjected, with a trembling voice.

"Aye, your mother—became one of us. The One Spirit took pity and gave her the ability to channel moonlight—as you do now. No matter how faint the moonbeams become, you shall always absorb their rays."

Diana remained lost in silent contemplation.

"Throughout the past ten years, Selene, your mother, faithfully served as our guardian, but she always took time to remind us that one day another more suited to the post would take her place. This new guardian would create the great miracle and lead us back into the daylight."

York knelt before the new Selene, kissing her hand with great reverence. "Selene, you are the one. Only you are capable of achieving this miracle. It is the One Spirit's wish that you succeed. Remember, Nero is formidable, but you can overcome him. All the angels will help you, and most importantly, "he added with a sly wink of the eye, "you shall always have me about!"

Quite unexpectedly, Diana leaned forward and kissed York full on the cheek.

The merry elf nearly stumbled back against a fallen log, so surprised was he by the act. His face flushed red for a moment before he called himself to attention.

"'Tis time for work!" he cried, leaping boldly in the air. "Allow me to show you how I create miracles!"

"You mean someone is about to play a dangerous prank?"

"Yes, oh yes, to be sure! If we hurry the prankster will merely see her plans backfire. Hence, she shall never know what might have been. Quickly, my lady, give me your hand!"

As Diana met York's firm grasp, she caught a glimpse of the old cottage in the glen. It appeared very dark and lonely, almost as if it were beckoning her to return and set everything right.

"Not yet, my lady," York tenderly whispered. He understood the pain she was experiencing only too well. "'Tis too soon, I fear. To return now would only cause them greater pain."

Diana knew he was right. She cast one more look at the cottage then followed her elfin guide toward the miracle that was to be.

CHAPTER 11

David Moss stood perfectly still, as the evening breeze kissed his tear stained cheek. Laughter filled the autumn air, but he could not hear it. Instead, his thoughts remained trapped within the chilling waters of Crescent Lake.

An occasional sigh escaped David's lips, while his clear, blue eyes remained fixed on some far-off point. He almost saw them: the gang of boys that ruled the neighborhood surrounding Hillside Drive. They were running through the streets, oblivious to sorrow or loss. A cry of life escaped their lips as they passed by him. They were not much older than she was…had been…

David eventually left his post, walking in zombie-like fashion across the street, past the gang, past the neat row of houses tinted by streetlight, and finally, up the weed-choked hill that overlooked a comfortable span of open fields.

"What's wrong with him?" asked a stocky boy with a shiny moon face, as he gave David's older brother, Jim, a good-natured poke in the arm.

"Don't tell me you haven't heard!" crowed a grainy voiced girl, who proceeded to push her way into the group. She was surprisingly tall and thin and looked almost as tough as her voice sounded. Her clothing, consisting of torn jeans and a black leather jacket only heightened the impression. Yet, if the gang members had looked into her face, they might have detected a trace of recently shed tears.

"Here comes the croak of doom," crooned Jim, as Jenny threatened to push him aside.

"Listen, Jim, I was there—I saw!"

"What is she talking about?" cried Johnny as he and two of the younger gang members crowded around her.

"She's gabbin' about what happened at Crescent Lake last night," muttered Jim, as he moved away from the group. The dim form of his brother beckoned him forward, but reputation, or perhaps it was cowardice, held him firmly in place. Jim, the gang's undisputed leader, was tough—that is tough for a preacher's son. Everyone knew better than to cross him, so they simply left him alone. He liked it that way.

Suddenly, Jenny's voice demanded his full attention.

"Yeah—I am!" she yelled just loud enough to reach David's ears. "It's his fault she's dead—and he knows it! That's why he is acting so strange!"

"Shut up, Jenny," warned Jim between a set of tightly gritted teeth.

"You know it's true," she whispered just loud enough for everyone to hear. A faint smile momentarily played upon her lips.

"Shut it!" he said, grabbing her by the shoulders.

"Ooooh! Violence!" schreeched Chris and Ken in mock glee, as they circled around the two forms locked in combat.

"Bug off, jerks!" Jenny spat at their faces. Jim drew Jenny's arm behind her until she gasped in pain." Yeah—get out of here guys. Leave us alone."

They had just begun to drift off toward the hillside, when he paused to bark at them, "Leave my brother alone. Got it?" The words were uttered as a statement, rather than a question.

Knowing better than to cross Jim's authority, the gang quickly changed course in favor of an apartment complex that lay nearby.

Jenny looked up at her captor with an intent gaze. She was glad to be standing there next to him, even if he was hurting her arm. He was tall for his fifteen years and strong.

It was hard not to marvel at his strength, as he easily pinioned both hands behind her back. Yes, she wanted to impress him—to say anything that would make him notice her.

"Listen, Jen, you're all right, but if you start messin' around with David's mind—watch out."

"Are you threatening me, Jim Moss? Oooh, I'm scared," Jenny taunted, while trying to loosen his grip from her arms. "Like you'd really hurt me," she said, slowly twisting her face up to his, certain he would not be able to resist her charms.

Was she actually waiting for a kiss? Jim laughed, then tightened the grip around her arm, until she cried out in pain. "Listen, girl," he said, I know you—and I know what your snobby friends do. This is just a friendly warning. Stay away from David or you'll be sorry."

Without uttering another word, Jim pushed Jenny away from him. She landed hard upon the pavement, skinning her elbow in the process.

"I'll show him," she muttered into the night wind.

An old oak tree stood nearby overlooking the ripe autumn fields. Jenny scurried up the trunk until she reached a vantage point high in the boughs. She could just detect David's solitary figure standing in the darkness below. What could she do to make him squirm? The moon casually directed a few stray beams onto the remnants of an old well, prompting her response. Jenny remembered how a young girl had fallen inside during the spring rains. The child had remained trapped for hours until a local rescue squad managed to haul her out. Eventually, the well was filled to avoid any further mishaps. Now it had reopened—no doubt as a result of last night's storm.

As Jenny paused in mid-thought, a brief smile played upon her lips. Could she do it? Could she really be that cruel? The answer appeared simple enough. David deserved it. Because of his foolishness, Kelly had almost drowned. Instead, it had been Diana. Diana…yes, that was it!

At the mere mention of Diana's name, a plan began to take shape in Jenny's mind. The moon, well pleased with her prompting, withdrew behind a foggy mask of clouds, and darkness enveloped the fields once more.

Lost in the endless blur of night, David allowed images of the Sherwoods to flood his mind. The bright sunlight was shining on Daniel, as he played his flute in the open meadow, Diana voicelessly mouthing words at his side.

"The moon shines;

The mists climb;

Twilight fills the air;"

David could not believe his ears! That was Diana's song! Surely, this was real, not some awful trick of the imagination.

"The pines know;

The stars glow;

Through darkness gleams despair;"

This time the words were whispered directly into his ear. David's heart began to thud against his chest. Perhaps there still was hope! Perhaps she wasn't dead!

A soft hand brushed against his cheek, then was gone.

"Daylight brings;

Eternal wings;

That they alone can share."

Certain that the voice was originating from somewhere behind him, David whirled around hoping to catch a glimpse of Diana's misty form but was met with nothing but darkness. The words seemed to fade upon the wind until only a distant sound of humming remained. He could almost distinguish the faint outlines of a girlish figure.

"Diana, is that you?" he whispered.

A shadowy silhouette materialized before him. Was it truly Diana? There was only one way to find out.

David had just started toward her, when something jumped in front of him, blocking his path. A muffled shriek pierced the veil of night, followed by a hint of merry laughter and the patter of dancing feet.

"W-w-who is it? Who's there?" David cried in confusion.

"It's me, little bro, just catchin' a snake," laughed Jim between muffled cries.

"Jim?—I thought I heard—oh, never mind. Who's that with you?"

"Just Jenny."

"It figures…" David's voice trailed off into silence.

"Why don't you go home and catch some sleep?" Jim suggested as the stifled cries gained in strength. "I'll see to the snake."

David paused for a moment, allowing a tear to slide down his cheek. "Whatever she was up to—go easy on her, all right?"

Without waiting for a reply, David shambled off in the general direction of the place he called home.

"How'd you like to be dropped down a well, Jenny, hm?"

"MMJIMMM!" she cried, as his hand tightened across her mouth. Jim easily lifted her in his arms and allowed her feet to dangle over the gaping hole.

"I'd just love to let go—oops!" he teased pretending to almost lose his grip.

"Nooo!"

Once again laughter filled the air. A gentle breeze, or something of that sort, tickled Jim on the vulnerable spot just under his chin, forcing him to smile. At that same moment, something also brushed against Jenny's cheek, but instead of giggling, she screamed.

Jim smiled at the frantic girl, who suddenly appeared quite different from the nasty snob he knew so well.

94

"Who's there with you, Jim Moss?" she cried in a breathless voice.

"Relax—it's just me."

"No—there's someone else! He just tried to tickle me!"

"Right, Jen. Whatever. I'm in a good mood, so I guess I'll let you go—you and whatever else is around," he said with a chuckle.

After gently placing her feet upon the solid earth, he added with a sneer, "Get outta here—before I change my mind."

Jenny did not wait to hear another word. She rushed up Hillside Drive, and into Brandt court before stopping to catch her breath. After a moment she turned back toward the hill only to find Jim still laughing at her. She would never live this down. The humiliated girl stomped through a set of iron gates that graced the entranceway to her house, pausing only to fasten the latch. Arrested in mid-action by an overwhelming need to look back at the oak tree she had occupied not so very long before, Jenny met with something of a surprise. A strange, young man was chuckling at her from his post on a low hanging bough!

Jenny flinched in surprise, but the young man only laughed louder, waving his hand in greeting. That did it. Within the span of a heart beat, Jenny had cleared the patio door and locked it fast. Was it possible she had been dreaming? Never before had she ever seen anyone that looked so foreign! Why, he almost reminded her of an elf— the kind that were found in fairy tales!

Once again, her eyes were drawn to the oak tree, but the young man was gone. The large branch lightly swayed in the breeze, even as a drop of dew nestled against her cheek. Perhaps it had only been her imagination...

CHAPTER 12

"York, do you really think it was wise to show yourself to Jenny?" asked the new Selene, as she nestled into a crooked bough overlooking the point.

"Surely you jest. I did not force Jenny to see me. She did that all by herself. Oh, do not look at me that way. You know what a creature of mischief I am. Wisdom, I fear, is not one of my special gifts."

York punctuated this remark by merrily drumming his heals against the ancient trunk.

"York—"

"You did not even comment on my good deed. I came to the aid of your friend David. You do remember that!"

"Of course, I do, and yes, you were wonderful, but—"

"Thank you, my lady!" the little elf cried, as he whirled around with unbridled glee.

Diana sighed. Selene had warned her about this. York simply refused to take anything seriously. When would he learn that existence was more than one big joke?

"Don't count on that happening anytime soon," whispered a mysterious voice that originated from everywhere and nowhere at once. "York is too old and too stubborn to ever learn that lesson!"

"I heard that, Miriah!"

"Miriah? Please, show yourself," suggested the new guardian. "I am afraid we have never met."

There was a subtle tinkling in the air. "Can you not see me? I am right here!"

Selene scanned the surroundings but saw only a branch or two rustling in the wind. "So—you are guardian of the wind."

"Yes, that's me! I never take mortal form. Being one with the air is simply too grand!" the bodiless voice cried, as it whisked around Selene time and again.

A smile spread across Selene's face. She was about to reply when Miriah whispered diligently in her ear, "Beware the master prankster, Lady, for he will certainly lead you astray!"

A single cry of "Miriah!" pierced the air as York pursued the invisible wind, leaving Selene quite alone. A sigh escaped her lips. York could not be changed to fit her own personal whims. At least, this gave her the opportunity for some serious reflection. There was so much to think about in this new existence—so much to explore.

Selene had not been at this task long when a bright star caught her eye. Its beauty drew her heavenward until she soared above Whispering Pines. There was something about the brilliant sphere that seemed to communicate all the secrets of the universe. Seeking to learn more, Selene flew toward the celestial orb. She had not traveled far when it dropped from its native haunt and began to plummet.

"A shooting star," Selene sighed with admiration. "How lovely."

As the bright light halted before her, a gentle kind of warmth seemed to emanate from its crystalline interior—a light that filled Selene with a joy she had never experienced before. This was how the guardian of the constellations offered greeting to the new Selene. Stella was her name, and a delight she was to behold.

Soon the twilight guardian became aware that everything around her was equally bathed in the luminous glow. Many earthbound angels quickly joined in the conversation. The very sound of Stella's laughter, penetrated their souls with all the brilliancy of a diamond. It was easy to see how her sparkle wore off on every spirit she touched. No doubt, Stella was a favorite among the earthbound angels. Why, then, had not she been chosen as the new Selene?

After Stella had returned to her post high in the sky, Selene puzzled over the question for some time. Thankfully, this angel did not appear to harbor any form of jealousy. At least nothing in their conversation gave her reason to believe otherwise. Still, something made her ill at ease. There was a difference about this angel—an oddity she could not define. Selene paused in mid-thought. Stella had never actually spoken one word during their entire conversation. Every bit of knowledge had been transmitted through the angel's brilliant light. Was Stella actually mute?

Once again, Diana was left pondering the real possibility that earthbound angels were far from the perfect souls she had imagined in childhood. Indeed, there appeared to be at least one flaw in every earthbound angel she had met so far. Although some of the imperfections were more obvious than others, Selene questioned why they were present at all? Could this mystery somehow be linked with the miracle she was supposed to perform?

Yes, that must be it! She, Diana, acting as Selene, would help every spirit find a sense of peace, but first, it was vital she help them accept their own personal differences. Only then could they comprehend their individual importance when it came to enacting miracles.

Pleased by this new insight, Selene thoughtfully determined that it was time to set the miracle in motion. Who, then, would she help first? The answer was easy. The one spirit who appeared to be in need of immediate attention was Brenda. Perhaps if she—

"What is it?" hissed a fuming voice, which perfectly suited Brenda's flame colored locks.

"I was just thinking about you."

"Really? No kidding. What do you want?"

"I would like to know you better," came the honest reply.

"Why?" the insolent girl practically spat in her guardian's face.

"Because, there is something special about you."

"Cut the crap," Brenda exclaimed, as a small burst of flame shot from her fingers, singeing a hapless pine. "I don't play into that sweet talking game like you do."

Selene broke into laughter. "I'm glad you think I play it well. I've had very little experience in that line." She paused, looking deep into the girl's amber eyes. "It's nice to see you do have a sense of humor, Brenda. You should try sharing it more often."

There was a flaring of the proud nostrils. "What are you—my mother?"

"At present, I am your friend. Why not tell me what makes you so angry."

Brenda spat in response. "I'll tell you what it is—its you and people—I mean spirits—like you who think they have to know everything!"

"I don't have to, or even want to think about knowing everything. I just want to help," Selene simply explained, reaching out to touch Brenda's hand.

A chuckle escaped Brenda's smirking lips. Perhaps a simple burn would make her guardian back off. The scheme fell flat, however, as the harsh flames could not even begin to penetrate Selene's soft, blue glow.

"Brenda, tell me how you became so hurt inside," Selene whispered, clasping hold of the fiery spirit. The stubborn girl shook her blazing locks in reply.

"Please, Brenda, I want to help."

Perhaps it was the steady, blue gaze, or the simple exchange of warmth as their hands entwined, that finally put Brenda at ease. Down came the barrier she had erected, if only for a moment. Selene placed a protective arm around Brenda's shoulders until the spirit's breath broke forth in jagged sobs.

"Why not share your thoughts with me?" she suggested hopefully.

Finally, the words came, slowly at first and with a great deal of difficulty. "I am—was—I mean—what you—or some would call a b—well, you see—my mother wasn't married when I was born so—" the voice faltered as the amber eyes remained fixed upon the ground. "Life wasn't easy for us—my mother and me—with no man around. Sometimes we were hungry and cold. What hurt most was the way kids at school treated me—you know—made fun of me for being a—"

"Fatherless child," Selene offered, as she squeezed Brenda's hand in a show of support.

"I went through most of my life without having any real friends—except Stormy, my dog."

For a moment, Brenda's eyes brightened at the memory of her one, true friend.

"He was a Collie—like Lassie. We found him abandoned at the pound. They were going to—you know—put him to sleep; so Mom said we could take him home and keep him—and we did. I really loved him," she confessed as a tinge of mist crept into her eyes.

"Well, anyway, who should show up one day, but my father. I was about fifteen then and had never seen him before—not even a picture, but there he was on the doorstep—this big, important business man..."

Selene heard the familiar edge creep back into Brenda's voice. She would have to tread carefully or the firebrand might erupt once more.

"My father took me out of the dumps and showed me a world full of beautiful things. He even let me bring Stormy along..."

As Brenda drifted into another silence, Selene sensed that they were no longer alone. Someone was listening nearby—someone interested in the story Brenda had to tell.

The fire maiden continued with her discourse before Selene could investigate any further.

"Then one night, all my hopes and dreams were stripped away with a flash of light. The man who offered me those beautiful things decided it was time to end my life forever. He—he was the one who killed me!" Brenda shrieked, as a mass of flames rapidly eclipsed her form.

Mystified by the unexpected revelation, Selene questioned why the One Spirit had chosen a teenager so troubled as Brenda to become an earthbound angel? In that moment, the fragile mask she had adopted as guardian instantly dissolved, leaving only a confused girl in its place. She reached for Brenda but was met with angry bursts of flame.

"Hush, Brenda. Calm yourself," Diana offered as a last attempt to regain control over her ward. She could feel her patience wearing thin. The girl was obviously paranoid. The words, "I am certain it was only an accident," escaped her lips before she could check their progress.

"You don't understand! Oh, yes, you pretend to—like they all do—but none of you have any idea what happened! It was no accident! My father killed me!"

Brenda rapidly conjured the cloak of a mythological firebird, known as the Phoenix around herself, then disappeared in an explosion of flame.

Diana stood dumbfounded. How could she have allowed this to happen? Why hadn't she listened to Brenda's warnings? Why had she not understood? Leaning back against a crooked ledge of rock, Selene willed her eyes to fall shut. When would she ever learn to be patient? This was her own personal flaw, and it had to be addressed quickly. Any delay might jeopardize her future success as the twilight guardian.

"Do not be so downcast, my lady," came the familiar elfin voice. "Brenda will heal in time."

"York, why do you think certain spirits have a far more difficult time adapting to their new existence than others?"

"I know not, my lady. The amount of belief they hold in the One Spirit, as well as themselves, may have something to do with it."

"You are wiser than you know, York," Selene offered with a smile. "There is one more question I wish to ask you, Little Elf."

York flinched. This made Selene pause. She recalled witnessing a similar reaction to the nickname once before. York's merry dimples disappeared and his bright eyes sought the floor. She had done it again. How was it that the wrong words poured from her lips with such ease? Now her dear guide was hurt. What a mess she was making with this new position of authority.

"Why did you call me that?" York cried as he stamped his foot in frustration. "You never called me that before. Is it possible you do not fathom how much that name offends me?"

"No, I did not realize that you dislike it so much. I meant it in a friendly way, not as an insult. You are always such a cheery guide, and you love to flit about so much— the name just seems to suit you."

York sighed in resignation. "I am sorry, my lady. How could you have known? What was it you wished to ask?"

At that moment a series of pulses overtook Selene, indicating that it was time to lead the angels back into the twilight mists.

Upon returning to the sacred haven, Selene still puzzled over York's nickname. How could the harmless endearment have the power to offer such pain? Perhaps one day they would discuss the matter. Until then, it was better to focus on other topics of concern.

"York, what can you tell me about the missing earthbound angel?" Selene began, "I believe you called her Mara, guardian of the waters."

The familiar twitch returned to York's lips, indicating that the question obviously disturbed him in some way. Well, there was no help for it. She had to press forward.

"Can you tell me where Mara is now?"

"Forgive me, my lady, but you have a tendency to ask very difficult questions. In truth, I do not know where she is," he confessed with some sorrow. "She has been missing since the day Nero placed the curse upon us."

"Mara crossed him when she tried to send my mother into the light."

"Aye. I believe Nero holds her captive in his realm."

"Then it is my task to find her and set her free."

Suddenly, a pulse overtook Selene with such force, that her elfin guide leapt backward in shock. A transformation unlike anything York had ever witnessed began to unfold before his eyes.

"Now, I understand," she whispered. Turning her luminous gaze on York, she said, "I must leave you for a time. Do not worry. I will return before twilight."

York began to tremble. How did she propose to cross over when it was still daylight? While he was still grappling with this question, the words: "Never Fear, Little Elf," came to him, then he noticed that she was gone.

CHAPTER 13

A steady flow of rain beat against the lonely cottage whose clouded windows overlooked Crescent Lake. Such was the promise of life renewing itself: a promise all but forgotten by the family locked within. Diana Sherwood had been dead for an entire week, and a dull sort of ache hung about the place like a heavy shroud.

No window could be opened to usher in even the slightest hint of fresh air, for Daniel was very ill. What began as a slight case of bronchitis, a normal reaction to the accident, soon developed into pneumonia. That was when Michael asked Dr. Schilling to oversee his son's recovery.

The good Doctor had seen this type of decline before. Knowing human nature a little too well, she began to worry. Daniel's illness had nothing to do with proper treatment. The true source lay much deeper. After all, she had been there that night. It was virtually impossible not to see Daniel's tortured face trapped within her mind's eye. A part of him had died along with his sister; a part that had to be revived before the body would follow suit.

How changed the once happy prankster appeared to even the casual observer. No one could speak to Daniel and expect any kind of civil response, that is, no one but Michael. Daniel stubbornly ignored all of his old friends when they came to visit. Even David Moss received nothing but an icy stare.

Time lost all meaning for the Sherwood family as they drifted in an endless sea of pain. Michael no longer noticed when one day came to an end or another began. All days were the same without Diana. The once proud shoulders began to droop, and the brisk step slowed in pace. Michael's face, however, remained unreadable. Dr. Schilling shuddered to imagine the actual thoughts that were raging in his mind.

An endless torrent of autumn rain had made recovery of Diana's body impossible for the better part of the week. Once the weather finally improved, a gritty band of volunteer policemen arrived at Michael's door offering assistance for the sad task at hand. Although it went against his principles, Michael decided to let them assume authority so he might better focus on Daniel.

Allowing himself a moment of rest on the living room sofa, Michael glanced at Selene's picture. If ever he needed guidance from the twilight guardian, it was now. Perhaps he should will the colors to speak to him as they had done when the painting was first created. And so he began the summons—eyes racing over the familiar outlines with fervent intent. There was a sudden stirring in the air. Something pulled Michael closer, drawing him into the very depths of the painting. Suddenly, he was at one with the brilliant creation. It was then the longed for voice whispered to his soul.

"Michael, you must be there. Only then will you know."

In an instant, Michael was back on the sofa, shaking. Thrusting both hands through his unruly hair, he wondered if he were going mad. Had the voice been real, or merely the vivid remnant of a daydream? There was only one way to find out. Crescent Lake beckoned to him, and he could do nothing but answer her call.

Michael shook his head in order to regain vision. Someone was talking to him.

"It's good to find you resting, if only for a moment," Dr. Schilling said. The only reply she was offered appeared in the form of a half-smile. "Michael," she continued, "I am afraid we must talk. Daniel's condition is worsening, and it is because he does not care what happens to himself. You must speak with him."

Michael rose to his feet and walked toward the large picture window. "It's not that easy."

A frown graced the Doctor's normally smooth brow. "Well, you have to make it that easy. This is no time to feel sorry for yourself. Daniel is growing worse. If things don't change, he could—"

"I don't want to hear it!" Michael roared, more at himself than Dr. Schilling.

"You must!" She produced a handful of unused pills to better drive the point home. "Here, look what I found underneath Daniel's mattress."

"You mean he's been—"

"Yes, I'm afraid so." She offered a sad smile, then continued in a warm voice, "Look, I know you are tired. You've had very little opportunity to rest since—"

"How do you expect me to rest?" he cried in anger. Upon observing her hurt expression, Michael softened the blow by adding, "I'm sorry. I know you are right. I'll have a talk with him about this."

"That's all I ask," the good Doctor replied, as she placed several discarded pills in his hand. "I'm going outside for a breath of fresh air. Don't worry. I'll be back soon. Perhaps then, you can get some shut eye."

"Thanks," Michael whispered, as he mechanically shuffled down the hallway toward his son's room.

Dr. Schilling looked after him a moment, then thoughtfully returned to the world outside.

Upon entering the sickroom, Michael was struck by the supreme effort it took Daniel to draw breath. There was no question that his condition had worsened. What else could be expected if he refused to take his medication? It pained Michael to watch his son sleep so fitfully. The confrontation would have to wait. That meant any thought of visiting

Crescent Lake must be put out of mind. The risk was simply too great.

After clasping Daniel's hand within his own, Michael began to pray for his recovery. Surely the Creator would grant him this request. Michael paused in mid-thought. Someone had just entered the room. Opening his eyes, he found Kelly Branwell gazing upon Daniel, a tinge of regret coloring her expression.

It might be generous to suggest that a metamorphosis had occurred within the spoiled socialite following the accident. Kelly did, however, appear to show genuine concern over Daniel's health. Every day, she managed to visit for at least an hour. Sometimes, she stayed even longer. Michael never questioned her motives. He was too concerned with his own plight to think about Kelly. Something about her appearance at that precise moment seemed preordained. At least Michael took it that way. The still, small voice inside told him she should be trusted. After all, Dr. Schilling was just outside. They would look after Daniel, while Michael slipped away to keep his appointment with Crescent Lake.

"Kelly, I have to speak with the search team. Can you watch Daniel for a few minutes?" Michael asked, offering her a brief smile.

"Sure. Go ahead. We'll be all right."

"Thanks. Dr. Schilling is just outside. If anything happens—call her."

"I will, Mr. Sherwood. I promise."

After pausing to thank Kelly again, Michael exited the cottage for the first time since the accident. It was not long before he stumbled across Dr. Schilling who was enjoying her brief lunch nearby.

"I saw Kelly go in," she said, between bites of her sandwich. "Maybe you should visit the fellows down by the lake."

Michael swallowed. She had made it easy for him. "That is exactly what I had hoped to do. Will you keep an eye on things inside?"

"Of course. I'm almost finished."

Michael nodded and with a wave of his hand, he was on his way.

It did not take long for the peaceful silence, that had enveloped the Sherwood cottage to be disturbed by a sharp series of coughs, issuing from Daniel's weakened frame. He tried to inhale, yet met with little success. Only a thin stream of air trickled into his starving lungs.

Kelly quickly appeared with medicine bottle in hand and began ladling the thick syrup down Daniel's throat. This proved no easy feat for she had to catch him between gasps.

"I'm all right!" he literally choked, pushing the spoon away. The slight exertion brought on another extended coughing fit. Daniel, giving into the spasm, fell against the wooden headboard for support.

Kelly scurried across the room, retrieved Diana's pillow and propped it behind her ward's head.

Daniel grew livid. "Leave her things alone!" he cried.

Kelly's face contorted in pain. He still blames me, she thought. His hatred is so great that he can't even bare to see me touch her things. How can I show him that I am sorry about everything?

She gently tried to raise Daniel from his hunched position so he might breathe with less effort but met with little success.

"Just leave me alone!"

Kelly fought hard to hide the tears that misted her clear, blue eyes—tears that did not escape Daniel's notice.

"Kelly," he whispered, softening a bit, "just go away for a bit—" It was evident he wished to say more but was cut short by another intrusive cough.

"Daniel, you are sick—you need to—"

"I don't care! Just leave me alone!"

Kelly leaned against the wooden bedpost in an effort to gather courage for what she was about to say. "I know you miss her, but—"

"I won't hear this!" Daniel screamed, covering his ears. Another series of coughs soon threw both hands against his chest.

"Daniel, listen to me! You have to stop blaming yourself for her death—or you'll never get better!" Kelly cried in exasperation.

Daniel turned from his attacker. So what if she was a Senator's daughter! He didn't have to hear this! Curling himself tightly between the sheets, he hoped she would take the hint and go away, but Kelly refused to comply. "—And you have to stop blaming me! We didn't kill her! It's not our fault!"

That was it. Daniel threw caution to the wind. He would do or say anything to make her stop. Grabbing Kelly by the wrist, he pulled her face close to his. "If it wasn't your fault, then whose was it? She died trying to save me— and why?"

Now it was Kelly's turn to pull away, but Daniel's hand only tightened around her wrist. "Why did I fall in?"

Kelly's face contorted in pain.

"WHY DID I FALL IN?"

Her trembling lips remained frozen, which angered Daniel even more. "When will you get the message? We don't want you here! Now get out!"

Kelly ran from the room. Why had she ever let her father talk her into this scheme? What good could it accomplish? People were not going to blame them for Diana's death, even if Daniel thought otherwise. So what if this charity work helped him gain a few extra votes in the community! Nothing was worth this pain! Now she was forced to wait in this house of death until her father arrived to take her home. Weak and confused, she collapsed on the sofa and allowed the tears to flow.

Daniel could hear her sobbing as he buried his face in Diana's pillow. He felt weak…so weak with the tears blinding his own eyes. Soon his head began to spin. Casting the pillow aside, he saw the room expand before him. He was falling down a long, dark tunnel. An image of Diana pillow-duelling flashed across his mind. Yes, it had happened in this very room. If only he could make her come back…if only…Daniel's eyes flashed open. Someone was watching him. Chills coursed up and down his spine causing his throat to tighten until he could no longer breathe. What was happening? Why couldn't he force oxygen into his aching lungs? Daniel made one last attempt to breathe and felt no surprise when the effort failed. He was dying. There was no way to stop it from happening. All he had to do was let go.

There is nothing in life quite so precious, or so taken for granted, as air. Daniel consumed the elixir with quick, greedy gulps. It soon became evident that he was stationed at the window seat—the window thrown wide open to usher in cleansing air. Only one explanation came to mind.

"Diana, is it you?"

A soft mist drifted through the room. Daniel watched in fascination as it magically began to boil like the contents of a caldron. If this was Diana, she had most certainly become a witch. It was then he heard her laughter.

"I am no witch, Danny," she said, taking shape before his eyes.

"Diana—" Daniel tried to cry out, but instead the words came as a whisper. Was it really her, or just some figment of his imagination? "There is no need to be afraid, Danny. It is me," the figure said in a voice that sounded quite different from the Diana he knew.

"You saved me twice, didn't you? At the lake and—"

"And just now. Yes, I did," she simply replied.

Daniel placed his good arm around his sister's shoulders, then balked at the sensation. It felt like he was touching a cloud! Everything about this new Diana seemed unreal, and Daniel could not help but feel disturbed by the realization.

"Danny, I am here in spirit, not flesh. I will never take that form again."

Daniel's eyes filled with tears. "Then, you are—" he stopped short, unable to say the hated word.

"I am one of them now."

"Are you, Di?" he asked, brightening a bit. "What's it like?"

"I will tell you about it at another time. Now, I must ask one, maybe two, favors of you."

"I'll do anything for you, Di!"

"First, you must cooperate with Dr. Schilling and regain your health."

Daniel could not help but sigh. "I promise."

"You had another close call just now, and I am afraid that was my fault. I should have come sooner. I planned to —but time passes so quickly there," she explained with a solemn bow of her head.

"That's all right, Di," Daniel replied, with just a trace of his mischievous smile. "You must be awfully busy."

"Yes, we are…" she said, wondering how much she should actually tell him. "Danny, when you recover I—we will need your help in solving a problem that has long tormented those who dwell in the Land of Twilight Mist."

"You have problems there?" Daniel asked, as he leapt to his feet. It was not difficult to guess where this new energy had come from. "I'll help you now!"

"No, not just yet," soothed Selene as she escorted him back to bed.

111

"First, you must regain your strength, both of body and spirit. You will need to be very strong to accomplish everything I will ask of you."

"I promise—it won't take me long, Di. I feel better already. See, I can breathe fine," he eagerly demonstrated by inhaling very deeply.

"Good," she replied with a knowing smile. "I will return in one week's time, then we will discuss the zany adventures that await Sir Laugh-a-lot."

Daniel chuckled as he snuggled back into the comfortable warmth of his bed.

"I leave you with one last thought, Danny. Forgive others, as you are now able to forgive yourself."

She paused only to place a familiar, yellow scarf in Daniel's hands. With this action, a beam of light traveled up the length of his body. At that moment, Daniel knew that he had been healed.

"Forgive others, as you now forgive yourself," he echoed, until both eyelids fell shut. What had she called herself—Selene? Sleep overtook him and he knew no more.

Selene softly kissed Daniel on the cheek, then approached the old family room with silent tread. There she found Kelly still sobbing on the green sofa. It was imperative the girl not see her.

"I will not question your motives for coming here," she whispered in Kelly's ear, "but perhaps you should. What is it you hope to accomplish? Absolution? You are no more responsible for Diana's death, than Daniel. Be patient. He will forgive you in time. Only believe, and it will be so."

CHAPTER 14

Minutes slowly lengthened into hours as Michael sat on the shores of Crescent Lake, waiting for some sign that might confirm his convictions. The search crew had found no trace of Diana's remains. That did not surprise him. Soon they would be forced to call off their efforts due to impending twilight. He could wait that long—and, if he were right…

After sobbing beyond the point of exhaustion, Kelly fell into a waking nightmare where ghostly images demanded her attention. What was it they were trying to tell her? Everything seemed so real, but deep down inside, she knew better. This was nothing more than a daydream—an occupation expressly forbidden in the Branwell household. If ever she breathed so much as a word of this to her father, punishment would follow. It was best, then, to ignore the voices inside her head. That was the only possible response her father would accept.

Wiping her tear stained eyes on a nearby pillow, Kelly paused to consider the many questions that still plagued her mind. Why had she been sent to watch—no spy—on Daniel? Was her father actually threatened by the Sherwoods in some way? Everything seemed so jumbled in her mind.

An unexpected patter of bare feet forced Kelly to open her eyes. She was surprised to find that Daniel stood beside her—and that he looked surprisingly well.

A heavy sigh escaped Michael's lips. There was still no trace of Diana—none at all. Why then, did the dark fears still continue to whisper their counsel? What if they did find her? What then? He would be forced to admit that Cynthia was dead, and so was her daughter…

Michael began to pace along the shallow hillside. What had he done wrong? Was it essential that an artist be forced to live a miserable life, or did the grand scheme go much deeper? He had tried so hard to live simply, free of unnecessary material desires that might cloud the mind. He had to be free to create, didn't he? And now he was, with the exception of Daniel, free. Was this what he truly wanted? Had he actually wished his own daughter dead?

A shudder raced up Michael's spine. Where had that come from? All he had ever wanted was to have a family that he could call his own. Now his dearest hopes had all but faded into darkness—and he was left to ponder such questions alone.

How many years had passed since Cynthia's disappearance? Did he really want to remember? Perhaps it would be better to ask if he had any choice. Everything in his entire existence pointed toward this neglected path. What could he do but follow?

Michael sighed. How long had it been? It was time to look reality square in the face. Perhaps he could best do that by centering on his children. Daniel was—had been—a little over a year old at the time, and Diana, his sweet Diana, a dazzling three year old. That was ten years ago—ten long years. The length of an entire decade stretched between them and the lost woman that had haunted their dreams.

The clouds broke forth and wept anew upon the battered search team. Michael listened as they railed at the thoughtless elements. Yes, he understood that the men were angry, but so what? They had not lost both wife and daughter to the lake. They had no idea what it felt like; no comprehension of what lay behind this supposed disaster! An inner voice roused Michael from his thoughts, forcing him to glance at the old oak tree that stood near the crest of

Lookout Point. The decaying branches all but reached out, seemingly beckoning him to a gentle embrace.

As he drew closer, a stream of light merged with the empty husk. He could not help but gasp as the two entities merged in a blending dance that made them one and the same. Michael's eyes grew wide with wonder. The somber hues of decaying gray had been replaced by a rich harvest of red and gold. It was at that moment he saw her. There, inside the very heart of the tree, stood a woman with hair of flame. Silently, she gained in definition until the entire structure erupted in one great burst of light. When Michael's senses finally cleared, he saw her as she had always been, intently whittling away at a long, slender piece of wood underneath an abundant canopy of a rich, healthy boughs.

"Cynthia?" Michael whispered softly, so she might not detect the catch in his throat.

As she turned toward him, all the light from the tree seemed centered in her eyes. "See how it takes form?" she said, indicating the gleaming wood. "It's time you had a new easel."

Michael began to tremble as she wrapped him within a loving embrace. What was happening? She seemed so real! The soft familiarity of those arms as they twined about his neck, nearly drove him mad! It did not take long for his senses to rebel. Breaking from her in confusion, he found himself trapped within the depths of her hazel eyes. They appeared so all knowing. Could she actually read his thoughts?

"I know you are discouraged, but you must continue the work. It is easy enough for others to judge you with their sharp criticisms, but you must know within that the work is good—as I know it."

Michael wanted desperately to speak, but no words would come.

"You must see Moss, and soon," she whispered, allowing her lips to touch his. "Arm yourself with the necessary tools for the days and nights ahead, then let her go. You must let her go—as I did. One day things will be different."

Without wasting so much as another word, Cynthia walked into the crystal waters until she could be seen no more. The phrase, "Believe and she will come back to you," hung thick in the air.

Michael shook his head, desperately struggling to regain some sense of equilibrium. Someone was speaking to him.

"Sorry to bother you, Sherwood, but—uh, it's getting late and we'll have to be packing up for the evening."

When Michael's eyes finally regained focus, they fell on Tom Delaney, a well meaning, if somewhat awkward policeman. Michael smiled for a moment: a forced smile that seemed all too unnatural for his brooding features. Perhaps it was because he did not use those muscles very much any more. Allowing his expression to relax, Michael gratefully clapped the exhausted policeman on the back. "Go ahead, Tom. I'm afraid I've lost all track of time."

"That's understandable," Tom replied, with an embarrassed shrug of his shoulders. He couldn't bear to imagine what must be going on in Michael Sherwood's mind. After all, seven days had passed, and there was still no trace of Diana's body.

Tom offered Michael a brief nod, then hurried back toward the other volunteers. He found himself thoroughly absorbed in the sound his boots made, as they squished through the sticky, brown mud when Michael drew his attention.

"There'll be no need for you to come back again."

The tired workers paused, tools still poised in hand. Their expressions registered a mixture of confusion and gratitude.

"I've decided to leave her in peace," he softly explained.

A strong hand came to rest on Michael's back with such firm intensity that he could not help but flinch at its weight.

"Easy, Sherwood," soothed Senator Branwell's resonant voice. "I just stopped by to collect my wayward daughter and heard voices down here, so I thought I'd see if I could be of any assistance."

Michael bit his lip, and somehow managed to remain silent, while he carefully scanned the black eyes for any trace of real compassion. It came as no surprise that he found none.

"Michael—uh, Mr. Sherwood, here, has decided to— let things stay the way they are," Tom supplied, hoping to relieve the tension that had accompanied Branwell's unexpected arrival.

"Then I take it she has not been found?" Branwell asked the ruffled policeman most pointedly.

"No, Sir," Tom replied, in an embarrassed, almost apologetic tone.

"My sympathies, Sherwood. Though we little know each other, I have no doubt that this was a very difficult decision for you and your son."

Michael offered no response, so the Senator continued, "I was speaking to Reverend Moss about you the other day. We came up with some ideas that you might find interesting." Michael tried to turn away, but Branwell stayed him with a firm grip on the arm. "It concerns a new foundation in Diana's name—"

That was it! What right had Branwell to speak with Moss or anyone about his daughter! "You came to 'collect' Kelly, I believe," Michael said rather curtly. The very sight of Branwell made him ill. His whole demeanor seemed pre-rehearsed. He could now appreciate Kelly for what she truly was: a misunderstood child who had been spoiled since birth. Branwell, on the other hand, presented a figure Michael refused to tolerate, especially at this difficult time in his life. "She's in the cottage. You can "collect" her there. I'll be along directly."

Branwell inclined his ruffled head, ever so slightly, then without another word, marched off toward the cottage. One thought consumed his being, as he drew near the top of the hill: Sherwood had to be dealt with and soon. A charge of child abuse, or endangerment might prove the best option, considering everything that had happened. It would, however, be difficult to make it stick. Sherwood was well respected in the community—and across the country. Still, he had little other choice. Michael had to be taken out of the picture before it all came to pass.

"Diana is the one," he whispered to the breeze. "I knew it long ago."

At that moment, a cold, stream of electricity whipped through the boughs overhead.

"You should be more careful, Branwell. It would serve you well to keep your thoughts hidden from me—now, that I know who you really are," Selene's bodiless voice rang soft and deep as the sea.

"Don't be so quick to cross me, little one. You forget, this is my realm!"

"Not for long, Nero. As you so wisely put it—the time is at hand!" Without further pause, the current passed directly through his being, leaving a sharp, burning sensation in its wake.

Branwell whirled around in surprise, his arms flailing about like some great bird, clipped down in mid-flight. He had never expected her to challenge him so openly. It was imperative he not allow it to happen again. After ascertaining that the angel had indeed gone, he bent his steps toward the Sherwood cottage, fully aware that a declaration of war had just been laid at his feet.

CHAPTER 15

A warm rush of wind ushered Selene back to her favorite haunt near the hollow oak at Lookout Point. It was time to rest, if only for a moment. After leaning back against the decaying trunk, her eyes fell shut. She had set the wheels in motion. Now Nero—Branwell would come to her.

"Well, I am waiting. You did plan on telling me what happened today, did you not?" York's perky voice chirped in her ear.

Selene opened her eyes to find the little elf settled in a tangled bough directly overhead. It was obvious from his beaming face that he could not contain his excitement.

"Are you certain you really want to know?" she asked rather playfully. "There are some things better left unsaid."

York leapt from his unstable perch, landing directly at her side. "Do not tease me. I wish to know everything that happened. If words fail you, why not tell me with your thoughts?" he suggested, quickly tapping his brow.

After careful consideration, Selene placed her hand on York's shoulder, then gazed into the depths of his brown eyes. The message flowed instantly between them without any assistance from author or recipient.

"Today, I made contact with the Spirit which dwells within us all. That is what you saw earlier when I went into the strange trance. I suddenly realized that all the answers I sought were here."

Selene motioned toward her heart.

York's eyes shone with a brightness she had never witnessed before. He was proud of her. That made Selene happy, although she did not know why.

"The One Spirit revealed many things to me. Did you know that I have the ability to travel between worlds whenever I wish?"

The little elf gave an anxious start, but Selene quickly calmed him with a smile. "Remember, I was not present when Nero condemned the earthbound angels to a twilight existence. No limitations have been placed on me. All I need do is contact the One Spirit and the transition is made complete."

York wiggled so violently that Selene feared he might burst at the seams. Only the sheer force of her hand kept him from enjoying the freedom found in the misting air.

"Then you did travel into the daylight!" he cried with glee.

"Yes, and I spoke with Daniel. He has promised to help us once his recovery is complete."

Once York finally managed to break from Selene's grasp, he danced a merry jig around the ancient tree. "You traveled into the daylight! Oh, how I miss it! You will take me with you next time—that is if—"

"I will take you tomorrow, if you wish."

With one, swift movement, York planted a kiss on Selene's forehead, then just as abruptly, disappeared.

Selene puzzled over this momentarily, then called out, "York, I have more to tell you. Please, come back. This is important!"

The glowing elfin figure reappeared at the very spot he had last occupied. "Yes, my lady," he coyly replied.

Selene drew close, then, after placing her hand upon his brow, she continued, "I saw him today, York—the Dark One. Why didn't you tell me he now goes by the name of Branwell?"

York bit down on his lip, hard, forcing the dimples into retreat. "I feared you would confront him," he honestly replied.

"I see," she continued with a smile. "Well, you were absolutely right. I did just that."

"Selene—" York cried as he leapt into the air, "that may have been unwise!"

"I had no choice. The Spirit prompted me to do so. Branwell already suspected who I was—am. You see, no body has been found."

"Nor, will be," York completed her thought, still trembling quite noticeably as he returned to earth. It took no small degree of effort for him to place his hand upon her brow. Once accomplished, however, the thoughts poured from his being, like water rushing through a dam. "'Tis time I tell everything, Selene."

York bowed his curly head, relishing a final moment of silence, before the horrors began.

"Nero and I lived during what you think of as the Dark Ages—though he existed long before that. He goes by the name of Branwell, because at one time he was known as Bran—a Celtic God."

"A God? How can that be? He is neither good or—"

"Selene, please—be careful of your thoughts. When the Celts worshipped him, he was known as Bran the Blessed—because he was good."

"Then what happened? I do not understand—"

"There is good and evil within every being. Often these traits exist in equal proportion, but with Bran the one so dominated the other that a split occurred. For centuries the evil lay dormant until it was set free by an act of wickedness executed upon the ancient Deity. It was then the evil took control and cast the good into oblivion. Now only the evil remains…"

Selene shook her head in confusion. "Then he too must be saved—"

"Think not on it, my lady. Your purpose is to free the earthbound angels."

"But—"

"Please allow me to continue with my story. We may have little time before he decides to strike."

There was a moment of silence during which Selene considered the many paths before her. Then after a nod of consent, she breathed, "Of course. Go on."

"I was once a performer—part of a seven member troupe led by my father, Nab. He taught me how to dance before I could even speak. We traveled from place to place performing dances, mimes—anything that might please an audience. Unfortunately, we often received little for our efforts. We were—what you might call—poor. The people we entertained often could not afford to pay with money, so they offered food and drink instead. That did not trouble me at all, though—as long as we made people happy. I have always found great joy in making people smile."

Selene was hardly surprised by this confession for she knew York to be the kindest of spirits, even if he did relish the occasional prank.

"Time passed very pleasantly, until my father noticed that I was rather small for my fifteen years. Why it took him so long to realize this important fact, I shall never know. I was always aware of the difference between myself and other lads, but never let it bother me. Something about me seemed more like a sprite than a young man. I could do things that seemed magical, such as read minds and make objects disappear. Hence, Nab became worried about my future with the troupe. The other members feared I was a victim of enchantment and wished me gone. I know not why they were so afraid. I was simply a child who possessed gifts few understood."

Selene offered his hand a warm squeeze in a show of support.

"One morning I went for a walk by a beautiful lake that lay just beyond a great forest—"

Her eyes widened with the question that all but hung on her lips—was it Whispering Pines?

"Nay, t'was a British forest that lay not far from a village where we had entertained the night before. I remember it well, for I had been especially good that night. A sense of giddiness overtook me and I began to dance a jig around the lake. I shall never forget that moment—t'was beyond all imaging. My feet barely seemed to touch the ground. Something greater than my own self led me through a series of complex steps I had never seen before. You of all beings, Selene, understand what I speak of."

Selene nodded in gentle affirmation.

"As I continued to dance, two squirrels appeared, along with a russet fox, a raven and a fawn. They watched my every move with rapt fascination. I fancied I had somehow managed to enchant them.

When the troupe finally arrived to gather water for our day's travel, they met with a curious sight. The animals were dancing with me! Each followed my intricate steps with an almost uncanny precision—as if they too were being guided by a higher force. Even the raven took part by remaining carefully perched on my shoulder, governing our progress. Naturally, the troupe was delighted with what they saw. They jested that I had placed a spell upon the pretty creatures just as a woodland elf might do. From that day forward I was known as the Little Elf. It was quickly agreed that I should remain a member of the troupe, provided that I perform with the animals."

"How very generous of them," Selene suggested, slyly winking her eye.

York momentarily displayed his dimples, then continued with his tale. "I was feeling very happy and not a little tired, so I sat down upon the bank and gathered these new friends into my sleepy arms. The troop soon departed. That was when I realized we were not alone. Instinctively, I turned toward a great oak, just beyond the glen, and was met by a pair of frightfully dark eyes. The animals were startled and huddled close to me for protection. It was then I heard his voice."

'Beware, Little Elf. Remember to whom you owe allegiance. Any attempt to mock me, or cross me again will constitute a severing of our ties. One day I will call. You will have no choice but to heed the summons.'

Selene, I had no idea what those words meant. Was this some practical joke played upon me by the troupe? As time passed, the dark eyes faded from my mind; and with the help of my animal friends, I soon forgot them altogether. Those dear, little creatures became my life.

Soon the act drew large crowds of people far and wide, who actually paid money to see me dance with the wild animals. They brought me such luck! Each was uniquely gifted in his or her own way. The two squirrels—they were husband and wife—always gossiped among themselves. I called them Tell and Tale—not very original I am afraid," York confessed with a slight shrug of his shoulders. The corners of his eyes crinkled in fond remembrance. "Both Tale and Tell were very possessive of me. They demanded to be carried on my person, whether it be in an open pocket, or a satchel, so they might scrutinize any stranger who passed our way.

The fawn was a rather shy, young lady, who possessed some extraordinary powers. She seemed able to read human thoughts, so I named her Morgan, after the mysterious enchantress you find so fascinating. Morgan would not allow any human to touch her but myself. One look in her eyes told me whether or not I should avoid a situation. She truly understood the difference between good and evil. In fact, she saved me on more than one occasion with her simple gift.

The last two members of our entourage were very independent in nature. Sly, as you have probably guessed, was the little fox. He did not need companionship like the others, unless we were practicing or performing. He would often leave us for hours at a time, only to return with a peace offering such as a fresh rabbit for dinner. Then, there was Caw, the raven. After securing a perch upon my shoulder, she would remain firmly anchored there for a good part of the day. Caw had this trick of staying so still that many people thought she was a stuffed toy. But, when they tried to poke her—just to make certain—she would scream out at the top of her lungs until the hapless intruders left her in peace. Caw was determined to watch after me both day and night, and so she did—until the end…Oh, how I loved the animals! Together, we brought such joy to people—or so I like to think…"

"I am sure you did, York," Selene affirmed with a smile. She watched as the brilliant gleam that fired his eyes, slowly dimmed, until it was replaced by the cold, cruel glare of fear.

"One day after a perfectly wonderful performance, a young man, who turned out to be a royal page, invited me to perform for his king. I had never danced for royalty before —so I jumped at the offer. The animals and I prepared for weeks, hours on end, with very little sleep in between. Finally, the day of our performance arrived, and the entire troupe accompanied me to the Kingdom, that lay near the sea. I remember the air was fresh and clear, yet I felt uneasy, as if some storm lay brewing just ahead. The animals seemed oblivious to the sensation, so we journeyed on. That evening, at the performance, they were nothing less than spectacular, executing their steps with grace and vigor. I felt as if I were gliding on air. Scanning the audience, I met with a swirl of bright, happy faces that seemed to float before my eyes. Then, I happened upon the dark robes of the court adviser. The page had spoken of him with a mixture of awe and fear. I need not tell you, Selene, that this was Bran, in another form. The page informed me that he had done a great many things of an unspeakable nature. One look told me this had not been a lie.

Even then, Nero looked very much as he does today. As I gazed into his dark, glittering orbs, I was reminded of that haunting experience by the lake. The animals became skittish. No doubt, they also sensed his malice. Thankfully, the dance soon ended, and we were met with thunderous applause. Both king and court begged for more. Naturally, I was only too happy to comply. Sometime, during the course of the encore, I became aware that Bran (Nero) had disappeared. I relaxed, temporarily forgetting the fear, and so the evening sped on.

When we finally could dance no more, the King offered our troupe rooms in the servants quarters. It was decided that the animals should be housed in the royal stables. This left me feeling a little anxious. If I accepted the King's hospitality, the animals and I would be separated for the very first time since we met. Nab convinced me that it would be foolish to refuse the King's wishes, so I complied.

Bidding the animals goodnight, I noticed how determined they were that I should remain with them. Even Sly curled around my ankles in an effort to prevent my departure. Dear, little Morgan pleaded with gentle eyes, but that night I refused to listen. I was pleased with my good fortune and wanted to share it with father and the rest of the troupe. Hence, I locked the animals in their private stalls, then sang them to sleep. It took quite a long time for them to doze off, but they were tired and could not help it. Only Caw remained awake. Her midnight eyes never left me as I crept out of the darkened stables and closed the door behind me."

There was a tensing of York's features as he struggled to maintain composure.

"On my way back to the servant's quarters, I began to experience a strange sensation, as if hidden eyes followed my every step. I called out to the presence that was stalking me: 'What do you want?'

An icy breeze curled against the back of my neck, indicating the unknown pursuant was nearby. My hair stood on end. The voice made its presence known. 'You know the answer, Little Elf. Think back—think back to the beginning. You chose not to acknowledge me this night, therefore, I cease to acknowledge you!'

Everything melted into one shade of black almost suffocating in its intensity. The sound of angry winds roared across the cliffs and into a raging sea. I heard them calling out to me, beckoning me forward with their siren's song until I deemed myself ready to join forces with the swirling foam below. Then, I remembered my father and the animals. I could not leave them. Our bond was too great. It was their love that called me back to life.

As my thoughts cleared, an unearthly scream shattered the night. My fear grew to terror. I ran toward the royal stables with a faltering heart but knew it was already too late. My animals friends were gone. I searched the stables a second time, hoping, praying I would find a clue that would lead me to them. Something made me pause at an inner stall I had not noticed before. There, on a wooden peg, which used to hold feedbags, hung the severed head of my beautiful Caw. I was horrified, for I felt certain she had tried to warn me that something terrible was going to happen. If only I had listened. It did not take much to imagine what became of the others. While lifting the senseless head from its final perch, I noticed a faded bit of parchment tied about the neck. It said: 'Do not grieve, Little Elf. You will soon follow.' My thoughts flew to Nab and the troupe. They were also in danger. I ran toward the castle knowing full well that it was already too late. It was not long before I noticed six forms hanging from the trees."

He paused to press his companion's hand. "They were oak trees, Selene. Nab was still alive when I reached him. 'Black magic—'tis him,' he croaked, gasping for breath. 'The wizard—I would not let him take you back—ruuun…'

His feet danced the waltz of death, and then he was gone. There I stood completely alone for the first time in my life, knowing full well there was nothing I could do. My brain was reeling, but somehow I moved forward. It was vital I make sense out of what Nab had told me. I did not remember ever having met Nero before—not even in childhood. What could he have meant?

As I fled deeper and deeper into the heart of the forest, lightning filled the skies; and I was forced to seek shelter under an oak tree. This turned out to be a foolish mistake for a large branch was struck by lightning and crashed down upon me—pinning me by the chest."

Selene's eyes burned with tears that stubbornly refused to fall. Such a fate had almost claimed her the night of the storm.

"'Remember me, Little Elf?' Nero asked, appearing in a wicked flash of light. 'Is it possible you still do not know who I really am? Surely, your conscience tells you.' It must have seemed odd to him, but I did not understand. Reading the confusion on my face, he graciously chose to remind me of everything I had forgotten.

'Who do you think your real father is? Hm? Surely, not that imbecile Nab? Let me ask you another question—why do you think the animals came to you? Because you are so special? You see, I can read your thoughts. They came to you because I sent them. They were my creations—life brought forth from my dark work, not as you thought, from the Spirit of light. You do not enjoy hearing me say that, do you, Little Elf? Rest assured, you will not have to listen much longer. It will be over very soon.'

"Nero offered something of a sad smile, as he continued, 'It pains me to see you this way, but remember, I am not the one who forgot! Yes, I created you. That is why you are not like other children. You were to be my right arm—my Little Elf—capable of performing magical feats to aid my endeavors. Since you chose to forget me—those gifts were never fully realized. What a shame. It is partially my fault, I will admit. How could I have known Nab would turn out to be such an idiot? He refused to follow my instructions and turned you against me. You grew too independent. You even had the gall to insult me. Do you remember that? Think. I once visited you in disguise—the dark man at Caerleon. A true son would have recognized his own father even then! I offered you immortality, and how did you repay me—with thankfulness? Nay. I was offered a reception that I will never forget! Aye, now I see you do remember! At least that allows me some sense of satisfaction, York. That is the name the idiot gave you, is it not? Remember when they were going to throw you out of the troupe? That night you breathed a prayer for assistance. Who really heard you? Not the Spirit! Who sent the animals? It was me all along! Me—whom you chose to deny! Well, Little Elf, I have decided to be merciful and offer you the gift of immortality once again—only because it pains me to see you laying there like some crushed poppet. You may continue to walk this earth in a manner more glorious than you ever dreamed possible. I will give you anything you wish—even send those silly animals back, but you must agree to serve me and the shadows of darkness. It is your decision, Little Elf. Choose wisely.'

"I need hardly tell you that I refused him, Selene. I denied him with every bit of strength left in my shattered frame. You can imagine what happened next. He left me with this final warning: 'Foolish elf, our paths will cross again, and when they do we will be sworn enemies. What a charming family we make, Little Elf. You will serve the powers of light, even as I rule by darkness. Defy me then, and I will thrust you into a land of no return for all eternity.'

York paused with drooping countenance. "That is my story, Selene. I died full of pain and confusion. Yes, I had triumphed over darkness but felt no joy. The fear that my parentage made me evil blotted out everything else for a time. Thankfully, the One Spirit lifted me into the world of light. As the years passed, I healed ever so slowly."

Selene was overcome with compassion for her dear guide. "York, how you must have suffered when you learned the truth. Your story has taught me many things— not only about yourself, but also concerning the other earthbound angels that remain in the stage where suffering still occurs. That is why we are earthbound. We are still bound by our previous lives on earth."

She paused for a moment, pondering whether or not to ask the question that preyed upon her mind.

York made it easy for her. "Go ahead, my lady," he said. "I will answer as best I may."

"What trick did you play on Bran? What could you possibly have done that angered him so much?"

"I am ashamed to say it, but during the performance he spoke of—in the city of Caerleon—I did the only thing I could to make him look foolish. You must understand—he was threatening to take me away from Nab—and I had no idea who he was—"

"You played a trick on him and somehow forgot as the years passed?"

"Aye, I cannot explain it, but 'tis true! When he grabbed me by the wrist, I momentarily tapped into his dark powers. Somehow, without my participation, Bran was stripped of his courtly guise and thrust into a large, gaping hole in a hollowed out oak. Everyone laughed and thought it a fine magician's trick. To this day—I do not know what happened. I certainly wished to be rid of him, but I never dreamed of shaming him in such a way. The Druids, the holy men of the times, used to consider the oak tree very sacred. Perhaps, through the act, I was trying to help reclaim that which was once sacred in him."

Selene smiled with appreciation. "The One Spirit was with you even then."

York nodded in affirmation. "Selene, it is your destiny to battle the Dark One. Please remember that he is absolutely evil. He will not hesitate to strike those you love. That is how he will weaken you before the attack. You must keep a constant watch over Daniel and Michael at all times. Keep angels guarding them always. If you wish, I will take charge of—"

"York, "Selene whispered, as her fingertips brushed his downy cheeks, "You are in great danger, perhaps even more so than I. He will be waiting for you. Hasn't he already warned you of what lies ahead? Bran will surely strike at you because of your connection to both of us."

"Aye, we are connected, my lady. Believe me, I will do everything in my power to protect you and your family from him—" York paused in mid-thought. He whirled around as if listening to something of great import.

A sharp tremor rushed through Selene's frame. It was the Dark One. He had captured a new prey. In a moment she understood that it was one of their own.

CHAPTER 16

Forrest slid through a sea of ancient boughs, weaving a path through his darkened sanctuary. Onward he climbed, swinging through a thick network of limbs knotted by time, all but oblivious to the discord that swirled in the air. Whispering Pines was his home—the only place in which he felt entirely at ease. There was no need to be embarrassed or shy about anything in this green cathedral. Among his woodland friends he was more than just a timid, fledgling spirit: he was their guardian.

"We're special in the Spirit's eyes, my friends," Forrest gently reminded his wards, upon nestling against a moss covered bough. How peaceful, how serene it felt lying in nature's womb! What a perfect wonder it was to be heralded a woodland guardian!

After a moment, he noticed how very quiet the trees were that evening. "What's got into you, friends? Why are you so still? I'll bet you're just hot and tired, aren't you? Not a breeze anywhere to fan your boughs. Don't worry, it can't last much longer."

Upon shifting his position, Forrest caught sight of the dazzling stars that sparkled within the deep, purple sky. He had always loved the stars, even when he was just a boy.

"Can you see that, friends? There, up above! Look at the heavens. Just part those needles and see what I'm talking about. That's right. Do you see them?"

The pine boughs lightly swayed back and forth as if in answer to his question.

Forrest smiled. The midnight sky reminded him of another time, when he and his father had watched the stars. Forrest had been sad, so sad that his father had lead him out into the freshly plowed fields, determined to demonstrate that life still held beauty...

A rustling of needles stirred Forrest's muddled senses. Something was wrong. His friends were trying to offer him warning. Leaping from his moss covered perch, the woodland guardian beat a hasty ascent up the King Oak. At that moment two shimmering lights appeared across the horizon, demanding his attention.

"It's the Lady," Forrest whispered to himself, before calling out to his wards. "The new Selene is coming to ask our help, friends. She's going after—the Dark One."

Several pines shivered in knowing response.

The restless moon witnessed everything. She knew it was her duty to warn Bran, yet something made her hesitate. This night could be the beginning of the end: this night, he was evil itself. Silently, she allowed the dark clouds to drift across her bright sphere. Tonight she would watch, nothing more.

Forrest looked up. They were almost upon him. A kind branch lifted him higher, so he might better welcome the two shimmering forms as they entered his domain.

Selene smiled in greeting, barely pausing to offer instruction. "We will need your assistance this night, Forrest. An innocent has fallen victim to the Dark One. Tell the angels that they must be ready for our call."

"I will, brave lady."

Forrest proudly saluted the guardian, as she and her guide sped away. He would do everything in his power to help save the earthbound angels. They were his new family, even if he was too shy to verbally admit it.

Scurrying across the treetops, Forrest watched the beacons of light disappear from view. Come what may, he and the earthbound angels would be ready when they returned. Now it was his task to prepare them for what lay ahead.

"We are very near, my lady," York chirped in Selene's ear. "I feel certain he has not detected us yet. There is still time to—"

"York, you can hardly think of backing out now, after we have come so far!"

The little elf paused in mid-flight, securing his lower lip between his teeth. "I know him, Selene. I know what he can do. I cannot bare to think of him destroying you in such—a ghastly manner."

Her smooth brow darkened ever so slightly. "I see. You have no faith in me, Little Elf."

York flinched as if struck a blow. "It is not that—I just—"

He stared at her with pooling eyes, unable to voice the sentiments locked deep within his being. He loved Selene, there could be no doubt about that. Yet how could he ever hope for her to return such feelings? It was far better to remain mute on this point.

"No matter," she said, recommencing flight, "I will show you."

The smitten elf said not another word but followed closely at her side.

Soon the charcoal outline of Senator Branwell's mansion rose to greet Selene and her companion, offering just the hint of a shadowy smile. It was a beautiful structure, beautiful in a malevolent sort of way. Shrouded with a veneer of normalcy, evil seemed to permeate the air around its foundation. Rumor suggested that Branwell had brought it piece by piece from Virginia. In any case, there was little time to sit and ponder the mansion's origins, for its master would soon be aware of their presence.

Calling on the twilight mist, Selene asked its assistance in transporting them inside so they might better escape detection. In practically no time at all, a thick blanket of purple engulfed their beings. It lent them a kind of invisibility that allowed easy access through a window that had been left slightly ajar. Onward they trod, through the wide foyer that led directly to a darkened staircase. This intricate structure seemingly begged notice as it spiraled a path through each and every floor of the mansion.

Although the energy radiating from upstairs felt far from tranquil, Selene knew it was the cellar that demanded her attention. She could almost hear a silent cry for help emanating below. It was then the images of a dark-haired woman began to flood her senses. So violent were these visions, so utterly lacking in warmth, that Selene was forced to grasp the railing for support. Was this a plea for help, or merely an elaborate scheme Bran had concocted to lure them into a trap?

"There is only one way to find out," York suggested, easily reading her thoughts. "Shall we proceed?"

Selene smiled at her wayward guide, then offered a quick nod of her head.

Downward she plunged, headfirst into the suffocating darkness, never once glancing back to see if York followed at her heals. There was a certain ease with which she navigated the lightless spiral—an ease that took her somewhat by surprise. Surely Bran sensed their approach. Why, then, did he remain hidden from view? What kind of game was he playing? Why did he not just simply attack?

The cellar itself was perfectly sweltering, with little in the way of breeze to stir the stagnant air. So thick was the blackness that met her eyes, everything appeared wrapped within an ebony shroud. Where was the dark-haired angel, and more importantly, where was the creature who held her captive?

Unable to endure the crushing silence any longer, Selene turned to her guide for answers. "York, can you see him?"

"No, my lady, but I feel him all the same. The Dark One is here. Alone."

"Then it is a trap."

"I hardly think so," hissed a shapeless voice from somewhere in the darkness. "It was you that challenged me."

A distant rustle of wings filled the air. Selene tried to counter the sound by moving in the opposite direction, but sharpened talons seized her arm. It was then he began to chuckle, a chuckle that seemed to originate from the very bowels of the earth.

"Selene, do not give in!" York cried in despair. "Fight him with all your being!"

Anger welled within the twilight guardian's soul. What did York think she was trying to do? Did he believe that she would simply hand herself over to the dark tyrant? Thus, Selene doubled her efforts against the force that remained cloaked in shadow.

"Why not show yourself, Bran? Could it be that you are afraid to face me in the light?"

A wave of bitterness slipped from the darkness, hurling Selene against a roughened stone wall. There was a brutal snap as she hit the unyielding structure, followed by the increasingly familiar chuckle. No doubt Bran found her plight highly amusing. Paralyzed from head to toe, Selene's terror grew to mammoth proportions. This caused a sudden shift in attack. Darkness eclipsed her senses. Unable to see, hear, touch or smell, Selene felt very lost and alone. Where was her guide? Why did he remain so silent? Had he also fallen victim to Bran?"

"So, you are worried about him, are you?—the Little Elf? How touching. I must admit there is something about York that twists its way into the soul. That something is me. We are eternally linked through time. He is the one who brought you here. How does that make you feel?"

Selene chose not to answer, so deep was her level of despair.

"Did you know," Bran continued in a somewhat amused voice, "it is only through my grace that he still continues to be? York is a misplaced child of darkness..."

Bran sensed the dilation in her pupils so he continued, "Oh, so the thought has crossed your mind. Was he so transparent? Never fear. He will be corrected."

A chill rushed up Selene's spine, lending a kind of agony to her captivity.

"Why do you shudder? There is no use trying to hide your feelings from me, Selene. I have watched you throughout time. It is quite useless to fight me. I have already won. Indeed, the darkness is coursing through your soul at this very moment. That is why you cannot move. Once the transition is complete you will be mine. You are already stronger than the other earthbound angels, think of what we will achieve together."

"No!" she screamed into the darkness that held her tightly in its vice-like grip.

This time the little elf could restrain his voice no longer. "Selene, heed not his words! Free yourself!"

"York, where are you?" Selene cried in agony, vaguely aware of an ice cold sensation working its way up her limbs.

"Forget him. He has betrayed you. I know all your strengths and weaknesses, thanks to him," the bodiless voice mocked her from within.

"I don't believe it!"

"Perhaps you will change your mind, once he returns with your earthly family."

"What—?" Now the chill centered at her heart, burrowing into its very core.

"Oh, yes, he will bring them to me. In fact, they will join us very soon."

"No—it can't be!"

"You would have it differently? Join me, Selene. We will catch him together."

137

Selene renewed her struggle against the heavy darkness that suppressed all avenues of light. Where was the One Spirit? Why could she not sense the great presence any more?

"Remember, Diana," stirred a voice from the not so distant past. "Remember what I told you."

"We are now one," hissed Bran, "there is nothing you can do but give in to the inevitable—"

"YOU ARE MISTAKEN. SELENE AND I ARE ONE. SHE IS THE CHANNEL OF LIGHT."

An exquisite brilliance blazed through the musty cellar, striking Bran full in the face. He tried to seek shelter behind an old bureau, but this proved useless, for the great essence followed him everywhere.

It was then the One Spirit showed Selene aspects of her powers she had never experienced before. Light issued from her frame with such intensity that all fears melted in its wake. Suddenly, she was reborn, an agent of mercy, capable of offering compassion and vengeance in equal proportion. Lifting her arms high, she watched the light spill from her fingertips. This was how she would defeat the Dark One.

York did not try to hide the look of awe that crept over his normally playful features. This was not Diana Sherwood of the little cottage in the glen, or even his precious Selene. No, the vision, that rose before him, was the perfect fusion of Lady and the One Spirit. She had indeed become the channel of light!

"HEED MY WARNING, BRAN. SHE IS THE ONE WHO WILL BRING MY CHILDREN BACK INTO THE LIGHT."

A violent explosion ripped through the lower basement showering every shadowy inch with a purifying radiance.

The next events unraveled so quickly that York could hardly tell how they came to pass. Somehow they had exchanged Branwell's abode for the fresh, open air, the angels of the twilight mist beaming around them. Selene did not choose to speak at this time. Instead, she merely smiled, aware that they had won a decisive victory.

When Bran finally awoke, he felt absolutely numb. Never before had he experienced such absolute power. The fact that it came from his arch nemesis made him seethe inside. Selene was far more lethal than he had ever imagined. It was imperative that she be destroyed soon, before her power increased. Yet, how was such a feat to be accomplished? The Spirit always watched over her. That left only one option. He must strike against those she loved. They must be brought down until only she remained.

Moving up the twisting stairs, he questioned what should be done about Kelly. There was no doubt in his mind that she had already betrayed him. That made what he was about to do relatively simple.

With a brief flick of his talon-like fingers, Bran sealed Kelly's bedroom door shut forever. A moment of pity rushed through his heart, upon realizing that she would never leave that room again. She had shown such promise.

"Well," he said, with a sigh, "I have lost other children. There will always be time for more…"

"The Dark One is coming," Selene began in a steady voice as the angels gathered close, "—coming for each of us. We must be ready for him to strike at any time and in any manner. Our efforts will determine the future, for not only ourselves, but those we serve."

Dawn had all but filled the sky. She could tell by the look of concern stamped on each and every countenance that they had a great deal to accomplish before the next twilight. It was essential that she teach them how to face their greatest fears.

"Remember, the One Spirit is stronger than Bran!" she continued, eyes aglow. "After he has been defeated, we will be free again, free to help others by the light of day!"

Caught by the clouds of doubt that still colored their faces, Selene decided to offer a demonstration, "York, give me your hand!" she cried, rising into the glistening air.

A wave of surprise swept over York's elfin face, indicating that he was thoroughly ready to comply. Pressing his palm against that of the twilight guardian, he gasped at the bright stream of light that easily engulfed him in its brilliant glow. York somersaulted off the boughs of the King Oak and spun dramatically through the open air.

Selene could not help but smile. This was the York she loved so well. Now, he too would be able to help others by the light of day. She had seen to that. The sight of his restored spirit almost made her dizzy. Yes, she was afraid for him, but it was time to let him go. He would never be completely whole until he faced his greatest fear.

"Now York," she said, "you have your wish. Go into the sunlight and guard my brother well."

With one swift motion, the little elf caught hold of Selene's hand and brought it to his lips. "Thank you, my lady, you cannot know how much this means to me."

He offered a sweeping bow, then without further ado, disappeared into the brightening air.

Filled with a new sense of hope, the angels twittered wildly amongst themselves. Selene allowed them but a moment of frenzied joy, before she resumed command.

"As it is with York, so will it be for all of you. We need but one more twilight to make the transition complete. Now I must call on another brave soul to remain behind this day. Who will it be?"

Several angels stepped forward, not the least of whom was Proudfoot, but Selene's eyes ultimately bent on those of the woodland guardian.

"Forrest, give me your hand."

The shy, woodland spirit could not speak. Out of all the earthbound angels, she had chosen him!

"Will you remain behind to assist York," she continued without missing a beat, "or take his place should the need arise?"

"But, Lady," interjected Proudfoot with some surprise, "Should not I be the one who—"

Selene never allowed him to finish. "I wish Forrest to remain so he might guard this realm from attack. Whispering Pines will play an essential role in our strategy. We can not risk losing it to Bran."

With no small sense of pride, Forrest knelt before Selene as she offered the gift of transformation.

"Forrest, I ask you to watch over York and my family, even as you safeguard this realm."

"I will, Lady," he softly replied.

Selene could not help but notice the light that sparkled in his dark eyes. Perhaps this quest would offer Forrest the healing he so desperately needed. Perhaps this quest would help him regain a healthy dose of self-confidence.

"I'll stay too, Lady!" cried Brenda, already down upon her knees. There was a certain expectancy in her expression, a haughtiness as it were, that practically demanded the twilight guardian's approval.

A firm prick of uneasiness told Selene that this request should not be honored.

"I need you with me, Brenda," she quickly offered. "There are strategies we must discuss that only you will understand." Selene was going to say more to soften the blow but stopped short. Bran had left his malevolent structure and stood waiting just beyond the outer fringe of Whispering Pines.

"Forrest, can you feel him?" she asked.

The shy spirit nodded in reply.

"He is near. Do not let him trick you with his cunning ways. Trust the power of your inner strength. The One Spirit is with you now and always."

Forrest smiled, then assumed his post on top of the King Oak.

Pausing only to draw breath, Selene stretched her arms toward the brightening sky, "Great Spirit, thank you for helping us to make this crossing one, last time."

The familiar throb of moonbeams instantly pierced Selene's frame, painting everything a soft shade of blue. One by one, the angels entered the gateway, intent on making their last journey to the land that had held them captive for so very long.

"Tomorrow," Selene whispered, "tomorrow, we will see the sun shining in all its glory upon the earth."

Selene paused, counting the pulses that clung to her for support. Three were missing. It was then she knew that Brenda had somehow managed to remain behind.

CHAPTER 17

How wonderful it was to experience the first rays of daylight! York could barely contain his joy. Oh, how he wanted to be out in the glen dancing amongst those gleaming rays, but that would have to wait. Selene had made him Daniel's guardian for a reason. Once the battle was over, then there would be time enough to revel in the sunlight —or so he hoped.

York opened the window screen and dreamily lifted his elfin features toward the sky. He was all too aware that these might be the last moments of peace he would ever know. Soon his father would arrive. One of them must experience defeat. A chill coiled its way around his spirit. How much longer would he have to wait? And what of her? Would he ever see Selene again? The question pierced through him with all the sharpness of a blade. It was vital that he put all such feelings aside. The Dark One might very well use them to his own advantage.

A slight stirring roused York from his silent reverie. Daniel was finally breaking through those last fragile cords that bind mortals to the world of dreams.

York could not help but chuckle. Daniel was up to his old antics again. Why did he always shut his eyes against the morning light? Did he not realize how very precious light was to all existence? The fact that a pillow found its way over the boy's sleepy face only caused him further confusion.

"Come now, would you block out every last ray of sunlight on such a fine morning?"

To say that the Little Elf's voice had an unsettling effect upon Daniel would be something of an understatement. Sheets and covers flew off the bed in varying directions, landing in little heaps upon the floor. A peal of elfin laughter echoed throughout the room. York could not help himself. Perhaps it was the fact that the pillow remained tightly clasped in Daniel's arms.

"I dare say I startled you. Well, you will forgive me that, Daniel. I simply could not resist!" York twittered with glee. Deep down inside he knew that this was going to be fun!

Daniel cautiously peered over the foot of his bed at the strange figure that occupied Diana's window seat. "Who are you?" he cried in surprise. "How do you know my name?"

"I know a great deal more about you than your name!" York boasted, rising up until he hovered in mid-air. He could not resist showing off in front of Selene's brother.

Daniel struggled to hold back the gasp that hung about his lips. "You—you are one of them!"

"Right! I was sent by she who was your sister—whom we now call Selene."

"But, why didn't she come herself? Why did she send you instead?" Daniel did not mean to be unkind, but the words slid off his tongue before he could check their progress.

York chuckled to show that he was not hurt. "She sent me because the others need her guidance this one last twilight."

"What do you mean—one last twilight?"

It was at that moment York realized how very much he would have to explain to Daniel. "I see I must tell you everything," he began with a sigh. "Your sister obviously did not have enough time when she last paid you a visit. Well, the first thing you should know is that I am to be your guardian. That means you must trust me in everything. Do you understand? She has sent me to protect you."

"Protect me—from what?"

"From the Dark One."

"He's the one that—"

"—Locked us in the Land of Twilight Mist. You see, I can read your thoughts!"

Daniel shook his head. This was too real to be a dream. He analyzed the seemingly fragile figure before him and then said, "I don't get it. Why did she send you?"

"Because we are very much alike—you and I. We both enjoy playing pranks on unsuspecting victims, and we are very good at it too! Yet, each of us must learn that tricks have a nasty way of backfiring."

Daniel turned from his guest to hide the tears that welled in his eyes. He was drawn back to the seemingly innocent prank he had played on Kelly. That prank had cost his sister's life. A lump formed at the back of Daniel's throat, and he began to cough.

York instantly saw his mistake. Before the situation could grow any worse, he somersaulted through the air and landed at Daniel's side. "'Tis time to be rid of that cough forever. Here, take my hand."

Daniel met his companion's sparkling eyes, unable to stay the single tear that slid down his cheek.

York was surprised to find something of Selene's persona reflected in her brother's gaze. "Do not grieve, Daniel. It was meant to be. Now she is a great help to all in need."

Daniel glared at York. What made him think that others needed Diana more than her own family? Once again he summed up the merits of this so called "guardian angel." Why had Diana chosen this one? He seemed so unqualified.

"What about my father?" he finally asked. "Will you be helping him too?"

York's features twitched ever so slightly. Guarding Daniel would not be so easy as he had hoped. "Nay," he exclaimed, "someone far greater than I watches over him."

Daniel's expression looked skeptical.

"You do not trust me, do you, Daniel?" York carefully asked.

His young ward offered a half-hearted shrug in reply.

"Well, I cannot blame you. After all, you know practically nothing about me."

"No, I don't," came Daniel's honest response. He stared into York's twinkling eyes with growing skepticism.

"Come, we have little time for this. Give me your hand," York said in a firm, commanding tone. "I will tell you everything—and even cure that last bit of bronchitis. Afterwards, you may decide for yourself whether or not to trust me."

Clasping hold of York's outstretched hand, Daniel was surprised to find that a wave of thoughts transferred easily into his mind. His eyes grew wide and a smile curled about his lips.

Forrest paid little attention to the beautiful sunrise that kissed the upper boughs of his beloved pines. His concentration had to remain completely focused on the Dark One below.

"What is he waiting for?" Forrest silently questioned his dear friends, whose needles sheltered him from the Dark One's gaze. "What is he thinking, planning—scheming? Why is he just standing there beyond the circle of your boughs? Does he think he can spook me with that wicked face, or is he already casting some evil spell?"

A soft breeze brought the unexpected image of Forrest's long dead father before his eyes. There he stood—tall and proud—against the Virginia skyline. This day he was tending the magnolia trees just outside the master's plantation. A better gardener could not be found within hundreds of miles. The rustling of pine needles, or perhaps it was magnolia blossoms, yanked Forrest from his dream world. The Dark One smiled below. Forrest was not to be fooled. The memory had originated in the dark realm.

Daniel's hazel eyes literally beamed with excitement. He understood so many things that could only have been guessed at before! How wonderful this adventure was going to be! No wonder Diana had chosen York to be his guide! The Little Elf's humble visage now garnered a tremendous amount of respect in his young eyes. Where once stood a pale, wiry fellow, there now appeared a very accomplished, not to mention mischievous, spirit. The only thing that troubled him was the fact that York seemed to be in love with his sister.

Reading Daniel's thoughts, York struggled to hold back the unnatural flush that painted his cheeks. "Aye, 'tis true," he explained. "I have loved her for a very long time—even before we met."

"But how could you know before?"

"I have always known her soul."

Bittersweet memories rushed through the autumn landscape and into Forrest's mind. His father was chopping wood, just outside the grand plantation. It was obvious he had worked long and hard that day for great beads of sweat clung to his brow. Thankfully, darkness would fall soon, then he could be with his son. The simple thought caused his massive shoulders to tremble and the dark eyes to mist with tears. Franklin was alone now. Lizzie would never grace their humble cabin again. The master had seen to that.

A sharp crack of the whip startled Franklin Senior as it lashed out at the log on which he sat. There was no time to shield his eyes from the fragments of bark that flew into the air.

"Work day's not over yet!" rang the metallic strains of the master's voice.

Franklin Senior rose with one swift movement, mumbling an apology along the way. The master's eyes never left him until the final tasks were done. Soon the sun drifted behind a column of purple hills and the familiar strains of "Quitting time!" filled the air. Now, he could go home. Franklin paused to bow his head before the master, then breathed a sigh of relief when there was no further reprimand.

All sense of joy drained away as he passed by the old well. It had remained stone dry for more years than he could remember. The master now used it to house runaway slaves until their owners could be notified. Thankfully, there had never been any occasion for the master to use it on his own slaves. Perhaps this was because no slave belonging to Wooddale Plantation had ever successfully escaped his reign. Franklin's step quickened at the thought, until he crossed the cabin's threshold.

Young Franklin eagerly received his father with a supper of good, strong porridge waiting on the table. He silently watched his father eat until the bowl was clean, then shared a rare smile with the one person he loved so well. It made him feel proud that he could help his father, if only in this small way.

There was little Franklin Senior could do but watch his son with thoughtful eyes. The time had come. It had to be attempted this night before things became even more difficult.

"Come along, son," he finally said, "I want to show you something."

Young Franklin happily complied. Together, they walked through the master's moon drenched fields, hand in hand. It was a very special moment for them both. They had not felt this close for a long time.

"Do you see that star up there, Franklin? Father asked, pointing to the largest, brightest sphere on the horizon.

"Yes, Pa."

"That star guided those three Kings to the baby Jesus."

"How do you know, Pa?"

"See how fine and bright it shines—so full of hope and promise—like its telling you to follow."

Franklin's eyes grew saucer wide as he searched his father's expression for some hidden meaning behind the words. None was to be found. "Yeah, I see it, Pa." Something about his father's voice made him tremble inside.

"That's where your mother is right now," Father whispered, placing a firm hand on Franklin's shoulder, "just beyond that star."

"Is she?" Franklin asked. He desperately wanted to see his father's eyes, but the strong arms held him firmly in place.

"Yes, son, I know it. She told me on the last day we were together that if the master sold her, then she'd send up her prayers to the Lord so he'd make a star that would shine so bright—I could not help but find her."

Franklin heard how difficult it was for his father to keep the tears at bay. Clasping that trembling hand within his own, Franklin offered what little comfort he could give. "Do you really think she's out there?"

"I know she is."

Father gently turned Franklin to face him. As he did, the slight hand fell from his grasp. "Now, listen, Franklin. You have to be strong. I'm going to follow that star until I find your mother, but you have to stay behind for now—just until we find some safe place far from here. Then, I'll send for you."

Once again, Franklin searched his father's eyes. This time, they were close enough that he could study them carefully. He did not want to forget this moment, in case they would be separated for a very long time. When words failed him, Franklin threw his arms around his father's neck and held on tight.

They stayed huddled in this position for quite some time before father kissed Franklin on the brow, and without so much as another word, disappeared into the darkened fields: his path undoubtedly bent toward the evening star.

Seven twilights slowly faded, giving way to seven lonely sunrises, as Franklin patiently waited for some sign that his father was still alive. The familiar drone of hunting dogs echoed in his ears day after day. Each time he prayed that the Lord would keep his father hidden from the men, and each time they came home empty handed.

As the sun burned an orange path across the horizon, signaling the beginning of the seventh day, Franklin heard the eerie strains of the dog's cries again. This time they sounded different, and that scared him. Franklin huddled behind the cabin door until his hand involuntarily slipped open the latch. Carefully, he peered through the tiny crack, just wide enough to allow a beam of light entrance. Something out in the fields made him force the door open wide until day light flooded the dingy walls. Franklin stood horrified, his legs rooted to the ground. There was his father bound with chains around his fine, strong wrists, ankles and neck.

Franklin could not breathe. His heart beat so frantically that he feared it might leap from his chest. What would they do to his father? When the master saw him, what would he do? There was only one way to find out. He had to be there. Maybe he could help his father in some small way. Maybe if father saw him, he would know everything was going to be all right.

An unexpected burst of courage carried Franklin out the door and into the early morning light. He was running, running toward the ragged group of men huddled around the empty well. They were hurting his father: mercilessly beating, punching and kicking him in the ribs, face and legs until blood stained the emerald grass. Somehow the crowd magically parted to allow Franklin's entrance. The master was staring at him from behind a pair of dark eyes—eyes that pierced the very core of his soul. Franklin shook his head in confusion. He had to help his father. Blood coated the beloved face, altering the features beyond recognition. There was blood everywhere, swimming before his tear-filled eyes, reeling in his fiery brain. How could he hope to help his father when he was drowning in a sea of blood?

Forrest gasped for air. Darkness swirled around him, heightened by the sound of raven's wings.

"Bran!" Forrest cried in recognition, but it was too late. The vision had been a trap.

"At last you understand, Forrest. Now you belong to me."

"Forrest!" York gasped, tumbling from his air-born perch, onto the hard wood floor. There the Little Elf remained, shuddering violently, as if suffering from a terrible shock.

"What's wrong?" asked Daniel, rushing to his side.

"Forrest, the other spirit Selene left behind—the guardian of Whispering Pines—is gone."

"What do you mean—gone?"

"The Dark One has vanquished him!"

"That means he'll be coming for us next!" whooped Daniel, with a great deal of excitement. He quickly armed himself with a sturdy baseball bat and a length of rope.

York stared at him with wonder. He had no idea what good such weapons would prove against Bran but admired the boy's spirit anyway.

"Why don't we trick him, York? It would be better than sitting around here waiting for him to strike. Why not take the battle to him?"

York froze in mid-air as a flicker of impish delight crossed his lips. All fear left him at that moment. He had Daniel to help him through this. Hadn't Selene told him that the young Sherwood was to play a great role in the miracle ahead?

"Aye, he will not expect that!" York cried with elfin glee.

Daniel smiled. He clasped the elfin hand in a show of friendship without fear or pause.

"We can do this together! I know we can!" Daniel said, as he raced for the door.

"Stop! I know a much easier method," declared York with a hint of his trademark giggle. "Catch hold of my hand and hang on!"

Daniel readily complied. Before he could even cry out with wonder and delight, they had already cleared Whispering Pines and were spiriting through the early morning air.

CHAPTER 18

There was a coldness to the woodland guardian's new abode—a pitch-like dankness that stifled all avenues of light. Is it any wonder that his thoughts continued to linger far in the past? At least the past offered seeds of hope. In his present environment, hope was a luxury indeed. Sometimes, he could almost hear a distant voice calling out to him, before it faded into nothingness. It was his mind playing tricks on him—of that he was sure. After a while, he stopped listening altogether.

"Forrest? Forrest? Can you hear me? Oh, come on—I know you're down there! Answer me!" crackled a raspy voice from somewhere beyond the hungry darkness.

This time the captured angel awoke with a start. The distant echo still welled in his ears. Feebly lifting his head, he tried to determine where the sound originated. When this failed, he fell back against the slime covered wall. Who was he kidding? There was no one nearby—no one to help him escape. He was imprisoned, just as his father had been, in the pit of an abandoned well.

"I must have been dreaming. All those people and places—my father—the master—they've been dead for a long time. How could I have been so blind? I knew Bran would try to deceive me—and still fell into his trap."

Forrest tried to rise, but was instantly checked by a sharp snap of metal. The Dark One had chained him to the moldering floor. What was Bran trying to do? Did the cruel master actually intend to make him relive his father's death?

"Well," the forest guardian thought with determination, "I won't let it happen. I'll just become one with the air and easily slip free!"

Filled with a strong sense of determination, Forrest leapt up, but sadly remained suspended in mid-air. It hardly seemed possible that the chains could hold an angel so completely in their wicked grasp.

"Do not even think of escape," Bran's voice echoed in the darkness. "You will never leave this place. It is your own private hell."

Forrest struggled against the chill that icily crept up his spine. There could be little dispute that Bran comprehended the captive mind very well. Where there is no ray of light, all hope fades. Forrest understood that implicitly. Would he ever see the misty strains of twilight again?

"Forrest, are you okay? Answer me!"

There it was—that same voice again! This time it sounded extremely impatient. Forrest shook his head. Perhaps he wasn't dreaming. There was something familiar in the color and tone of that voice, but he was far too overwhelmed to settle on any positive identification.

"Forrest, answer me—or I'll have to make things very uncomfortable for you with my flames!"

"Bren—Brenda, is that you?" Forrest was so excited that he momentarily forgot his rescuer. Instead, he turned toward prayer. "Thank you, Spirit, even when I fail you—"

"Forrest," Brenda cried in wild exasperation, "listen to me!"

"Sorry," he offered, stopping in mid-prayer, "How did you—?"

"Never mind how," she interjected, growing more and more impatient, "just listen to me. We don't have much time. He'll be back soon. I'm going to burn through this thing he's sealed you in. Stay as low as you can—got it?"

"That won't be too hard," Forrest replied, "I can't do anything else. He's chained me to the floor."

"Don't be stupid—I mean foolish," she quickly amended. "Just disappear out of them."

"I tried that already. It doesn't work," came the frustrated reply. Forrest felt so helpless, so utterly useless, bereft of all spirit powers.

"What's he done this time?" she muttered to herself, against a set of tightly clenched teeth. Well acquainted with the Dark One's tactics, she knew better than to ponder the answer. Delay was fatal. If she waited much longer, he would be upon them! "Get ready, Forrest—I'm coming through!"

Forrest listened with great expectation to the sharp hiss of fire as it kissed the unholy seal. Unfortunately, nothing happened. Not even the tiniest ray of light could be detected through the heavy enclosure. A sigh escaped his lips. The Dark One had foreseen the possibility of such a rescue and planned accordingly. He would remain trapped throughout time—just like his father. And why not? It seemed only fitting. He had failed Selene when she needed him most. He had even lost sight of the One Spirit.

Somewhere amidst this increasing despondency, a small finger of smoke trickled through a crevice in the seal. Forrest sat up. Was he dreaming again—or had Brenda actually managed to pass through the fiend's barrier?

"Yes, it's me, Forrest," Brenda reassured her shaken comrade, as the smoke gently curled about his neck. "I thought I'd better warn you before flaming up, or else you might suffer another scare." There was a distinct edge behind her voice that did not escape Forrest's notice. It took little effort to understand that she was worried. Indeed, there was good reason for that.

A wave of horror swept over the captive spirit as the entire chamber came alive with Brenda's fiery glow. Everything about it reminded him of the legends he had heard about hell. Beneath him, black pools of stagnant water festered, lapping away at his exposed limbs. Strange insects scattered up the walls in all directions, desperately seeking sanctuary from the foreign light.

"Hurry, Brenda!" he cried. "You have to get me out of here soon, or I will go mad!"

"Try them now!" she hissed as the flames consumed her form. Forrest lost no time in leaping up from the murky floor, but his escape was cut short by the sharp snap of chains.

"You see!" he exclaimed, "The Dark One has put some spell on them—or me. I can't make myself disappear!"

"Okay, okay, calm down," she said, trying to ease his fears. "I'll get you free, but you'll have to trust me on this —and you'll have to hold still no matter how hot it gets!"

Forrest swallowed nervously, then gave Brenda the signal to begin. A slender tongue of flame flicked toward the chains that bound his wounded feet. He could almost feel the scorching fire as it brushed against his leg, yet there was no real pain. Another tongue lapped away at the wrist constraints. Steam began to rise from the water beneath him, but still, nothing happened. He was trapped in the well —perhaps forever.

"Never, my son. You will never fester here. Not while I still have a say!"

That voice—could it really be? "Father?" he whispered, almost half afraid that it was true. A warm laugh answered in response. Yes—yes—it was him!

An unexpected snap of metal brought Forrest back to reality as his legs slipped free of the molten restraints. With a renewed sense of strength, he forced the wrist chains apart. How easily they fell to the floor, reverberating with a metallic clank. He was aglow—with love and light! Nothing could contain him—not even Bran's hateful fury.

"Father, Bran will answer for your death," he said in a booming voice. "I swear it."

Forrest was about to offer Bran a direct challenge when Brenda arrested him in mid- speech.

"Not yet," she cried, "We must wait for twilight. At twilight nothing will save him."

Without further ado she melted before his eyes, altering into the mystical firebird known as the Phoenix. Forrest's respect for Brenda swelled at the sight. She was glorious to behold—a sight truly divine. The strong wings rhythmically rose and fell until they touched the crest of the well's summit. It was then the creature began to spin.

In no time at all the Phoenix burrowed through the blackened seal, allowing daylight to flood the chamber below. Forrest did not wait to see what would happen next. He was free! The light of day once again kissed his brow, but there was little time to enjoy the sensation. Whispering Pines demanded his attention. It was vital that he keep her protected until twilight, then the others would join him in defeating the Dark One. At that moment he saw Brenda, the rescuer, hovering nearby. She looked different somehow, perhaps softened through the act of kindness.

"Thank you, Brenda," he whispered, clasping her hand with great warmth. "Now, I have something that my father never did—a second chance. This time I won't fail."

"You mean, we won't fail," the fire maiden added with firm conviction.

Forrest did not catch the look of concern that painted her brow. It was not yet noon. They had seven hours of daylight left before Selene's return. Could they hold on that long? There was only one way to find out. In a flash, they were spiriting toward Whispering Pines.

CHAPTER 19

Kelly awoke to a curiously dark room almost devoid of light. She puzzled at this but was diverted by a faint rustling sound that originated at the terrace door. Something was outside! No, she kept reassuring herself. It was only the nightmare still haunting her thoughts. Once the sun rose she would feel better—unless this was not a dream.

A familiar prick of fear wound its way up Kelly's spine. She had seen this all before—not once, but many times. It was a recurring nightmare. The realization made Kelly's heart pound within her chest. What was it trying to tell her? Certainly some message could be found within the core of the dream. She had only to observe the symbols and images before her. The difficulty lay in the fact that this was not easily accomplished since everything appeared shrouded within the darkness. Kelly froze. Suddenly she understood what was different about her room. The terrace window, that always offered a perfect view of the sky, was gone!

Fumbling through a lacy mass of coverlets that graced her Victorian bedstead, Kelly listened to the familiar creek of it ancient frame. Well, at least that was normal. The realization spurred her forward. With a growing sense of determination, Kelly threw her legs over the edge of her bed and called out to her father. There was no reply. This struck her as being odd. Where could he be? It was not often he went for early morning walks. Perhaps he was just outside. As both feet hit the floor, they met with a kind of burning sensation. Assuming that her feet were still asleep, she walked on.

Kelly slowly padded through the darkness toward the terrace door. It was her favorite place to recuperate after an especially bad dream. Somehow she always found a measure of peace in the tranquil autumn air. She had only to open the door and then everything would become clear.

As Kelly paused to touch the brass knob, a sharp stab of pain met her fingers, forcing her to pull away. The door magically opened of its own volition—just wide enough for a wicked tongue of flame to lash out in anger. A cry escaped her lips as she slammed the door just in time to escape the onslaught. In that brief moment of illumination, Kelly saw that her entire room had changed. The haven of her childhood was gone. Only a dark, colorless sphere, devoid of all windows and doors, remained. The terrace appeared to be the last familiar thing left in the room and even that was off limits to her. What had happened while she slept? There was no longer any way to enter the rest of the house!

Kelly could think of nothing beyond seeking shelter on the wrought iron bed. Without further pause, she began to run. Suddenly, something tripped her at the heels. As Kelly's body hit the floor, a stinging sensation ripped through her senses. Had someone actually poured acid on the hardwood while she slept? She had little time to ponder the question, for a sharp set of talons clamped about her wrists making escape impossible. Something terrible held her in its grasp and refused to let go.

"Father—Father, help me!" she cried struggling to break free.

"He cannot help you now, my dear," answered a pair of frightful eyes that seemingly blazed into her very soul.

"Oh, my God! Someone—anyone help me!" Kelly screamed at the top of her lungs. There was no answer. What could she do to escape? One thought crossed her mind. She knew little of the Holy Bible but did remember a fragment of the famous psalm. Perhaps if she said it, the fiend would go away.

"The Lord is my shepherd," she began with a trembling voice, "I shall not want."

"That verse will do you little good against me. I know you too well, Kelly. There is no conviction behind the words."

An involuntary gasp escaped Kelly's lips as the psalm died in her throat. All at once she understood. "Father, what have you become? Why are you doing this to me?"

"Do not be so naïve, Kelly. You know who I am and it should be perfectly obvious why I am doing this."

"I don't understand! Please explain it to me!"

The talons hurled Kelly against her bed. "You chose to pity the Sherwoods—a betrayal of the worst kind. Do you have any idea who they really are? They were sent to destroy us, and now you begin to side with them. How could you do this, Kelly? How could you do this to me? You realize what the punishment is for such a betrayal."

"No..." the trembling girl whispered.

The talons stroked her cheek in fond remembrance. "Betrayal is always punishable by death," the dark spirit said.

Kelly gasped for breath as the oxygen drained from her lungs.

"Do not act so surprised. You betrayed your own father. How should this be answered?"

"I never meant to betray you—I swear!" she sobbed into the boiling air.

"Perhaps not," he said, scanning her face for any trace of deception. "Yet, how can I ever trust you again?"

The dark creature's answer endowed Kelly with new strength and vigor. Perhaps she could beat him at his own game. He still obviously cared for her in some small way, or she would be dead. All she had to do was find some means to utilize this weakness against him, then she could reclaim her freedom.

"Think what you like!" she cried, breaking from him with new conviction, "I never have and never will betray you in any way!"

"I almost want to believe you," he said with a sneer. "Remember, I can read your mind."

Kelly shook so violently that he softened a bit. "Oh, do not worry. I expect you to lie. You are, after all, my daughter." The spirit chuckled in such a diabolical manner that Kelly's hair almost stood on end.

Upon achieving this desired effect, he continued, "There is one small thing you can do to reclaim my trust, child. You can help me defeat them. Daniel is beginning to trust you. Destroy him and I will let you live."

"What do you mean? Daniel hates me!"

"I think not."

Kelly watched in horror as his long, thin lips twisted into a crooked smile. He looked repulsive at that moment, utterly demonic in intent. One tapered finger reached out to caress her delicate tresses. When she tried to pull away, he latched onto the roots and held fast.

Kelly screamed in pain, "Stop—you're hurting me!"

"That is the general idea. Like attracts like. You wound me—and I will do the same to you."

"I don't understand. Are you suggesting that Daniel actually cares what I think or say?"

The dark spirit continued smiling at her with a kind of malicious glee. Kelly couldn't breathe. Why did he not answer her question? There was obviously more involved here then he cared to reveal. "Who are you—really?" she cried from the depths of her soul. "Don't say Stuart Branwell!"

"Surely you know by now," he replied with the same leering grin. "Search within. The answer lies there. I will keep you here forever, Kelly, unless you consent to help me. Oh, and just in case you are thinking of escape—let me show you what lies beyond that threshold."

The terrace doors burst open to reveal a perfect torrent of flames. Kelly tried to turn away from the sight, but the dark spirit held her fast.

"Look deep into the flames, Kelly. Tell me what you see."

Kelly blinked back the tears that were blinding her eyes. How was she supposed to see anything? There was smoke everywhere! Suddenly, her vision cleared. From out of the funeral pyre rose a familiar figure. It was that of Daniel Sherwood melting into dust.

A terrible scream filled the air. Kelly fell back against the precious safety of the bed and pulled the tousled covers over her body, but it was no use. The eyes still found her. No doubt those fierce orbs would haunt her even in the land of dreams.

"You were my favorite child, Kelly. Did you know that?"

Kelly looked out through a tiny opening in the covers. Stuart Branwell was sitting by her side.

"You showed such promise," he hissed, as his claw-like hand brushed against her cheek. "Perhaps, one day I will forgive you."

"When, father?" Kelly pitifully whispered.

"How dare you call me father!" he cried, throwing her back against the wrought iron headboard. Kelly wreathed in pain.

After a moment of necessary silence, he continued, "I'll forgive you when I decide you are worthy. You must prove yourself to me, and there is only one way to do that."

The image of Daniel perishing amongst the flames flooded her senses so violently that there could be no doubt what form her penance must take. He wanted her to kill Daniel Sherwood.

"You must strike him down—undo the wrongs you have committed against me—then and only then will I consider reclaiming you as my child."

Michael Sherwood awoke with a start, his head thudding against the pine headboard Cynthia had carved so many years before. Something was not right. Someone was in the cottage.

The gun cabinet lay no more than a few feet away, sporting a thick layer of cobwebs that coated its withered exterior.

Brushing off the dusty stragglers, he considered how much they reminded him of tiny spirits as they drifted to the floor. Perhaps he was giving them the freedom they so desperately desired.

Michael shook his head. Where had that come from? There was no need to ponder. Such images were a regular part of his life ever since Cynthia's disappearance. Now Diana had joined her in the unknown. Try as he might to forget, they were always there. Always…What was he doing? This was no time to reminisce. Someone was in the cottage!

Slowly, carefully, he edged toward Daniel's room with the rifle clutched tightly in his hands. The door stood wide open. Had he left it that way the night before? Michael could not remember. One thing was certain, Daniel could not have opened it in his condition. There was nothing left to do but enter and face the unknown.

As Michael crossed the threshold, his eyes scanned the room for any signs of intrusion. None were to be found. Only a shower of warm sunshine spilled through the open window and onto Diana's unused bed. Everything else seemed normal except the fact that Daniel was nowhere to be found. The bed stood unmade, and the covers were left in a tangled heap upon the floor.

Michael's heart began to thud against his chest. Where was Daniel? He couldn't have just disappeared! Forgetting any attempt at caution, Michael rushed into the family room but was met with the same unearthly stillness.

"Danny, Danny, where are you?" he cried between muffled sobs. "Danny, answer me! You're not well enough to—"

The frantic plea was instantly checked by a stream of blue light that flowed from Selene's painted image. Michael's senses told him that this must be a dream, but deep down inside, he knew otherwise. He had seen this so many times before. The last bit of strength left his trembling limbs, and he fell to the floor. Sensing his pain, the shimmering light spilled over his brow.

"Do not worry, Michael. Daniel is well," soothed the gentle voice he knew so well.

"Cynthia…"

"You cannot stay here any longer. It is not safe. Trust me. You must leave immediately."

"What do you mean I must leave? I don't understand. Please—tell me where Daniel is!"

"You will know soon enough. If you can still trust— reach out and follow me."

The blue light offered no further direction but spun a deliberate path through the screen door and out into the bright daylight. What choice had he but to follow?

CHAPTER 20

Kelly awoke with a start. There it was again: the distant sound of thunder, mingled with a faint rustle of raven's wings. Her eyes flew open, afraid of what they might find. Thankfully, he was gone. Everything else appeared unchanged. One solitary shade of darkness still filled her room, yet somewhere beyond the living nightmare, Kelly sensed a familiar echo. What was it trying to tell her? If only she could think.

Again it called out to her—the distant echo that drifted through her mind. It was louder this time but still too muffled for her to decipher.

"K—!"

Kelly remained perfectly still. Perhaps it was a trap the dark spirit had set to test her loyalty. She had no desire to face his wrath again.

"Kelly—it's me!"

The message expanded into shades of a human voice. Thankfully, it did not sound like her father, yet she had to be careful. It might be a trap.

"Kelly—can you hear me? It's Daniel!"

The trembling girl rose halfway, the covers still twisted around her frame. How could she be certain that the voice really belonged to Daniel? Perhaps if she spoke with it, the answer would become clear.

"Danny, is that really you?" she softly whispered.

"Aye, 'tis he," chirped a perky voice from not so very far away.

Kelly screamed, forgetting all previous caution. After a moment, when no attack came, she whispered, "Who's there with you?"

"No time to explain. We're here to help!" Daniel cried. "You can speak to me through my friend. Don't be afraid of him. His name is York."

Tears pooled in Kelly's eyes. Something deep inside told her that this was Daniel and that he had come to save her. How could she ever have treated the Sherwoods so shamefully? Kelly paused in mid-thought, remembering what she was supposed to do.

"Are you quite alone?" asked a friendly voice at her ear.

Kelly inhaled abruptly. Could this creature also read her thoughts? Regardless of the answer, she had to be careful. At this point there was no one she could trust, but herself. "I think I am alone, but I'm not sure. He was here before and he may come back soon. You had better take Daniel and—"

"Do not speak, my lady. Just think. I will know what you wish to say. Have you seen him recently?"

"Yes, but—you must leave! Believe me—it isn't safe for any of us!"

"Please, calm down," York said, as he softly touched her shoulder. His form was still invisible to her untrained eyes, and she trembled at the sensation. "Fear not. I have no intention of harming you. Use your thoughts to tell me everything. Did he hurt you in any way?"

The gentleness of York's voice softened Kelly's heart. This gave her courage to ask the one question that plagued her thoughts. "Who is he—really? Your name is—I'm sorry—I've forgotten it—I'm so scared!"

"I know how you feel. My name is York, and I too have experienced the brunt of his anger. You ask me who he is, my lady, but if I told you—you might not believe me. Search your conscience, and then you will know."

"Yes—you're right! I already know the answer! He's my father!" Kelly sobbed into her pillow. Once again, she felt the soft touch of a comforting hand. This time it lit upon her brow.

"Hush! He is also known as the Dark One. You do not believe me? Has he not imprisoned you in this very room?"

"I don't understand what is happening, York. Are you really here, or am I imagining you as well? If you truly want to help—then find a way to get me out of here!"

"Are there any doors or windows you can see?"

"There used to be, but everything is black now. I can't see a thing. The terrace doors are still there, but he has filled them with flames!" At that moment Kelly lifted her eyes and was surprised to find a slight, young man hovering over the mattress.

"He will use your greatest fears against you, my lady. That is how he strikes at all of us."

Kelly could not help but gasp at the sight. This creature was not human either. Was he a demon sent to trap her, or simply a figment of her imagination?"

"My lady, you can defeat him—if you really put your mind to it. Just remember that it will take every last bit of strength—"

York's voice came to an abrupt halt. Although his image still floated before Kelly's eyes, York's true essence remained outside the terrace door.

"My lady," York quickly instructed, "start reciting any prayer you know."

"Are you crazy? He's sure to come back if I do that! Besides, I have already tried that and failed. He knows I do not believe."

"Well, you must change your point of view. Try again, and this time believe the words with your heart, mind and soul. Quickly, now. We have little time!"

York heard the tearful sobs escape Kelly's lips, as he rapidly scanned for any trace of weakness within the sealed door frame. Daniel had already used the end of his trusty baseball bat to pry away at the structure with little success. What scheme could they come up with to set her free?

"York—Danny, are you still there? Please, don't leave me. I'll try again. I promise."

Something about the sound of Kelly's voice struck Daniel especially hard. Suddenly, he understood that Diana's death was not her fault. In that moment, words of encouragement escaped his lips. "Go for it, Kelly! You can do it! I know you can!"

York turned to Daniel with a look of surprise and nodded approvingly. Selene would be most proud. His own dear, precious Selene…

The Little Elf swallowed hard. He must not think of her. Not now. The facts were plain and simple. He would do the task set before him and then move on. That meant he had to find some other means of admittance. The front door was the only viable option. York could not ask Daniel to accompany him in this dangerous game. He would have to proceed alone.

"The Lord is my shepherd. I shall not want," Kelly's voice burst through the darkened recess of her room.

Daniel flashed a smile at York and then joined in. This was the moment to act. Bran could do no harm if they were saying the psalm. In a flash York swept through the front door. What was it the One Spirit wanted him to do?

"Come on, Kelly," Daniel cried with great enthusiasm, "louder! Really show him that you mean every word of it!"

"He maketh me to lie down in green pastures," they exclaimed together. "He leadeth me beside the still waters."

A force greater than Daniel's own self lifted him off the ground, and with one swift motion, hurled the baseball bat at the door. Daniel was flung in the opposite direction. He watched as the bat passed directly through the frame and was absorbed into inky blackness. There was a moment of eerie silence before the screaming began. Bran had returned.

"No one is here! Leave me alone!" Kelly shrieked.

Daniel leapt to his feet. He was about to dive at the door when York appeared, blocking his path. "'Tis done, Daniel. Everything is in order. The rest is up to Kelly."

"What do you mean?"

"The Spirit has given her the option of freedom. You helped her earn it—with your fine words of encouragement. If she takes it, she will be free of him forever. If not, she must remain his minion. The choice is strictly hers. Now we must be off! Bran will be after us!"

In a flash they were spiriting through the air.

Daniel was stunned by their sudden flight. It took him a moment to register the full import of what had happened. Once the truth hit home, he began to thrash against York. This forced the Little Elf to zigzag across the horizon.

"Good, Daniel," York thought to himself. "Keep that up. Surely, this will draw the Dark One's attention to us!"

"Let go of me, you coward! We can't just leave the battle like that!"

"I do not expect you to understand, but the Spirit has prompted me to do this. Bran is too strong for us there. We must meet him on equal ground."

"Are you crazy, York? He'll kill her! The Spirit surely does not want that!"

"Nay, he will not kill her," York explained to the angry boy as they landed upon a thick bough. "He will follow us. Trust me. We are his true prey, not Kelly. She is only important in this because of her connection to you."

Aware that Daniel was still glaring at him, the boyish elf placed a steady hand on his comrade's shoulder, then explained, "Kelly is the trap the Dark One has set to capture us."

Daniel jerked his shoulder away. "Then why did we go there to help her?"

"Because your love and forgiveness has offered her the opportunity to be saved—if she has the strength to deny him. Do you not see the truth of this?"

"The only thing I see is that you are a coward! Only a coward would run away like that! Why did my sister send you? You must have worked hard to fool her. You had me fooled too. I thought you really cared what happened to us!"

York flinched ever so slightly. Daniel's words helped him remember how very cruel young people could be, especially when they felt betrayed. Well, it would all be over soon. The Dark One's arrival must set the true battle in motion. A wave of concern swept across York's face. Would he survive long enough to protect Daniel from Bran?

The young Sherwood noticed the sudden change in his guide's expression. At that moment he stopped quarreling and began to listen in earnest. A thin stream of perspiration trickled down his nose. How long would it take before the Dark One found him—found them both? Shafts of sunlight flickered through the tangled web of boughs, gently spilling onto Daniel's sandy hair. A great change had taken place inside him. Never had his mortal senses felt so sharp.

"He is approaching," whispered York," and 'tis still early. We must find a way to distract him. Oh, well, so much for sitting back and waiting for twilight. Why are you not smiling, young lad? You wanted an adventure, did you not? Now you will stand face to face with him!"

Although the Little Elf remained outwardly calm, Daniel could sense that he was worried. There was something in his guardian's eyes that troubled him immensely. They seemed sad, almost resigned. Daniel instinctively knew that York was seeing the future, and it did not look promising.

Suddenly, York snapped out of his silent revelry. "Daniel," he said, "Do you have any special friend we can trust?"

"You mean at school?" Daniel asked.

"I mean someone you would trust with your very life," whispered the Little Elf, his eyes still fixed on some far off point.

Daniel could not help but suspect that his friend was listening to instructions from another being. Something in that misty gaze told Daniel it was his sister. She was watching them from afar. She could—would help them when the time came. York's brilliant orbs fell on Daniel, flooding his soul with light and forgiveness. "I'm sorry, York," he confessed. "I didn't mean what I said. Really I didn't."

A smile spread across York's up-turned lips. "I know," he chirped with pleasure. There was nothing left to do but give Daniel a big hug. After a moment, he leapt into the air, and offered Daniel his hand. "Are you ready?" he cried.

Daniel firmly took hold and once again felt the familiar tingling sensation that always seemed to accompany the disappearing process. "I wonder if I'll ever get used to this?" he thought to himself.

"Fear not," York chimed, "after this day, you will not feel it again for a very long time!"

CHAPTER 21

Michael Sherwood awoke to the music of bird chatter filling his ears. It was a pleasant sound that drew him back to happier times when he and Cynthia had slept under the stars. That was before Diana had been born; before Daniel had fallen ill. Michael's eyes flew open. He suddenly remembered that Daniel was missing.

Struggling to focus his groggy mind, Michael saw sunlight streaming through the soft brilliance of stained glass. The door to an antique shrine stood wide open, welcoming the few brave sparrows that had entered to keep him company. Michael shook his head. His senses were muddled, but he recognized the familiar surroundings all too well. Try as he might, it was impossible to forget the many hours they had spent there in the past. This was the prayer chapel where he and Cynthia had been married.

The cool stone tiles on which Michael rested his head made an indifferent pillow at best, and his neck ached as a result. With the exception of the tiny sparrows that hopped about the altar, the chapel appeared deserted. At that moment he remembered the vision. Why had it lead him to Moss' church?

The sun's rapid progress across the sky, informed Michael that it must be well past noon. He had waited long enough. Regardless of what the blue light desired, it was time to find Daniel. He was half way out the door when a voice arrested his step.

"Now Sherwood, you didn't really plan on going without saying goodbye, did you?"

Michael turned to find Reverend Moss smiling at him from across the room.

"I kept wondering when you would turn up. Somehow I knew it would be today—and here you are."

Michael allowed his tongue to slide along the edge of his lips. They were very dry. Suddenly, he realized that he was incredibly thirsty. How long had he been there?

"What day is this, Moss?" he finally asked, almost afraid to hear the answer.

"It's Friday, October 23rd; but then you knew that, or else you wouldn't be here. Cynthia would be pleased that you remembered."

Michael felt the blood drain from his face. It was the tenth anniversary of her death. That was the message the light had been trying to convey. He glanced at Moss, who was smiling at him in a friendly manner. Why did it seem that he always understood more than he ever let on? Not knowing what it was he meant to say, the words, "Then you know why I am here," spilled from his mouth.

A fine mist covered the Reverend's eyes, and he began to sway. His mouth opened, but a voice issued forth that belonged to another soul.

"This day will decide more than your family's fate, Sherwood. There is nothing you can or will do about it but sit here and pray. Leave this holy ground and you too will become subject to the evil at hand. Do not try to assist your son. It is for them to do."

Moss' eyes rolled upward, and he fell to the floor. The poor Reverend's body trembled as if it had been charged with electricity, before finally slumping against the tiles. Michael ran to his side and tried to prop him up against the foot of the altar. After a moment, Moss smiled.

"Thank you, Michael," he whispered. "I don't know what came over me.

"Do you remember anything you just said, Moss? Anything at all?"

"No. I suddenly felt as if something had entered my body, and then I no longer had control over my voice or actions."

"You said this day would decide the fate of my family and that I should not interfere in any way. What did you mean? You told me not to help Daniel. Why would you say that? My son is all I have left! In case you didn't know — he's missing."

Moss' face blanched an even ghastlier hue. "Missing? Michael, something strange is happening here that I do not understand. I firmly believe that you must listen to what the voice said. It must have been a message from God—"

"—Or the devil! Why shouldn't I help my son? Why shouldn't I be there for him if he needs me? If you are so close to God, Moss, that He speaks through you—tell me that!"

"Interference of any kind is unacceptable," replied the same foreign voice that had issued from Moss. This time it originated from the entranceway.

Michael whirled around to find Stuart Branwell leaning against the doorframe.

David stood at bat, but was in no mood to play baseball. In fact, if it were not a required gym class, he would have refused to participate at all. Mr. Schuman had insisted, however, and so he waited—most impatiently—for Craig to throw the pitch. If only the bell would ring, then he could claim freedom. So much had transpired in the last week that school hardly seemed important any more.

"Strike one!" Jenny croaked over David's right shoulder.

Why did she always have to be around reminding him of what happened at Crescent Lake?

"Strike two!" came the same throaty reminder as the ball whizzed past his bat. "Hey, David," Jenny taunted, "Why don't you try swinging at the ball?"

174

"Jenny," Mr. Schuman said with a yawn, "let's keep the commentary to yourself."

"Don't listen to her, David!" cried Eric and Marty in almost perfect unison. They were just dying to come home, and David was their last chance.

David saw the final pitch coming and braced himself for contact. Well, it wouldn't hurt to try this time. Carefully tightening his slippery fingers along the molded wooden frame, he prepared to swing, then something curious happened. The bat lifted itself from his clumsy grasp and met the curve ball with a resounding "crack!" David was stunned. He watched in awe as the ball flew high out into the neighboring fields.

"'Tis a homer—if I ever saw one! Take flight, young lad! Do not delay!" cried a voice that David assumed must belong to Eric or Marty, though it sounded nothing like them. What could he do but comply? He traveled from base to base as the team cheered him on, his heart swelling with pride. Eric and Marty had already crossed home plate and were dancing in that funny knock-kneed manner that Daniel had taught them not so very long ago. Oh, how he wished Daniel had been there to see it! Craig was also jumping up and down, waving at him with shining eyes. He was trying to tell David that the diamond was empty. All the other participants had run after the miracle ball. Even Mr. Schuman could be found heading out toward the open fields.

"Wow!" cried an ecstatic Marty, catching David in a broad bear hug, after he walked across home plate. "That was super!"

"Awesome—really awesome!" added Craig, who was finally forced to admit some admiration for another player's skill.

David remained silent, staring out into space. Eric and Marty waited for a reply but received none. No doubt he was still dazed by the entire event. After all, such hits did not come along every day!

David's lips parted. He wanted to cry out, but only a faint whisper issued from his lips. "Danny," he said, "what are you doing here?"

The others did not hear him, for the bell rang, setting them free. Off they ran toward the buses, completely forgetting the miracle ball and the boy who had hit it out into the fields.

David remained standing on the diamond, alone, unable to believe his eyes. Daniel was walking toward him, grinning from ear to ear, as if his presence on the baseball field were the most natural thing in the world. A slight, wiry fellow approached at his side. David could not help but observe that the young man's clothes were quite unusual, almost ancient in style. It was only when Daniel embraced David in a broad bear hug that he knew it wasn't a dream.

"I'm sorry I was so nasty, David—it's just that—"

"I know. I miss her too," David softly volunteered. After a moment, his eyes returned to the young man who was dressed in such a funny manner.

York smiled in greeting. In fact, his entire face was beaming with joy. Suddenly, David understood.

"You did it. You're the one who hit the homer," whispered David, as his eyes grew wide. "Daniel, he's one of them. I've seen him before!"

"'Tis true!" York exclaimed with glee. He was about to say more when a young woman caught his eye. Would she willingly thrust all fear aside in order to help them?

Jenny Weiss ran breathlessly across the fields toward the baseball diamond. It was just too hot to be searching for David's miracle ball. Besides, there was a group huddled around home plate that literally begged her attention. They appeared to be discussing something in hushed tones. Perhaps it was a secret. Never one to miss out on new gossip, Jenny decided to join them.

"Hey, what's going on?" she called across the field.

"'Tis she!" York cried in a fit of delight. "Just the lady I wished to see!" The trio instantly parted to reveal the Little Elf in all his resplendent glory.

Jenny's feet came to an abrupt halt. This couldn't be happening to her again! It was the same elfin figure that had taunted her from the oak tree on Hillside Drive. All at once she began to tremble from head to toe. "It's him!" she gasped in horror.

"Fear not. I am your friend, York. Do not say you have forgotten me so soon," he pleaded, gently taking her hand within his own.

York's kind words made very little impact on Jenny, for her only response came in murmurs of terror. He had actually touched her! What was she to do?

"Forgive me, my lady. I did not mean to frighten you. The truth is—we need your help. Will you assist us?" York asked in a most charmingly elfin manner. Unfortunately, he forgot that at that moment he was hovering several inches off the ground.

In a fit of desperation, Jenny struggled to make some sense of the situation. What was this creature that haunted her both at home and at school? A ghost? No, that couldn't be. This thing seemed almost friendly—and it was smiling at her—just like before! There was something mesmerizing about the way its dark eyes shone in the afternoon light. If she could only learn to trust him…

She tried to mouth the word, "yes," but somehow the answer came out, "no," instead. The Dark One had claimed another victory.

York sensed the change and immediately understood what had happened. Her faith was not strong enough. Gently, he withdrew his hand from her arm.

It was time to run. Jenny set her heals in motion and promptly departed the scene. Thankfully, her house was no more than a few blocks away. Certainly, this apparition would not follow her there.

Upon reaching the final stretch, she cast one, last look at the baseball diamond. It was completely deserted. Had the entire experience been nothing more than a dream?

The chapel door flew shut behind Branwell, forcing several sparrows to shriek in fear. Michael turned to Moss for an explanation, but he was nowhere to be found. It was then he heard the Reverend's cries, punctuated by a set of fists hammering against the door. Branwell advanced further. No sooner had he done so than the tiny birds began to strike their bodies against the stained glass windows in a desperate bid at escape. Michael took a deep breath and held his ground.

"What is it you want, Branwell?" he asked in a surprisingly calm voice.

"An understanding," came the forceful reply.

"Go on. I'm listening."

The Senator's lips curled up into a half-smile that seemed to mock Michael. "Commit yourself to non-interference, and you will live. That's the least you can do for her."

Michael's brain was reeling. "Her?" he questioned in confusion.

"Don't play dumb. She brought you here. If she hadn't, you and your precious son would already be dead."

"Stay away from him," Michael warned as he stepped toward Branwell, throwing caution to the wind.

The wicked smile grew even wider. "It is not I who have hurt Daniel," he threatened. You are the one who will be brought up on child endangerment charges."

"What are you talking about? I—"

"It is already in motion. Just wait and see. Your life will become a living hell on earth. I promise you that."

Michael felt the blood churn within his veins. He couldn't believe his ears. Regardless of who Branwell was, he had no right to make such ridiculous threats. "I don't care what you do to me—just stay away from my son!" he cried in anger.

"There is no other way. He is a part of this. Just as she was—just as your daughter is!"

"Diana?" How can you even mention her name to me? It's because of your daughter's foolishness that she is dead!"

"Is that what you really think? How shallow. There is a much greater purpose behind her death than you can ever realize. Ask yourself who Diana really is—"

"My daughter!" Michael cried, as he lunged toward the dark image before him.

A mass of sparrows exploded against the window from the outside, ushering in torrents of daylight. Michael struggled to shield his eyes from the fragments of broken glass that shattered all around. At that moment he truly saw his opponent. It was no longer Stuart Branwell who confronted him, but some magnificent creature of darkness with eyes like burning coals and fingers that tapered into raw talons. Michael could not see the face, for it remained hidden behind a black, hooded cloak, the balance of which spilled to the floor. What could he possibly do against this waking nightmare?

Feeling hopelessly abandoned, he railed at the heavens, "What is it you want me to do?" It was then he remembered the ally who waited just outside the door.

"Branwell—Demon—whatever you are—you must leave this place now!" Moss cried at the top of his lungs. "To enter a holy sanctuary you must be welcomed by God!"

That was it, Michael thought. Moss had uncovered the key to conquering the beast!

A hideous scream ripped through the air as the Dark One staggered backward.

179

Michael never saw the blue light spill through the open window, nor did he witness the sparrows enter in its wake. They set upon the creature with a wild abandon, frantically tearing away at its flesh. The Dark One let out a howl of pain before finally taking flight.

Dazed and trembling, Michael watched the tiny birds chase a dark raven out the broken window pane before his senses failed, and he knew no more.

CHAPTER 22

Forrest watched the sun drift across the sky, silently wondering what steadfast guardian maintained its path. How strange it was to see his beloved pines bathed in amber and gold. Surely, some unknown spirit had orchestrated this glorious gift. If only its pleasure could go on forever. If only…a voice deep inside cautioned that he must not allow himself to enjoy the sight. Distraction of any kind could prove fatal. Bran lingered nearby, ready to strike, and twilight was still hours away.

The air hung full and heavy, without so much as a friendly breeze to fan the throbbing pines. Forrest heard their pleas for a few precious drops of life giving water but could do nothing to ease the situation. As guardian of Whispering Pines, he held no control over the elements. Selene, however, was another story. Once twilight fell, he felt certain she would send some repast.

A lengthening shadow fell across Forrest's brow, demanding his full attention. The woodland angel sat up with a start. Bran had arrived. It was crucial he not be allowed to enter Whispering Pines.

"Careful, Forrest, I know your thoughts," Bran's oily chuckle dripped through the angel's mind.

In an effort to pinpoint his adversary's location, Forrest scrambled up the tallest tree that he could find. Known simply as the King Oak, it was one of two such entities in the surrounding area. The other, long thought dead, lay at the crest of Lookout Point.

"Do you hear me, Bran?" Forrest whispered to himself. "This time I swear you will not enter."

"That is most daring, Forrest, considering you have fallen victim to me before. Do you suppose Brenda will bother to save you again? Come now. Be reasonable. Just how long do you think you can hold out against me? Remember, I have all eternity to wait."

Forrest cringed as the rumbling strains of laughter filled his ears. How strange—that the harsh tones sounded almost like thunder. Perhaps he should have read the signs. Perhaps he should have acknowledged the warning that screamed in his mind. Suddenly, it was too late. A sharp flash of lightning rushed down from the sky on a direct collision course with his lofty perch. Forrest barely managed to avoid this lethal blast by seeking shelter on the ground. Unfortunately, the King Oak proved not so lucky, for its thick trunk, pierced by the fierce bolt, was easily cleft in two. The woodland guardian watched in horror as a low moan broke from the heart of the dying tree. Gravity soon took hold, forcing the limbs further and further apart until the rift came to an abrupt halt four feet above its trembling base. The rumbling sounded again; this time from inside the sacred oak. Louder and louder it grew, drowning out everything else until the entire structure burst into flames.

"Why?—why torture the innocent trees?" Forrest cried into the thickening air. "They have done you no harm!"

There was no response.

Numbed by this senseless cruelty, Forrest followed the Dark One's winding path in and out of the shivering pines. It wasn't until he had reached the crystal stream, however, that the dark spirit appeared. He was waiting on a large, flat stone, his lips twisted in an upturned smile. There was something familiar about the expression that reminded the woodland angel of York.

"Very observant," Bran exclaimed in low, hypnotic tones. "The smile is the same because he is my son."

Forrest shook his head. This was a another kind of trick conjured to divert his attention. If he could just focus on

182

something beyond Bran's eyes—those eyes that threatened to pull him deeper and deeper into the pit. The gaping mouth loomed before him, threatening to swallow him whole.

A snap of twigs drew Forrest back to the present. The Dark One stared at him, smiling, analyzing his every thought. It was only when the menacing grin grew wider that Forrest knew something was about to happen. As if on cue, Bran became one with the air.

Bracing himself for an attack, the woodland angel struggled to determine what form the Dark one would take. Within the fraction of a heartbeat, he had an answer.

A pair of talons ripped through the air, slashing away at Forrest's eyes. He had barely managed to dodge the blow, when a huge raven appeared overhead.

"Quick, Forrest—move!" cried a raspy feminine voice.

Brenda had arrived to offer a challenge. A jet of flame shot through the air, easily engulfing the dark creature within a set of orange jaws. It greedily lapped away at the bird until a horrific scream shattered the afternoon lull.

"Now you know what it feels like to be burned alive!" the fiery spirit shrieked at her captive prey.

"That is splendid, Brenda! Let me feel your hatred! Let my power kindle your soul!" Bran's voice echoed through the air.

"Don't' listen to him, Brenda!" Forrest cried with increasing horror. "If you keep this up, he'll win for sure!" She seemed not to hear him for the flames increased two fold. What was he to do? There had to be some way to stop her. If only Forrest could think. Everything was happening much too quickly.

"Join me, child," Bran hissed through the blaze. "Do not struggle so. You were born for this purpose. Our lives are forever entwined. Remember, Brenda, there is no way to escape your destiny."

Forrest tried to muster a rallying cry, but it stuck in his throat. He felt hopelessly lost. One question beat in his mind—how much longer could Brenda hold out? A quick glance at the sky revealed that twilight was still at least an hour away. What could he do to shift the balance of power until then?

Scrambling up a nearby tree, Forrest shimmied along a length of bough. This put him exactly where he wanted to be: within inches of the fiery blaze. "Brenda, listen to me!" he cried at the top of his lungs. "You can't win with hate— it only makes him stronger! Let him go! We can still win this together! I know we can! Don't do this all alone!"

Unfortunately, these words did not achieve the effect Forrest had desired. Instead, Brenda's flames swirled even higher, growing into a huge, gaping funnel. In that brief moment, he saw what would happen. It was now his duty to save Whispering Pines.

A great explosion ripped through the woodlands as the first of countless trees were drawn into the fiery tornado. Forrest managed to avoid the sparks by seeking shelter on the woodland floor. Several tiny stragglers landed on the bough that had supported him and began an eerie dance of consumption. Before he could even manage to blot one miscreant out—another took hold. Soon a neighboring tree burst into flame.

Seeking momentary shelter near the streambed, the poor angel breathed a silent request for assistance. A gentle splash answered in reply. The water was trying to communicate with him. At that moment, he knew what must be done. Respectfully extending both hands toward the stream, Forrest watched in delight as the water flowed up the length of his body until it burst in a great explosion from his wriggling fingertips. The blaze sputtered and died. A first victory had been won, but the hapless angel could not let his guard down. He had to make certain that Brenda's funnel did not set all of Whispering Pines ablaze. If only he could find someone to help.

Suddenly and without warning, three figures appeared wrapped in a wave of light. Forrest could not believe his luck. York stood among them poised and ready for battle, Selene's earthly brother at his side. It was the third figure, however, that gave him some pause. What was the Little Elf planning? Why had he brought a child into the fray?

"I won't even ask where you found him," Forrest said, indicating David. "I think I know. Do you really understand the trouble we're in right now? Do you? Everything you see here could go up in flames if we're not careful—so take your friends to some safe place and—"

"That's why we're here—to help!" Daniel cried before York could even part his lips.

Forrest was about to protest, when he noticed marks of exertion stamped across the brow of his most curious friend. It was then he saw that the children were hovering in the air. York was assisting them all by himself.

"York, you are always such a show off! Here, let me help—otherwise you'll wear yourself out too quickly. Give me one of your friends; it'll be much easier that way!"

"With pleasure, young lad!" exclaimed York as he released David. The poor soul began to plummet toward the stream amidst a series of protests. Thankfully, Forrest came to the rescue, stopping David just short of watery contact.

"Thanks," muttered David, whose senses were still somewhat reeling.

"All right, we must get back to work!" Forrest cried with growing excitement. "Watch how it is done!"

A great burst of water flowed from the length of his hand, striking a pine in danger of consumption. The miscreant flames flickered then died away.

"Let me try!" cried an enthusiastic Daniel, who began directing water blasts in a most haphazard fashion.

David could not help but laugh at Daniel's awkward fire fighting maneuvers.

"Take it easy, Daniel," suggested Forrest. "We must work together on this. Remember why you are here. Wait—I'll show you again. This time watch carefully. You too, York!"

York could not help but smile at the transformation that had taken place in the formerly timid angel. Something far greater than fear was now controlling his actions. This was a fine example of the freedom all earthbound angels would claim once Bran no longer controlled their actions. If only —York paused in mid thought. Time was growing short. It was essential that he speak with Daniel immediately. The Little Elf had just opened his mouth for this express purpose when Daniel turned to him with a smile.

"Don't worry, York. Now I understand. I really do. We didn't run from the battle, we brought it to us."

"That's right, Daniel. The only way Kelly will ever be rid of the Dark One is to free herself. We could not do that for her."

"Do you think she has it in her?"

"Only Kelly can answer that," York thoughtfully replied. "Well, be that as it may, there is work to be done." The Little Elf quickly tapped Daniel on the back and then started off for a direct assault against the wicked flames. Together, they moved through the tree tops in an effort to stop new sparks from spreading. They had almost reached their target when York saw the ferocious funnel churning wildly in upon itself.

"Brenda—" he gasped, at once certain that it was she who had engaged the Dark One in personal combat.

Daniel never heard the cry for he was already on route to the horrific apparition with the express purpose of quenching its roaring flames.

The Little Elf could not believe his eyes. Was this some cruel trick of fate? If only he had taken time to explain. How could Daniel know that it was an earthbound angel, not the Dark One that conjured the fiery blaze? How could he know? There was no time for regret. He had to act quickly before the funnel blew apart.

Streaking through the air at breakneck speed, York caught Daniel by the arm and flung him into the depths of Whispering Pines.

There was a sharp churning of the air, followed by a fierce explosion. When the smoke finally cleared not one but two separate entities met the Little Elf's eye. A coal, black cloud seemingly devoured the sky, blotting out every inch of daylight. Against this oppressive backdrop rose a beautiful firebird stretching its wings in resplendent glory.

York immediately gathered his earthly friends into a sheltering thicket. After extracting a promise from both Daniel and David that they would remain there unless specifically called upon, the Little Elf met up with Forrest. Together, the angels quickly ascended to the highest point they could safely attain without detection. Only a half- hour remained until twilight. They had to help Brenda hang on until then. Needless to say, Bran was not about to make this easy.

A blaze of light burst from the dark, boiling cloud with uncanny precision and struck the Phoenix on her breast. She cried once, a long, ghastly, mournful cry, before begin- ning a downward spiral.

Forrest and York did not wait to see any more. It was time to set upon Bran. The ebony bird had seized Brenda and was in the process of wrenching her wings even further back, when a strange tickling sensation coursed up and down its spine. Whirling around to find the source of this discomfort, he was unprepared for the flaming bough that was thrust into his left eye. The dark bird shrieked in pain and his talons released command of its prey.

For a moment it seemed the poor Phoenix smiled, then she began to fall, her broken wings unable to stay the descent. As gravity took hold, the flames lashed inward, actively consuming the once noble frame. Just as it seemed she must hit the ground, the entire mass exploded in one great burst of light and was seen no more.

York cried out for Brenda, but knew it was too late. She was gone. He could only hope that one day she too would resurrect like the ancient firebird born of myth. There was nothing left to do but continue where she had left off. Bran had plenty of fight left in him. That meant York and Forrest were his next targets.

Suddenly, everything became deathly still. Sensing a change in the air, York and Forrest also followed suit. Retreating to the boughs of a nearby pine, the two angels watched as the inky silhouette melted away, leaving behind only the slightest trembling of breeze.

York shivered. Glancing up at the sky, he remembered that twilight was almost upon them. The time of reckoning was at hand. Forrest touched his shoulder and for a moment their eyes met. A look of mutual respect was exchanged between them. Yes, they had done well; but Brenda was gone and evil still lingered in the air.

A movement from deep within the eastern woods drew York's attention. Darkened weeds trembled, revealing an unseen presence. The Little Elf peered closely at the clump of bramble. Something was hiding there, afraid to come out.

"Fear not," York exclaimed in a kind, gentle voice, "I mean you no harm. Why not show yourself?"

A soft breeze rustled York's merry locks until they covered his eyes. As he moved to brush them aside, a doe entered the clearing and began to stare at him intently. York froze. His entire being began to shake. There could be no doubt that this was Morgan. York turned to Forrest for confirmation, but discovered that he was gone. It seemed safe to assume that the woodland angel was looking after

Daniel and David. That left him free to explore this new development.

With a flash of her downy, white tail, Morgan raced off into the depths of Whispering Pines. What could the Little Elf do but follow?

The trail grew narrow and ragged, making travel difficult at best. Indeed, York nearly stumbled over an obstruction blocking his way. It was then he saw a flash of rust. Sly had also joined in pursuit of the nimble doe. The giddy fox nipped his toes in greeting, then sped off ahead. York's senses began to protest. Everything around him seemed too real to be part of a dream or a memory. What was going on? Why had the animals reappeared after so long an absence? Regardless of the answer, one thing was clear—he had to save them from Bran. If that meant his own destruction, then so be it. York was all too willing to sacrifice himself in order to spare the others any additional trauma.

Upon entering the glen where the King Oak once stood so strong and proud, York's senses rebelled. Every fiber of his being told him to take flight and run in the opposite direction. There was great evil nearby: evil that was waiting to consume him. All at once York understood, and still he did not run. It was time to face his father head on. Only then would he truly be free.

A bold stirring of leaves pulled York from his silent musing. This truly was a reunion of sorts. Two squirrels scampered up the length of his body until each found a comfortable resting place upon a shoulder blade.

"I have missed you too," York whispered as Tell and Tale burrowed against his cheek in a warm show of affection.

Soon all the old friends stood huddled around York, gazing upon him with twinkling eyes. The Little Elf could not gather them into his arms fast enough. They were all together again just like old times. It seemed almost too good to be true. They were all alive—that is all of them except—

"Caw!" shrieked a harsh cry from within the hollowed oak trunk.

York could just make out the faint gleam of her dark eyes. Caw was staring at him, pleading for help. She had been placed inside what York instinctively knew to be his own tomb—by the Dark One himself. This time he would save her from destruction.

As York leapt forward, Morgan blocked his progress, standing directly in his path. A strong warning blazed in her large, brown eyes. York desperately struggled to pass the delicate obstruction, but the look made him pause.

Caw cried out again. This time she sounded hurt. "Stand aside, Morgan," he said with quiet determination. "A spirit must meet his own destiny." Fully convinced there would be no further debate, York was unprepared for the doe to trip him at the ankles.

"Morgan, what is wrong with you? Can you not see that it is Caw?" he cried in frustration as his body thudded against the ground. He had almost regained his footing when Sly caught hold of one elfin boot and stubbornly refused to let go. York offered protest with a firm brush of his hand. He was growing more and more agitated. The sound of Caw's cries rattled his senses, until he could think of little else. His own sacrifice was nothing in the face of her suffering. Come what may—the animals would let him pass.

York paused for a moment, struggling against the sound that threatened to drive him mad. Why couldn't he think straight? What had happened to all his firm resolve? Bran was behind this. He had known that from the start. This was one, long elaborate scheme to banish him into the dark realm. Was this sacrifice truly necessary? Suddenly, the earth started to spin until everything around the Little Elf blended into one, long scream.

"York, help me—help me please!"

The Little Elf froze in his tracks. Now it was the strangled cry of Daniel Sherwood that issued from the oak's hollow innards. How could he have left Daniel unguarded at such a time? Hadn't he known that Bran would target him first? What would Selene think of his foolish actions—now that their worst fears had come to pass?

It never entered York's mind to stop and contemplate the consequences of mounting a rescue. He had to save Daniel no matter what the price.

The animals made another attempt to stay their friend's flight, holding him firmly in place from all sides.

"No more of this, do you hear?" York cried in agony. "You have to let me go!"

Always sensitive to their master's pleas, Tell and Tale tumbled onto Sly's shoulders, forcing him backward. Such was the fox's devotion that one elfin boot remained tightly clutched in his jaws. York instantly flew to the rescue.

"You did not guard him very well, did you, Little Elf?" taunted the dark, familiar voice York knew so well.

"Let me go!" cried Daniel as he attempted to reclaim his freedom. The Dark One violently drew him back into the unseen recesses of the tree.

"What will Selene think—when she finds you can not even guard her brother from me?"

Bran's well calculated words easily gnawed at York's soul. His own battle was over and he knew it. Only one thing remained to be accomplished: Daniel's release. Pushing all fear aside, the Little Elf peered down into the darkened hollow. What he saw there made his stomach churn. Daniel was struggling to free himself from Bran's unyielding embrace. The young Sherwood kicked and clawed at his captor with great determination, but it was all to no avail. In fact, Bran hardly appeared to notice the effort. The sound of his heavy laughter filled the air, forcing the very pines to tremble with dread.

"'Tis I you wish, Bran. Why not put an end to this once and for all? Release him, and I am yours."

"With pleasure, my son. He can do me no harm once you are gone."

York paused to choose his words well. "I have but one more request, then you may proceed. Before you claim me as your prize—you must return him to the others."

"You make far too many demands, Little Elf! Come here, or I will destroy you both!"

"York—don't do it!" Daniel screamed.

The prankster angel merely smiled as he held out his arms to receive Daniel. After setting the young Sherwood's feet upon solid ground, York offered him a warm embrace. "Do not grieve, Daniel," he said with a smile. "It was meant to be."

Daniel struggled to reply, but was thrown back against Morgan by a fierce explosion. The trembling doe instantly acted as a shield between Daniel and the wall of flames that enveloped the once vibrant tree.

"York!" Daniel cried in a voice far too feeble to be heard above the fierce roar.

After the smoke cleared, Daniel saw that the entire tree had been sealed with a pitch-like residue. Tears formed in his eyes. It was all his fault. How could he ever have allowed himself to be captured by the Dark One? More importantly, how would he ever explain this to Diana?

Forrest paused in mid-flight, a shaft of water still awaiting his direction. He had heard York's final cry, then the horrible stillness that followed. Try as he might to regain focus, all concentration faltered and the much needed water missed its intended mark. His thoughts flew to the boys. Were they still with him? A brief scan of the sur- roundings revealed David dousing a nearby tree, but Daniel was no where to be found. It was then he saw the truth. Brenda was gone. York was gone. Only he and David remained. Would they survive this seemingly endless day? At that moment, a soft mist kissed his throbbing temples. It was almost too much to hope for. Scanning the sky, he saw the first star twinkling in all its glory. Twilight had finally arrived.

CHAPTER 23

A soft, blue mist gathered around Daniel as he slumped against the moss-covered ground. Life, as he knew it, was over. He had brought destruction upon York—a destruction that could not help but condemn all the other earthbound angels as well. Why had Diana, Selene, asked his assistance? Why had she wanted him to join the fight?

Unable to stay his tears, Daniel allowed them free expression. He had not been in this attitude very long when it became evident that someone was watching him. It was then he looked up to find the twilight guardian's eyes upon him.

"Diana!" he gasped with joy, impulsively throwing his arms around her translucent form. This time it came as no surprise when he met with the familiar touch of mist.

"You have been very brave, Danny. Even more so than I ever imagined. I am so proud of you," she gently whispered in his ear.

"York's gone! The Dark One got him! I'm sorry, Di. It's all my fault. If I had just listened—"

"You needn't blame yourself. I saw everything."

"But, Di, you don't understand. It's because of me that he's dead!"

"You forget one important fact, Danny. York cannot be killed. He is a spirit, remember? Now calm yourself, and listen to what I have to say. Everything that has happened is a part of the One Spirit's great plan. Do you understand?"

"You mean that killing York was planned!"

"He's not dead, Danny. At least not in our realm. You see—his soul remains trapped inside the King Oak."

"Then we must help him!" Daniel cried, leaping to his feet.

Selene held Daniel fast with a touch of her hand. "I am afraid it is not that easy. In order to rescue him, we must first bring the Dark One down."

"How can we do that?"

"The Spirit will teach us the way. Listen to the guidance that lies within you."

After taking a deep breath, Daniel shut his eyes. Selene could not help but giggle at the look of impatience that adorned his brow.

"It does not work that way. You cannot force the Spirit to speak with you," Selene chuckled, despite herself. At that moment, she seemed no different than the sister Daniel so fondly remembered.

"To hear the voice, Danny" she continued, "you must relax and believe."

"It's hard to relax at a time like this! Where is he now? I mean the Dark One."

"He's right here watching us," she calmly replied.

A low chuckle rumbled from just beyond the blackened oak. "Is that the best you can do?" it taunted. "Where are the others, Selene? Why aren't they here to help you and Daniel at such an important time?"

Selene remained perfectly tranquil while the laughter continued to grow.

"I'll tell you why no one is here to assist you—they are all serving me. Those who would not, met with, shall we say, rather unpleasant endings."

"I have seen their so called endings, Nero—or do you prefer Bran? You bear so many names that it is difficult to know which to use at any given moment."

Bran smiled. "How true. That is all part of the deception. Let me make a proposition. We can end this now. Join me, Selene, and I will offer Daniel his freedom."

Selene smiled and said nothing. She knew how to break down the Dark One's defenses. The One Spirit had shown her the way.

"Selene, you needn't worry about your earthly father. He will also remain free if—"

"If you hurt my father I'll—" Daniel's cry died amidst a roar of laughter.

"Hush, Daniel," soothed Selene, as she caught his trembling body within her soft embrace. "It is his way. He has no more power to harm father, than he has against yourself. Believe me, I would never allow it."

An eerie silence followed that seemed to drag on for an eternity. Daniel wondered where the Dark One hid himself. He turned to Selene for answers, but she offered none. Instead, she gently lead him to the King Oak's hollow remains. Daniel watched in a kind of daze as she placed both translucent hands against the column of charred bark and began to communicate with the Little Elf trapped inside.

"Do not blame yourself, York. You knew this must happen. You knew it long before I."

There was a moment of silence, during which Selene listened intently to a message that escaped Daniel's ears, then she replied, "Yes, I sometimes question how it will be accomplished. Forgive me, for saying so but, I do wish you were here."

She paused for a moment, then turned to Daniel with misting eyes. "York, would like to speak with you, Danny, before we leave."

Slowly, cautiously, the young Sherwood willed his fingertips to touch the blackened trunk. It took a few moments for Daniel to dissect York's words from the series of screams that erupted inside the tree. The Little Elf was suffering a great deal of pain. If only he could help shoulder some of that torture—perhaps then the tears would leave his eyes.

York would have none of this. "Come now, lad, do not be downcast. This prison cannot hold me forever—"

The elfin words were cut short by another hideous shriek that seemed to shatter the very woods with its force. Behind it rang an echoing current of laughter.

"You delude yourself, Little Elf. I plan to keep you here forever!"

"Danny," continued York as he struggled to be heard above the wicked current of mirth, "You are the breath of life and the eyes that guide. With your help, we will disarm him. Now, listen, you must—"

The rumbling voice grew to such a frenzied pitch that it completely drowned out York's further instructions. Daniel shook his head in confusion. He had no idea what he was supposed to do. Bran had seen to that. Those dark vibrations rushed out into the heart of the forest itself, causing squirrels and birds to squeal in fear. Bran had terrified them all: all except one.

"Remember, Danny. He cannot harm you," Selene said, as she caught him in her arms, "if you truly believe in the power of the One Spirit."

"Never forget that you are mine, Daniel," hissed Bran's fierce voice from inside the hollow. "Come, join your father and mother—they are with me even now."

Daniel was about to pummel the blackened tree when his eyes settled upon Selene. How magnificent she looked at that moment, how utterly strong in her command.

Selene stared at the Dark One with an expression that was almost undefinable. Her misty lips curled into a half-smile, pondering some secret known only to herself. Clasping hold of Daniel's hand, she rose into the air.

Before the young Sherwood even knew what had happened, they stood together on Lookout Point, next to the decaying oak tree. All the hours they had spent there together as children came flooding back to him. So much had changed since then. Did Diana—Selene still remember their childhood games?

"Well, Sir Laugh-a-lot, the quest is about to begin," she offered in response to his unspoken question. "Only this time you will be searching for a far different Grail."

Daniel snickered. It pleased him to know that she still remembered. Perhaps one day when this was all over, she might be coerced into engaging in another pillow duel.

There was a catch in the air, followed by a chorus of giggles. Stirring from his thoughts, Daniel realized that they were no longer alone. Indeed, dozens of angels were hovering nearby!

"So, these are the angels of the twilight mist," he said, with more than a little awe.

"Yes, Danny, but after tonight, you must not call us by that name anymore. Tonight we become part of this world again, and that means, we must seal the door to the Land of Twilight Mist forever."

"Seal it forever—why?" Daniel asked in confusion.

Selene offered a warm smile. "Because it is not of this world, Danny. We belong here, don't you see? Perhaps I can make this easier to understand. We were created to protect and guide people. That land, no matter how beautiful it may be, is of his making. The Dark One conjured it to separate us from you and all other mortals."

"—But, if you can free yourselves from this curse tonight, why can't the door just stay open—so you can visit sometimes?"

The angels awaited Selene's reply with as much curiosity as Daniel. It seemed obvious that the thought of never seeing their home again filled each and every one of them with sorrow and regret.

"If the miracle can provide us with some means to leave the door open, and still assure us freedom, we will certainly take it," Selene responded with a knowing smile. "I love the Land too, but if the door does remain open—

there will always be the chance that Bran may find some way to send us back."

The angels twittered in perfect understanding. They had grown to respect Selene's opinion and knew that on this point, she was absolutely right. It would be far too dangerous to leave the gate open. They must simply learn to exist outside the purple hued world of twilight again.

"Can I see it, Di—just once?" Daniel cried, remembering the many stories his father had told them about the sacred place.

"I'm sorry, Danny. There just isn't enough time. Do you see how the moon changes even now?"

Daniel could only nod in reply. He was desperately struggling to understand everything at once, but it seemed to take more effort with each passing moment. Selene's lips continued to move, but he could no longer hear what she was saying. The only thing he could do was mumble a "yes" in reply.

"Her light is about to be dimmed, Danny."

"You mean by the Dark One?" he asked, striving to regain focus.

"No, by a perfectly natural occurrence: an eclipse."

The light of excitement filled Daniel's eyes. "Cool. I remember we learned about that last year in school!"

"We must use that moment to destroy every means of control he holds over our kind. The moon and I operate the threshold together. We earthbound angels must regain control over our destiny when she is at her weakest."

"So, you will use the eclipse to catch her off guard!"

"That's right. You see, at that moment, she will be unable to use her powers."

"—But, I still don't understand what I am supposed to do."

"Don't worry, Danny. You are the breath of life and the eyes that guide. The Spirit will show you. Just listen to the voice within."

Selene paused for a moment, as if indeed heeding the voice of another, then called out, "Ora, Starr, it's time to begin!"

The tiny spirit of light approached Selene with an air of indescribable joy. She stopped to peck a swift kiss on her guardian's cheek, then began spiriting over Crescent Lake. Daniel could not help but notice that she left a warm trail of light behind.

Stella remained characteristically quiet, allowing her smile to speak instead. Daniel observed how much the other angels admired her strong faith. She must be very special, he thought to himself, then wondered why. All spirits were special in God's eyes. He followed her progress as well—until she came to a stop directly opposite Ora. Together, they framed the moon.

What could their mission be? Selene had obviously come up with some elaborate plan. Why, then, was she waiting so long to let him in on the secret? At that moment his eyes fell on Crescent Lake. There in the tranquil waters, he saw the moon's pearly glow heightened by the presence of Ora and Starr, each spirits of light. Suddenly, he began to understand. They were there to aid Selene in the transformation. Their light would strengthen hers. It seemed so very simple. Why was he still having so much trouble maintaining focus?

Once again, Daniel felt himself drifting into unknown territory. When the purple mist finally cleared from his eyes, he noticed that the lake was in turmoil. Indeed, a series of angry waves slapped against the shore in hostile aggression. Something about the sight reminded him of the night Diana had died. Was this a sign? He watched in silence as thick, cottony layers of mist rose from the lake's turbulent surface, blocking out all trace of the moon's reflection. It was imperative he warn Selene, in case she did not see.

Picking up on Daniel's unspoken thoughts, the twilight guardian cried, "Keep an eye on the lake! Without Mara to guard this realm, we are most vulnerable through the water below."

The Dark One instantly shifted his attack to the heavens. Harsh winds and thunder began to pummel Crescent Lake. To make matters worse, Bran soon conjured an icy stream of lightning that appeared expressly intent on striking Selene. The angels saw this immediately. One after another they leapt in front of the blast, hoping to spare their guardian, but it was to no avail. The lightning easily sailed through them without eliciting any harm.

In a last attempt to head off calamity, the guardian encircled her being with a rush of blue mist. Even then, she saw it was too late. The lightning hit her head on. A hush fell over Crescent Lake as she plunged into the water and then became deathly still.

Michael Sherwood awoke with a start. Everything seemed so oppressively dark. Where was he? Why was he laying on the floor? Only a faint wind answered in reply.

"Diana. Find your daughter, Diana. You must go to her now."

Michael's heart began to thud within his chest. Something had happened to Diana! And Daniel—where was his son?

As a great shaft of lightning blazed through the broken windows, Michael fell to the floor, clutching his face. The pain was excruciating. He began to weep, not for himself, but Diana. She had been wounded. He knew it instinctively.

Rising to his feet, he rushed to the chapel door. He hadn't gone very far, when Cynthia Sherwood appeared, barring his path. A strong warning blazed in her eyes.

"That is not your destiny, Michael," Reverend Moss said as he placed a calming hand on Sherwood's shoulder.

Michael whirled around in confusion, then understood his mistake. Once he turned back, Cynthia would be gone.

"You must not interfere in the battle," Moss continued, showing no indication he saw the twilight image. "To do otherwise would most certainly spell your destruction."

Michael stared at him with an eerie fascination. Was it Moss or Cynthia speaking to him?

"I've come to tell you that I understand now," Moss explained. "When Branwell connected with me earlier today, I began to see things in a different light. Forgive me, Michael. I was wrong about Cynthia. The night she disappeared, I thought I saw her walking with the Senator. It was rumored she had accompanied him to Washington. Now I know I was wrong. Branwell has made that clear."

Michael's brain began to reel. What did Moss think he was doing? Why was he always standing between himself and bliss? There was nothing left to do but shake his head in confusion. It was useless, Cynthia had left him again. If only he could get rid of Moss. Flopping back against the tiles, Michael allowed his eyelids to flicker as the Reverend droned on."

"Cynthia never left Crescent Lake. She has always remained there." Moss was still speaking when Michael's eyes closed and his breathing slowed.

"I have to go now," Moss said. "Kelly needs my help if she is going to survive this night of terror. She has done no wrong."

Without speaking another word, Moss shut the door behind him.

After silently counting to one hundred, Michael soon followed Moss into the midnight air. It took little ingenuity to make certain their paths did not cross. Once out of the parish grounds, Michael began to run. Daniel and Diana had summoned him, and he was not about to deny their call.

CHAPTER 24

"Come on, Selene, get up!" Daniel cried as her limp form drifted amidst the swirling waves. The sight filled him with a kind of horror, born of memories from the not so distant past. Once more the icy waters of Crescent Lake would be her tomb, if he did not do something to intervene.

"Di—I mean, Selene—wake up! The angels need you!"

The lake seemingly heard his plea for it soon enveloped Selene in a liquid embrace. Slowly, gently, it escorted her toward Lookout point, pausing only to deposit the precious cargo into Daniel's ready arms.

"You are the breath of life."

Suddenly, Daniel remembered the prophecy. Something, an inner knowing perhaps, prompted him to breathe on Selene's forehead. Although this action made little sense, deep down inside he knew it was the right thing to do.

Time clicked away at an ever-steady pace, but nothing happened. Selene still remained motionless. He had all but given up hope when there was a soft flicker of her eyes. Daniel began to shake the lovely guardian until she was able to gaze full upon him. An unexpected gasp escaped his lips. The once sea gray orbs were completely devoid of color!

"Do not worry, Danny," she said, trying to ease his troubled thoughts. "I am all right, but Bran has blinded me. You will have to be my eyes while the miracle is in progress.

"The eyes that guide..." he whispered, finally understanding what the strange prophecy meant.

Selene offered a nod. "That's right. Now, we must get back to work."

"Is there still enough time?" Daniel questioned, glancing at the moon. "It's almost at full eclipse!"

"We will see."

There was a subtle stirring in the air. A wave of twilight mist rushed from Selene's image past the myriad of angels hovering overhead and onto the darkened moon itself.

"Danny, what color is the moon now?"

"It's bluish purple," he cried. "The same color as you! How did you—?"

"There is no time to explain," Selene interjected in a firm voice. "All is in readiness. We must begin now. Danny, be my eyes. Watch for Bran and let me know when he is near."

Suddenly, she was gone.

"But, how—" the protest died on Daniel's lips. She was already far away. Indeed, the tiny Ora was already in the process of leading Selene back toward her ring of angels.

Scanning the surroundings for the highest vantage point available, Daniel quickly decided to scale the old oak tree. Somehow, amidst a chorus of creaks and groans, he managed to shimmy up the main trunk. Finally, after breaking off a few leafless boughs, he possessed a clear, unobstructed view.

"Daniel, get down from there at once!"

The sound gave Daniel such a start that he almost lost hold of the decaying trunk.

"Father, what are you doing here?" he asked peering down at the form that seemed disproportionately tiny from so great a height.

Michael fought back tears of relief that threatened to color his eyes. "I might ask you the same question. You are supposed to be at home in bed recuperating!"

"I'm here to help Di!" Daniel exclaimed, indicating the beautiful twilight guardian that darted through the night sky.

Michael swallowed hard. His suspicions were confirmed in that instant. "What can I do to help?" he asked in a breathless voice.

"Watch for Bran."

"Who?"

"Stuart Branwell. He is also known as the Dark—"

Daniel never finished his statement for an eerie cry shattered the air with such force that it made his hair stand on end.

"I think we've found him!" Michael shouted above the mayhem. "Look at the water!"

As Daniel turned his eyes on the lake, a new horror began to unfold. Ferocious waves lashed into the air with a vengeance that could only be matched by the shrill whistle issuing from its churning core. Somewhere out of the very depths of this apparition, a watery funnel was born.

What kind of black magic was this? Daniel tried to cry out, but his lips remained frozen. Did Selene need to hear his voice in order to understand the warning?

A huge, gaping mouth opened in the turbulent center, forcing waves through its gullet before spewing the excess in wild disorder. Angels flew in every direction until they managed to surround the apparition on all sides. Thankfully, Selene had heard his thoughts.

"Great job!" Michael cried from the ground. "But, I'm afraid its far from over yet!"

Thunder and lightning answered in reply. Somewhere amidst the fury, the spout leapt up, watery jaws spread wide, narrowly missing its prey.

During this temporary diversion, the angels of light positioned Selene in a direct line with the moon. It took but a moment for her spirit to defuse, melting away until only a purple cloud remained.

"The thresholds between darkness and light are aligned," she cried. "Let the transformation begin!"

Casting a wary glance at the brightening moon, Daniel saw that the eclipse had ended. He quickly gave warning of the change, hoping that Selene could hear him. There was a certain fury in the way the lunar beams lashed out at the violet cloud that contained Selene's essence. Once the two entities met, however, they easily fused in common bond producing a glorious pearly light.

The first earthbound angel was summoned for transformation. Daniel instantly recognized the beaming Forrest as he approached the cloud. A strange twinge of guilt, however, kept him from thoroughly enjoying sight. He could not help but remember York at that moment. And what of David Moss? What had become of him?

"So this is where you have been hiding, Daniel Sherwood!" Forrest cried in a not so timid voice. "David's back at home in bed—where kids your age should be at this time of night. Oh, don't worry. He won't remember anything at all!"

Daniel felt somewhat relieved at the news. "Don't tell me," he said with a sigh. "It's better that way."

"That's right!" Forrest cried, as he leapt directly into the light.

This act caused a pronounced reaction in the Dark One. Instantly, Bran's spout hurled the waiting angels aside in an attempt to rise. Here was yet another device to cut Selene off from her connection with the moon. Water crashed against Forrest and the fragile blue cloud with such ferocity that it became impossible to determine which way was up and which was down.

"Stay with me, Forrest! Don't let him draw you from your purpose!" Selene's voice rang through the tempest.

"But, where is the light?" he questioned as water pummeled him from all sides.

"It's right here inside you! Can't you feel its glow?"

Yes, that was it! Forrest finally understood. Even if he could not see the light, it was still there. All he had to do was believe and the transformation would occur.

Forrest smiled, a big, broad smile free of fear and doubt. It was then he willed the cool, pale beams to pierce his soul, thereby dissolving every last bit of sorrow in their wake. Now he was truly free—free to explore eternity without trepidation! The first miracle of the night had been accomplished!

Instead of mounting another attack, the water spout ceased churning and abruptly dropped beneath the waves. A deadly stillness followed, yet there was no time to anticipate Bran's next move. One after another the angels raced forward to participate in the transformation before he struck again.

A sharp stab of fear pricked at the base of Daniel's spine. Something nasty was about to happen. How he knew this was unclear. Suddenly, his lips began to tremble, as a flood of darkness spilled across the sky.

"Selene!" Daniel cried at the top of his lungs. "Bran is trying something new!"

"Tell me what is happening." Her voiceless words rang in his brain.

"The sky is growing black and all the stars are fading away. Even the moon is in danger of disappearing before our eyes!"

Selene knew this was their last chance. If Bran somehow dimmed the moon's light, they would remain trapped within his boundaries forever. The miracle would stand incomplete. She had no choice but to continue. Ora and Stella still awaited transformation—and then there was York, Brenda and Mara who were far from her reach.

"Go ahead, Ora. I will be right behind you!" indicated Stella, keeping one eye on the stars as they faded from view.

Bran had almost succeeded in blackening the entire heavens, when Michael cried out, "Diana, transform them together or—"

The warning never fully escaped his lips for Bran decided that it was time to intervene. Michael could do nothing but stare at the lightning as it bore down upon him. Echoes of Daniel's screams rang in his ears, yet Michael's feet remained firmly rooted to the ground. All appeared lost until a sudden stirring of water drew his eyes to Crescent Lake. What Michael saw there made his heart skip a beat. Cynthia, his own precious wife, rose from the crystalline depths and with one swift motion pulled him into the unknown.

Lost in this unexpected bliss, Michael never saw the lightning shift course. Indeed, the crystal waters had already closed around him when the heated blast struck the dead oak instead. Once the smoke cleared, it was impossible for him to know that Daniel was gone, seemingly evaporated into thin air.

Ora had just drawn Stella into the healing shaft when darkness extinguished its radiant glow altogether, leaving the transformation incomplete.

"You have failed, Selene. Most impressive for such a novice, but now it is over: now you and your dependents belong to me."

CHAPTER 25

Selene remained perfectly still, without offering retort of any kind. It was imperative that she not give up—not when Daniel and Michael had all but sacrificed themselves for her cause. There was also the problem of the missing angels: Brenda, Mara and York. Could she abandon them to an existence of everlasting darkness? The many voices gathered in her head, clamoring for completion. Bran had to be brought down—no matter what the cost.

She paused for a moment, perhaps to gather courage, perhaps to better gage her capabilities, offering Bran a charming, if not indiscernible half smile. Although she could not see him, it was possible to read his mind. How typically bold of him to believe that the battle was over.

Suddenly, and without warning of any kind, she plunged deep into the chilling waters, trusting that the One Spirit would guide her way. Little did she imagine that the angels would not allow her to face such a nemesis alone. Little did she imagine that Ora, Stella, Forrest and Proudfoot would follow in her wake, but indeed they did.

Onward they sped, dodging visions of horror on every side. Bran's forces were mocking the angels—daring them to proceed into the unknown. Just as it seemed each must fall into madness, Crescent Lake evaporated, leaving a hollow chamber in its wake.

Selene could not see the change in her environment but sensed it all the same.

"It is the threshold that leads into his realm," Proudfoot volunteered in a low voice, hoping to augment Selene's limitations. "Three caverns lay directly before us—each with its own hypnotic pull."

"Yes, I can sense that," Selene replied. She paused for a moment, as if listening to some unheard voice, then said, "I am to enter the third chamber—alone."

This statement was uttered quite matter-of-factly, offering little, if any room for objection.

"No—you cannot!"

"It is folly to challenge him alone!"

"At least allow us to come with you!"

The angels protested in mass chorus, begging Selene to heed reason. She merely smiled and said, "It is my destiny. You must remain here to offer assistance when the time comes."

The many voices fell silent, respecting their guardian's wishes. Each watched with bated breath as she drifted forward, blind to what lay ahead, relying solely upon the Spirit's guidance to speed her way. Thus, Selene set out on the final leg of her quest.

After traveling for what seemed to be an eternity, she entered the third cavern. A cry of vengeance all but hung in the air, suffocating any attempt at escape. Bran was watching, waiting to see her next move. She could also detect the throaty whispers of a soul in pain. Would it be wise to stop and free a prisoner at this time?

"Why not? It cannot hurt to try. But, remember, you are alone in my realm. I have already returned your other spirits to the surface."

"Heed not his threats, my lady!" cried a familiar elfin voice, "I am here!"

"And I'm here!" snarled Brenda, who suddenly flared deep within a wall of pitch at her left side.

"And there is one other," sneered Bran.

With a flick of his talon-like fingers, he flung the unseeing guardian back against the sticky substance that oozed from the walls.

Try as she might, Selene found it impossible to free herself from this gooey prison. The blob-like restraints began to ooze into her eyes, nose and mouth until it seemed she must drown. Despair rose in her soul. Could a being like herself actually die more than once?

"Of course. Death can be attained time and again until the entire experience seems nothing more than a continuous string of expiration."

He was very close to her now, so close that she could feel his breath upon her face.

Suddenly, the voices began to speak all around her, offering council.

"Remember, my lady—"

"—The power lies—"

"—Within you."

They were all speaking at once: York, Brenda and the other voice, that she could not identify. They were reminding her of the essential truth that Bran refused to accept: the truth that she could defeat him any time she chose to call on the power inside her own being.

All at once a shower of light burst through the blindness, rendering her free of restraint. A look of fear registered in Bran's eyes as the entire cavern was bathed in a heavenly blue light. Selene could not help but gasp when he, Brenda and York faded from view. The One Spirit had healed her blindness!

"DO NOT WORRY ABOUT BRENDA AND YORK, SELENE. THEY HAVE EVOLVED TO A DIFFERENT REALM. CONTINUE ON YOUR JOURNEY. I HAVE SUPPLIED THE TOOLS THAT WILL HELP YOU DEFEAT BRAN. REMEMBER, THE EFFECT IS TEMPORARY. YOU MUST WORK QUICKLY OR THE BLINDNESS WILL RECLAIM ITS HOLD. GO, FIND MY MISSING CHILD."

Selene did not stop to question the Spirit's motives. She was simply grateful to find her eyesight restored, if only for this one, last quest. Allowing the great presence to guide her footsteps, she walked directly into the center cavern. Something was waiting for her inside: something that she did not want to see. There, at the very core of darkness, a light beckoned her forward. She could just distinguish a faint outline illuminated within a dazzling pool of green light. This was to be the test of her existence. Either she would emerge a victor, or remain doomed to an eternal servitude in the darkness.

"Why not move into the light, Selene? I want you to see my prize possession. I think you will be most surprised to find who waits within."

Selene sensed that Bran was at her side. He was escorting her toward the image. Something about the action reminded her of a wedding ceremony. Together they moved as one, arms linked in common bond. Her soul cried out to avoid what lay ahead, but Bran was a demanding bridegroom and pressed forward toward the ultimate prize. It was time to unmask that which demanded to be seen.

Off the mask came, unleashing Selene's worst nightmare. She blinked, certain it must be a trick of light. The image was still there. Every fiber within her being screamed that it was a lie; that Bran had conjured this vision to wound her at the core. How could Cynthia Sherwood, her own mother and the former Selene, be in league with the Dark One? At that moment she felt Bran's lips upon her mouth. He was claiming victory, and she had become his prize.

"Now you know the truth," he whispered. "She was mine long before you were born, just as you will be mine until the end of time."

"I always wanted to tell you, Diana," the brilliant form explained as it rose up before her, "but there just wasn't time. Do not be so downcast. You will find him a wonderful husband."

Something about that statement struck a cord within Selene. She knew only too well that Cynthia would never give her away to the darkness. It was time to reach within and claim the power once more.

Selene's eyes opened wide. Light surged from her glittering orbs and onto the false figure. Cynthia trembled and tried to speak but it was no good. The charade had ended. She gave a little cry, then clawed at the air, disappearing in its wake. In her place stood a familiar image—that of the often glimpsed woman with long, dark hair.

"Mara!" Selene cried in disbelief. She had found the lost angel!

Bran began to chuckle, well amused with his delusion.

As Selene whirled around to face the bridegroom, another beam of light shot from her body striking him full between the eyes. One look told her that Bran was momentarily frozen in time. Taking advantage of the situation, she caught hold of Mara's arm and spirited her toward the cave entrance, hoping against hope that the others were still there.

They had just cleared the threshold when all five angels eagerly showered them with praise.

"It's Mara—you've found her!" Ora cried with delight.

"Welcome back," Stella indicated, as she folded her sister spirit into a warm embrace.

"I fear we have little time for welcomes," Mara suggested as she looked to Selene.

"That's right," came the guardian's firm reply. "Is everything in readiness?"

"Both earth and woodlands have bound together to create the fourth cavern," Proudfoot declared with a reassuring pat on his comrade's back.

Forrest smiled. "It is now up to you, Selene."

All further discussion dwindled away as Bran stirred from his frozen sleep.

Selene turned to Mara and transmitted a wordless request.

"Yes, Selene, I will be the bait," the dark-haired spirit quickly replied. "Thank you for everything."

The twilight guardian offered a smile, then sped off after the others who had already taken their places.

Mara understood the delicate nature of her position. The success of the entire quest rested on her ability to draw Bran into the fourth tunnel. Could she do it? Did she still possess the strength necessary to block her thoughts?

With little warning, Bran appeared at the threshold. A smile played upon his lips. "How foolish of Selene to leave you behind after spending so much effort in mounting a rescue," he said in a bemused voice.

"Don't fool yourself, Bran. She has no idea that I am here—waiting for you."

"Come now—you expect me to believe that Selene does not know everything about her earthbound angels."

"I expect you to pay for your crimes!" Mara exclaimed, summoning a strong burst of water from the parallel dimension. Bran merely laughed as it swept him deep into the fourth cavern.

"Not very original, Selene, but then again I imagine you are fresh out of ideas. Why not send Mara to trap me in a cavern? You might even succeed in holding me for an hour."

Mara appeared before him and said, "That may be too brief a time for your reclamation, Bran. You have much to learn, and it cannot be accomplished in an hour." Before the Dark One could offer a reply, the water guardian began to circle around his form.

"How many bands make up the core of your existence?"

There was no response beyond that of a sneer.

"I see you cannot answer. Then know that this is the first band of reckoning. It will cleanse your dark past—in time. Escape is impossible. Open your spirit and allow the healing to begin."

Little Ora, all too eager for freedom, began her task at the precise moment Mara finished speaking. Her bright beams fell upon Bran as she cried, "The second band of reckoning offers something you lack in heart and mind. It is the gift of light. Accept, and allow its healing powers to flow through you."

Bran appeared surprised at Ora's apparent youth, but soon the twisted smile graced his lips, and he began to chuckle once more. The two angels tried very hard not to show their terror, even as his voice rang out with a vicious taunt.

"Is this the best you can do, Selene? Surely, I am worthy of a greater test!"

With one swift motion, Bran raised an arm above the water and flung a stream of black, sticky emulsion at Ora and Mara. Both spirits were instantly engulfed within the mire. The cavern grew dark once more and the river all but subsided from view. Water alone had not conquered him, nor had Ora's gift of light.

Selene knew it was her turn to make an attack. "There is a third band of reckoning which I hesitate to use," she said in a calm voice.

"Why hesitate, Selene? I would not."

"Because I pity you. No matter how evil you have become, I shudder at what lies ahead. You were once called Bran the Blessed by an entire race. Why not reclaim that goodness? Why not show us that it still exists somewhere inside you?"

A look came into Bran's eyes that Selene had never witnessed before. He paused a moment then, bent his knee in humble supplication. The act itself indicated that he was awaiting her command. Yet Selene could not bring herself to speak. It was essential Bran find his own way out of the darkness.

As time lengthened into what seemed to be an eternity, it became clear that the Dark One was uninterested in redemption. He was merely bating her—testing her resolve. Indeed, when Bran finally met Selene's eyes, he was already calculating her defeat. Only one thing stood between him and success. He had to physically cast her into oblivion. Once there, she would never torment him again.

Throwing every last trace of pity to the wind, Bran merged with Selene.

Caught inside a vortex that offered little hope of release, the twilight guardian felt her spirit falter. Bran was fighting her from the inside, governing her very thoughts. She could actually feel her soul being stripped away like petals torn from a flower.

Desperate for some means of deliverance, Selene drifted away into a sea of lost souls. Her eyes weakened and began to blur. Very soon the blindness would reclaim its hold, and she would be rendered an invalid once more.

"Fear not, my dear. You have entered the realm of oblivion. There is an inherent air of nothingness here, so you will not miss your sight."

Selene was surprised to find Bran standing next to her. Something about him seemed different, and that made her pause. Indeed, there was a lost look haunting his eyes that she could not understand.

"I have been locked here for centuries. Lost in a world where neither time nor past good deeds have any meaning."

"I do not understand. If you are locked in here, how can you function in the land of the living?"

"There are two parts to every being. One good, one evil. Each battles the other for dominance. In my case, the evil has so consumed the good that it may only exist in oblivion."

"I am sorry for you, but that does not explain why you have brought me here."

"The fact remains that there is only one hope for my escape. Bran knows that—which is why he sent you to me."

"Bran wants you to escape?"

"We wish to be whole again. Your love can make that happen."

"My love?" Selene questioned, as a laugh escaped her lips.

"It seems ludicrous, I know, but it is possible. You already love that which is best of me."

Selene scanned his face, then understood. "York..." she whispered, visualizing the merry faced elf she held so dear.

"And Brenda. She, too, is a part of my soul."

"That is why he—you tried to marry me earlier."

"There is no other way. We know you can bring us to destruction. But, it is your love that will offer redemption."

Selene felt his arms entwine around her waist as his lips brushed against her hair. It would be so simple to remain in this land of emptiness: to love and be loved, but that was impossible. She was guardian of all earthbound angels, and they depended on her for support.

"I can best help you by returning to the fight at hand. Please do not say another word. You are right. It is my love that will save you, but not the kind of love you imagine. Be patient. We shall meet again," Selene said, willing his gentle form from view.

Instantly, she was hurled back into the dark realm.

Bran looked surprised by her reappearance. This was something he had not anticipated. "So, you even refuse my good side? Well, there is no help for it then. One of us must perish this night."

"Before you strike, remember, it is love and freedom from oblivion that I offer your soul."

Bran began to laugh. "So, you actually believed him? Well, he must be a better performer than I ever imagined. Believe me, Selene, we do not seek your love. We seek only your destruction. Watch as it comes to pass!"

Before Bran could make good on this threat, a blinding wave of light shot through the threshold with harsh precision. Stella had unveiled her face. In that instant, a rush of solar power descended upon the dark spirit. Selene was cast aside as if she were no more than a rag doll as it hurled Bran into the farthest depths of the cavern. Bruised and battered, he struggled to regain his footing, but it was to no avail. The angels were already upon him.

"We are here to introduce your final bands of existence, Bran," Forrest and Proudfoot said in unison as they appeared on either side of the battered spirit, "for we are guardians of the earth and woodlands."

"The earth will nourish your new vision and allow it to prosper as you grow," declared Proudfoot, with head held high.

"And a tree will free you from your dark prison," exclaimed Forrest. "It will be your reclamation."

Unable to focus, Bran fell against the cavern walls and became trapped within a strange substance that held him fast against any means of escape. Something wet and sticky dripped into his mouth and eyes. It tasted like sap! A living darkness surrounded him on all sides! At that moment he understood. He was trapped within a tree, not a cavern. The tree of reclamation. That was why they had called each attack a band of reckoning. Just as the bands of a tree determine its age and character, the bands of reckoning represented his existence. Now he was trapped within a hell of his own making.

As vision slowly returned, Bran noticed a gaping tunnel that stretched out before him. At the end of this expanse waited a figure not unlike his own shape and form. Between them rushed the faces and images of those he had destroyed in life. The dark angel began to tremble, even as he clung to the tree for support. He had no wish to meet those lost souls again.

"Do you understand the bands of reckoning, Bran?" Selene asked, as her own vision began to fade.

There was no reply. "Of course you do. They are of your own making. Stella will remain nearby to help you incorporate the lessons they teach."

Bran tried to scream but could not. The sap made that impossible. He was now alone: alone with the horrors of his past. At that moment, oblivion seemed like paradise.

CHAPTER 26

When Daniel's eyes regained focus, he found himself lying face down in what appeared to be a lakebed. "Where am I?" he asked with a shudder.

Suddenly, events of the previous night came flooding back to him in startling detail.

"Why am I still alive?" he questioned the misting sky. "I was hit by lightning! I should be dead!"

The words faded upon his lips as he noticed the wet, purple earth that coated his hands. He was in the Land of Twilight Mist! Did that mean he had actually died?

Daniel scanned the violet horizon for answers but found none. A heavy sigh escaped his lips. Where was Diana—Selene? She would be able to explain what had happened. Again, he found himself answered with silence. A sharp pain tugged at his heart. Perhaps Selene had succeeded in closing the door on this world forever, and he was locked inside. How would he pass the days alone in this land of purple mist? And, what of his father? What had become of him?

Searching the lakefront once again, Daniel's eyes latched onto a large slab of rock not so different from Lookout Point. There, resting against an oak tree, was the figure of a man he had obviously missed before. Daniel blinked to make certain that his eyes were not deceiving him. The figure was still there. Perhaps he was dreaming, yet there was something so real about the man; something so familiar, that made Daniel pause. His heart began to thud within his chest. After a moment, he began to run. Each step brought him closer to the realization that it was his very own father who slept against the tree.

"Welcome to the Land of Twilight Mist, Daniel Sherwood," crackled a feminine voice from somewhere overhead.

"Who are you?" Daniel asked in hushed tones, as he searched for the identity of his invisible host.

"I am, Brenda, the guardian of fire."

Daniel could not help but gasp as the smiling angel materialized before his eyes. "York told me all about you. I thought you were—"

"—Dead? Well, spirits don't bite the dust so easily, Daniel. It takes a lot to keep us down. Isn't that so, York?"

A nimble form leapt from the old oak tree, landing gracefully on Lookout Point without so much as disturbing Michael Sherwood.

"Greetings, young lad! What has taken you so long? We cannot keep your father asleep forever!"

Daniel stood gaping in awe as York danced a merry jig.

"I know, I know, you thought I was imprisoned forever. As you can see that has changed. I am free again— free to travel to new worlds and beyond!"

"New worlds? Do you really mean there are worlds within worlds?"

"Don't confuse him, elf boy!" Brenda snapped playfully.

"I see you are still feisty as ever!" York quipped, preparing to dodge any fireballs that might come his way.

"We don't have time for this, Little Elf. Daniel and his father must go through the gateway now. See, how she is waiting," Brenda indicated, pointing toward the purple cloud that hovered over Crescent Lake.

"You mean I'm not—we're not—"

"Dead? Oh, no. Selene just put you here for safe keeping!" York replied with glee.

A wave of concern swept over Daniel's brow. He hardly dared to ask the question that plagued his heart.

"Yes, she will be fine, but only if you hurry!" Brenda responded, reading his mind.

"Thank God," Daniel whispered, as a small tear formed in his eye. He watched the pulsating cloud descend upon the old, oak tree, and lovingly wrap his father in its violet glow. How tender Selene was, how motherly. Suddenly, another shadow burst through the mist, claiming the place Daniel rightfully considered to be his own.

"Hurry, Daniel!" Brenda cried. "You must enter now!"

Daniel began to run. His fingers had almost brushed against the misty cloud when it disappeared altogether.

"They're gone," he sighed in bewilderment. Something, or someone had managed to take his place. "York, Brenda, did you see that strange shadow jump into the cloud just before I reached it?"

The two angels exchanged quick glances, but said nothing.

More than a little disappointed by the fact that they were basically ignoring him, Daniel yelled so loudly, they could not help but hear what he had to say. "Well, I guess you are stuck with me forever!"

"Oh, yes, Danny. Do stay. We wish you would. This is such a wonderful place to be. No school—no chores," York chimed in a sing-song voice, "but, unfortunately, 'tis not for you! I am afraid you will have to leave!

"How can I?" questioned Daniel, who was not very amused by York's insensitive reply.

"Selene will return for you soon," assured Brenda with a soft smile. "Come, we'll show you what Whispering Pines looks like in our world."

Daniel was about to offer a formal protest when each angel grasped hold of a hand and began to propel him toward the beautiful, purple forest.

"So, young knight, what have you learned from this quest?" York asked, trying to ease Daniel's obvious level of disappointment.

222

"I never really thought of it as a quest, York," Daniel replied with a sigh. "I was just there to help any way I could."

"He who seeks the Grail must never be surprised by the form through which it chooses to present itself."

"—But we were not seeking the Grail. We were seeking your freedom—freedom from captivity—"

"And what have you learned of freedom?" York questioned, trying very hard to keep his devilish grin at bay.

There was something in York's look that spoke to Daniel. Suddenly, he understood. "The answer lies in your heart," he said, with growing wonder. "That is where the Grail resides! There is no need to travel on a quest, for the Grail lies within!"

"Well said! Freedom was always within our reach. We simply needed to journey within to find the truth. Selene helped us accomplish that miracle. She was our gateway, and you were the key!"

Daniel's only reply came in the form of a perplexed frown.

"You confuse him with all your fancy words, York! Just tell him the truth of it!" Brenda snapped in good humor.

"Certainly he knows that Bran was defeated!" York bellowed to the winds.

"I'm not deaf, York!" Daniel cried, as he clapped both hands against his ears.

A moment of silence passed before he completely realized the significance of York's statement. "You mean we won?"

"Of course, we won!" York and Brenda cried together.

Daniel had little time to celebrate the new turn of events, for his eyes were drawn to the beautiful, blue light that steadily approached. "It's time, isn't it?"

"Yes, you must go now," whispered Brenda in a gentle voice. Daniel noticed that she seemed sad about his departure, and that pleased him.

"I'll miss you!" he cried, drawing both angels into a broad bear hug.

"Fear not," chimed York, reading his unspoken thoughts, "We will meet again. 'Tis a promise!"

"Your family needs you now, Daniel. Go to them. They're waiting for you," Brenda urged, gently pushing him into the light.

The words, "What do you mean by they?" escaped Daniel's lips, and then he was gone.

CHAPTER 27

Daniel was never exactly certain when the violet cloud had disappeared. All he felt was surprise at the sheer amount of green that met his eyes. Not even the slightest hint of purple could be found anywhere. This was Whispering Pines as he knew it. There could be no doubt that he was home.

Glancing around, Daniel expected to find his father anxiously waiting nearby, yet he was nowhere to be found. Daniel had taken no more than a few steps when a young doe blocked his path. Staring at him intently, she offered a nod of her head, then gracefully bound off toward Crescent Lake. Daniel could do nothing but follow.

Upon clearing the hill, the doe froze in her tracks. Daniel also came to an abrupt halt, his eyes rooted to a pair of figures seated beneath what had once been the old, decaying oak tree. In its place rose a majestic king oak, magnificently arrayed in a red coat of autumn splendor. It was at that moment Daniel fully realized that more than one miracle had transpired since twilight.

"York," he whispered to himself, "this is your doing."

A sleek fox appeared beside the doe and waved its tail in greeting. Daniel smiled. No doubt they were the Little Elf's emissaries on earth.

Suddenly, remembering the reason why he had come to the lake, Daniel's eyes returned to the two figures seated beneath the tree. Yes, there sat Michael Sherwood creating a new painting, quite unaware of his presence.

Daniel tried to speak, but his words were no better than a fractured whisper.

"Father—"

A smile of heartfelt delight broke across the artist's face. Yet, it was only when the other figure turned around, that Daniel began to run. Stumble he must, for the tears were clouding his eyes. Could he actually bring himself to say the name that had remained unspoken for so long?

The thin strains of "Mother" somehow escaped his lips, mingling softly with the misting air.

A long piece of wood slipped from Cynthia's pale fingers and fell to the ground. She could not gather Daniel into her arms fast enough. No words were necessary. It was their first embrace since Daniel's earliest days. Time lost all meaning as they clung to each other in silent communion. Soon their tears blended and became one.

Daniel's limbs trembled in a most annoying fashion. "Mother, is it really you?"

"Yes, Danny," she softly replied. "I am a part of the miracle you helped bring about," she whispered in his ear.

"Then—the miracle also involved sending you back to us?"

"Well," she explained with a knowing smile, "I was never really dead, Danny. The One Spirit placed me in a sacred realm until the true guardian arrived."

"Diana," Daniel whispered in a quiet show of admiration.

"Selene," Cynthia gently corrected, as she softly stroked his cheek.

"But, how will she ever come back to us?"

Cynthia smiled. "Remember, Danny. All things are possible for those who believe. Just look at me. I am living proof of that."

At that moment, Michael Sherwood caught his son around the waist and lifted him into the air. "Where have you been, young man? We were worried about you!"

Daniel threw a quick look at his mother, who simply shook her head in reply. The words, "He doesn't remember anything about it, Danny. It is better that way," rang through his mind. She was using that old spirit form of communication. Daniel wondered if one day he too would forget everything associated with the Land of Twilight Mist. He sincerely hoped that would not be the case.

Remembering the furry companions who had offered him guidance, Daniel glanced back at the hill. There stood the doe, straight and proud with a rusty ball of fur curled at her feet. Underneath the fox's paws lurked two squirrelish heads that poked out into the open air. They each paused to offer silent approval, then disappeared into the forest, taking their own separate path.

Daniel turned back toward the lake. It did not surprise him to find Selene hovering overhead. Indeed, she had been watching them the whole time. There was something about her appearance that startled him at first, then after a moment he understood. Her once gray orbs now shone with a brilliant silvery hue. The blindness was irreversible. She would never look on him with seeing eyes again.

"You really do look like an angel, sis," he thought, biting his lip to keep the tears at bay. He must not cry for her. Not after all they had been through together. "I'm gonna miss you. I hope you'll visit me sometimes, especially if you ever need my help again."

Selene smiled, then became one with the air. "You can count on it, Danny. I will always be near. On behalf of all the earthbound angels—I thank you."

"Danny, don't you want to know what's been going on around here while you were gone?"

Daniel looked into his father's eyes. Had he also seen Diana? The casual gaze seemed to indicate that he had not.

"What did I miss?" he asked, almost mechanically.

"We have some guests visiting right now that I know you will find of interest."

As if on cue, Reverend Moss strolled over the hilltop with Kelly Branwell in tow.

Daniel froze. What was she doing there? Didn't they know that she was Bran's daughter?

Reverend Moss' face broke into a warm smile. "It's good to see you, Daniel!" he cried. "We have been awaiting your return."

Daniel frowned, then looked to his mother for some kind of an explanation.

After placing a firm hand on his shoulder, she gently nudged him forward.

"I just got back," he replied in confusion. His eyes fell on Kelly, who smiled in return. "How did you pull it off?" he asked, after a moment. "How did you manage to escape him?"

"I didn't do it by myself—if that's what you mean. Reverend Moss saved me," she gratefully replied. "You see, there was a terrible accident. The mansion caught fire and..." Her voice began to waiver as her eyes sought the ground.

"The good Senator was lost in the blaze, Daniel," Moss explained in gentle tones.

"It happened last night after the eclipse," Michael added with a glance at Cynthia that clearly indicated he knew more than he was about to let on.

Cynthia picked up on his thoughts and continued, "The Reverend is going to have Kelly stay with his family until her relatives can be notified."

Daniel could barely hear what they were saying. His mind kept returning to York. "Kelly must free herself in order to escape Bran's control," he had said. What did this new turn of events portend? Daniel watched as Kelly walked over to the shoreline and casually dropped a golden scarf into the water. "I have no family to speak of," she said ever so softly.

"Oh, yes you do," Daniel thought to himself. It was vital that he keep a close watch on Kelly. Perhaps one day her heritage would not seem so disgraceful. Perhaps one day the darkness would reclaim its hold on her. Daniel mused on this for a moment, then let it go. Bran was imprisoned for a time. Some people might even think he had died, but everyone who stood underneath the old oak tree that morning, knew better. Someday he might very well return. Kelly smiled at Daniel. It was impossible to determine whether or not she had just read his thoughts.

CHAPTER 28

After bidding Daniel and her earthly parents goodbye, Selene sought shelter in the familiar Land of Twilight Mist. She could not help but feel sad at the parting. It made everything seem far too real. She was now alone in a world of darkness without friend or confidant. If only her dear guide still stood nearby.

One thought pushed all others aside, as she slowly picked her way along the soggy lake shore. Was York actually free? There was only one way to find out. She had to find the sacred oak and determine if York's spirit still remained trapped inside. What should have been a perfectly simple task proved to be incredibly difficult. Without the aid of her eyes, Selene found herself in a handicapped position. It was not until she stumbled over a set of knobby roots that the truth became clear. She had already reached her destination.

Following the root's twisted trail, Selene soon met with its sturdy trunk. A moment's contact taught her that York no longer dwelled inside. This left her puzzled. Where had he gone? When no answer appeared to be forthcoming, she plopped against the oak and began to consider her own plight.

What was her purpose—now that the miracle had been accomplished? There certainly was no need for her in the Land of Twilight Mist. What deeds would the One Spirit expect of a blind angel? Selene drank in the silence. Perhaps she would never hear the sacred voice again.

As Selene rested against the sacred oak, she became aware of just how knotted the roots felt beneath her hands. This was something she had never noticed before with seeing eyes. Gently tracing the long, narrow trails they wove with tapered fingers, she could almost distinguish a purple brilliance through her mind's eye. A small voice inside told her to use this knowledge as a means to reclaim sight, but she was simply too exhausted to try.

Down she plopped, face to the ground, hardly caring if existence ended at that moment.

"Fie upon you, my lady. This will never do. Groveling before the Little Elf is an unpardonable offense. What will you think of next?"

Selene sat bolt upright at the sound of the Little Elf's voice. Her hair hung in a garden of wild curls, offering a kind of shelter to each wounded eye. Reaching out toward the merry voice, Selene's hands met with the toe of an elfin boot.

"York?" she whispered, almost daring her senses to be wrong.

"'Tis I, my lady!" the Little Elf cried, scooping Selene into his wiry arms. He was careful not to allow any trace of pity to color his thoughts or voice. She must not know that he was afraid for her.

Placing the twilight guardian upon a soft, mossy knoll, York gently smoothed the hair from her eyes. He had to know the truth. Would she ever see again? One look at the silvery orbs told him the affliction was permanent.

"It's all right, York. I know the truth. From this moment on—I am blind."

"Aye, my lady," he softly replied.

"Well, I did get to see my family. The One Spirit allowed me that," her voice trailed off into the mist. It was all York could do not to cry.

"Remember, Little Elf, tears do not come so easily to those of us who dwell in this realm. Besides, there is no need to cry for me. I am thankful you are here and well. I was so worried, York. I thought I might never find you again, but I should have known better. My only regret is that I can not see you biting away at your lip right now."

York checked his progress with no small degree of embarrassment. Suddenly, a thought dawned on him. "Why think you that I am biting my lip?"

"Because I know you," she replied with a chuckle.

"—Or is it because that you can see?" he questioned, leaping to his feet.

"This is no time for jokes, York. I told you, I am blind. Bran—"

"Think, my lady. For a guardian of such intelligence, sometimes you surprise me. Of course you can see! You saw your family through the power of your mind's eye. Use it now to see me!"

"Not now, York. I am so tired—"

"Allow me to prove my point!" exclaimed the determined elf. It was vital that he help her recognize the inner power she possessed before all hope began to fade.

"Try it now. I know you can see me."

Selene struggled to pull away from York, but he held her fast in his arms. "I dare you to look at me," he challenged. "'Tis time you knew just how much Bran's curse has changed me. Perhaps then, you will not feel so sorry for yourself!"

"What did he do to you? Are you hurt badly?" she asked with increasing alarm.

"You must look at me to find out!"

Selene fell against the oak tree for support. Why was York being so cruel? Didn't he know how much she cared? Tears fell from her eyes as she began to imagine the cruel tortures enacted upon him by Bran. If only they could wash away the blindness that kept her from seeing the truth. At that moment she realized the significance of the action. She was crying. That meant a change had taken place in the Land of Twilight Mist, or perhaps it was merely a change in her own soul. A familiar voice drew her focus down into the core of her being. It whispered that there lay the key to all avenues of sight. She need only unlock the gate and claim what remained hidden from view.

She took a deep breath and waited. All was stillness and concentration. Suddenly, a door appeared draped in violet blue. Beyond it lay a wall of purple flame. Without hesitation, Selene stepped across the threshold to claim her destiny. Setting foot upon a trail of white light, she saw a dim figure waiting on the other side.

"Why, York," she sighed, "you haven't changed a bit—except perhaps to grow more mischievous than ever!"

York leapt to within a hair's breadth of her person and planted a lingering kiss upon her lips. "Well done, Selene!" he cried, momentarily forgetting his place.

Selene saw the blush steal across his face, before he quickly sought refuge in dance.

"If you can see me, then you can also choose to see everyone else who is here!" he cried in delight, quickly casting off any last trace of embarrassment.

"Everyone?" questioned Selene. Who else have I missed?"

The smiling image of Brenda came into view. "Then you have also been reborn."

"We all have, Lady Selene, thanks to you," Brenda exclaimed with a new tone of respect. "Even York's good friend here."

Selene rapidly trained her inner eye back on the Little Elf and found to her great delight that he was not alone. Indeed, a beautiful, black raven sat on his shoulder.

"Caw!" cried the lovely bird, as she flew to Selene's outstretched arm.

"I should have known," Selene whispered, stroking the ebony feathers. "It is so nice to finally meet you."

"The miracle made it possible, Selene. You made it possible. Your strength and guidance have set us all free!" Brenda exclaimed with joy.

"People will search for the good Senator, but no body will ever be found. It will almost seem as if he never existed," added York in a rather solemn voice. He wanted to be happy about Bran's imprisonment, but knew he could not. There was always the chance he would find some way to return.

"Almost," echoed Selene, reading his thoughts. "It still remains to be seen whether or not Bran learns from his mistakes. If he chooses not to change, then we may count on another reappearance."

"Let's not think of that right now," Brenda sighed. "We have other things to occupy our minds."

"True," Selene interjected, "The Land of the Living is now closed to both of you."

"Aye, but you may go there anytime, Selene. The angels will need your guidance," York added, in a reassuring voice. His face shown with pride. Oh, what a guardian she had become!

"We—my sister Brenda and I—will explore the new worlds that are open to us. Some day you may wish to visit us there—after you have taken time to rest," York teased ever so gently.

"I'm feeling better already," Selene exclaimed, rising to his hidden challenge.

"Then come with us now."

"All right, but only for a short time. Remember, the angels need me."

The three beings joined hands, as they rose into the misty air. Selene noticed with some amusement that Caw was once again perched on York's shoulder. There she would remain throughout eternity, or at least until they were called to battle the dark angel once more.

The End

234

ABOUT THE AUTHOR

Carol Weakland has written numerous theatrical adaptations of literary works including, *The Arthurian Trilogy,* a series of plays based on the legends of King Arthur. She is an accomplished live actress, performing the leading roles of such classics such as *Jane Eyre, Wuthering Heights,* and *The Scarlet Letter.*

She is a certified Reiki practitioner and teacher who deeply believes in the spiritual quest. ARCH studies and practices have also served to strengthen her belief in angelic guides. Carol's great love for animals is apparent in every aspect of her life.

Carol Weakland's novel *Morgen of Avalon: Dreamspell,* offers a new perspective on the beloved Arthurian myth.

For more information, including appearance schedule and other books, please visit: www.CarolWeakland.com

30679651R00135

Made in the USA
Middletown, DE
03 April 2016